Another One Bites the Crust

Oxford Tearoom Mysteries
Book Seven

H.Y. HANNA

CONTENTS

H.Y. HANNA

CHAPTER ONE

They say revenge is a dish best served cold... a good thing to remember when you're planning to murder a chef.

Not that I was thinking about murder and revenge as I wriggled around a changing cubicle in one of Oxford's top dress boutiques, struggling to get into a silk evening gown. I sucked my breath in and tugged vainly at the zipper again... Had I really put on so much weight recently? I'd always had a slim, almost boyish figure, and now that I was on the brink of thirty, it seemed that I was finally getting some curves, like I'd always wanted. The only problem was, I seemed to be getting them in all the wrong places! There was a distinct bulge around my waist and a lot of surplus padding around my hips...

I thought guiltily of the rich, buttery Chelsea bun I'd eaten last night—stuffed with cinnamon, raisins, and soft brown sugar, and drizzled with sticky icing—and the delicious sticky toffee pudding, oozing with caramel sauce, not to mention the slice of Victoria sponge cake, slathered in homemade strawberry jam and fresh whipped cream! They were all "leftovers" from the menu at my business, the Little Stables Tearoom, and, as usual, had been too tempting to resist. That was one of the occupational hazards of running a traditional English tearoom, I was beginning to realise—especially when you prided yourself on serving the best in classic British baking...

"Gemma? What's going on in there? Have you fallen asleep?" came my best friend Cassie's voice.

She flung back the cubicle curtain and stepped inside, looking effortlessly gorgeous in a simple white T-shirt and jeans that hugged her body. *Now, Cassie has curves in all the right places*, I thought enviously as I looked at her. A classic pocket Venus, what she lacked in height, she more than made up for in voluptuous beauty. I'd always wished that I could be more like my best friend—not just in the looks department but in general too. As one of five in a warm, rowdy family of artists and creatives, Cassie was a free spirit with a fiery temper and an earthy, relaxed approach to life—the complete opposite of me and my anxious concern for peer approval and following the rules, courtesy of my "proper" upbringing in a typically repressed British upper-middle-class household.

Yet, despite our differences, Cassie and I had been best friends from the moment we met back in primary school. And we had stayed close, all the way through university (luckily we had both got into Oxford, although we had been at different colleges) and even during the eight years when I had been away from England. When I'd decided to give up my corporate career to return to Oxford and open a tearoom, Cassie had jumped to support me, giving up her various part-times jobs to come and work at the Little Stables.

Now Cassie looked me up and down and said, with a best friend's blunt honesty, "You look like a stuffed sausage!"

I winced. "I could suck my stomach in," I said, demonstrating.

"What—the whole night? Besides, then you'd just look like a slightly thinner stuffed sausage."

I sighed. "Okay. I guess I'll have to try a bigger size."

"It's not just that, Gemma—this dress doesn't do anything for you. Makes you look all washed out."

I turned to look at the full-length mirror at the side of the cubicle and had to admit that Cassie was right. The shimmering navy sheath, which looked so elegant on the hanger, now hung limp and shapeless, the dark blue colour making me look pale and tired.

"It looked so gorgeous on the hanger," I said wistfully, fingering the silky fabric.

"Your hair doesn't suit this minimalist style either. You need something more feminine to go with this gown, to balance it out... more like my hair," Cassie added, tossing her dark, wavy mane.

I looked back at my reflection. I'd cut my dark hair into a pixie crop just before returning to England last year and, much to my mother's annoyance, had steadfastly refused to grow it out again. I liked the short, gamine style—I liked to think I might be channelling a bit of Audrey Hepburn—but now I wondered if it was too androgynous to suit any of the gowns on display.

I gave Cassie a despairing look. "What am I going to do? The ball is the day after tomorrow; we've looked in five places now and I still haven't found anything suitable!"

"Well, I did tell you not to leave it till the last minute," said Cassie. "You know what it's like during the ball season. Everyone snaps up the good stuff early. There's not a lot of selection left."

I made a rueful face. The thing was, June might have been ball season in Oxford, but it was also the height of the tourist season, with people flocking to the university city and the surrounding Cotswolds countryside to enjoy the local attractions during the glorious but brief English summer. With its prime location in a little village on the outskirts of Oxford, business at my tearoom had been booming, and taking time off to go ballgown shopping had seemed the least important of my priorities. With only Monday off each week, I usually spent it catching up on sleep, chores, and emails... but I was grateful now that Cassie had dragged me out shopping today. Although it did look like I might have left it too late...

"I suppose I could just wear that black dress I usually wear for work do's and cocktail functions?" I said, thinking of my LBD— "little black dress"— wardrobe staple.

Cassie looked aghast. "Gemma, this is an Oxford ball! Everyone will be dolled up and looking fabulous. The men will be in black tie... You can't wear a bog-standard work dress. What a waste!"

She was right. Oxford was one of the last places where you could really go to town and indulge in a Cinderella fantasy. The annual summer ball at the end of the academic year was a custom still followed by many of the Oxford colleges—as their grand quadrangles, elegant cloisters, and extensive gardens were transformed into a fairytale wonderland, whilst students and their guests enjoyed a night of music and dancing, games and entertainment. And dressing up in a ballgown—a real, floor-length, sweeping, romantic ballgown— was probably one of the best parts of the experience. Well, for the girls, anyway. Most of the male guests probably groaned at the obligatory dress code of "black tie" and I was sure many left it even later than me to rush around town and try to hire a black dinner jacket and matching bow tie for the evening.

I sighed as I looked at my reflection again. I hadn't been to a ball since graduating over eight years ago and I had been looking forward to reliving the experience. It did seem a terrible shame to attend such a special event dressed in my staid old black number...

"Hang on a tick," said Cassie suddenly. "There was something I saw on one of the racks..." She disappeared and returned a moment later with something pink and frothy draped over her arm.

"I'm not wearing that!" I said, recoiling as she held it out. "I'll look like a meringue!"

"Just try it, Gemma," Cassie begged. "Trust me."

I heaved a sigh and took the dress. However, when I surveyed myself in the mirror a few minutes later, I was pleasantly surprised. The simple strapless bodice highlighted the slim lines of my neck and collarbones, and moulded itself to my body like a glove. From the nipped-in waist, the dress flared out into a full skirt which, despite the layers of tulle, looked graceful and elegant—and nothing like egg-white confectionery. In fact, for the first time, I really did feel like I was channelling Audrey Hepburn; this dress embodied all the 1950s glamour of vintage movies like *Sabrina* and *Roman Holiday*.

"It's beautiful," I breathed.

"Told you," said Cassie with a smirk.

I grinned at my best friend. I should have trusted her artist's instincts. Then I glanced at the tag attached to the skirt and my smile faded.

"Bloody hell, did you see the price?" I cried.

"Yeah, it's a bit pricey... but it's made in Italy, with silk tulle—the best—and that's all hand embroidery," said Cassie, pointing at the delicate pattern of silver threads on the bodice.

I shook my head. "Cassie, I can't spend so much money on a dress that I'll probably only wear for one night."

"Aw, come on, Gemma! The tearoom has been doing really well lately—you've even given me and Dora a raise—I'm sure you can afford it."

"Yes, but I shouldn't be spending money on something so frivolous. I should be investing in something for the tearoom instead."

"You've spent tons on the tearoom already. When was the last time you bought something for yourself?" Cassie demanded. "Ever since you got back from Australia, all you've done is focus on the business. It's high time you treated yourself a little. Yes, the dress is a bit expensive but it's hardly going to break the bank. And you look absolutely gorgeous in it."

I gazed at my reflection in the mirror, feeling myself waver. Cassie was right again—I *did* look wonderful in the ballgown. The soft pink shade seemed to bring out the warmth in my skin, making my complexion glow and my eyes bigger and more luminous. I thought suddenly of my boyfriend, Devlin O'Connor, and imagined his blue eyes lighting up as he saw me in this dress...

"All right! I'll take it," I said suddenly with a smile.

"Great!" Cassie beamed. Then she glanced at her watch. "Hurry up and change—we need to get you some shoes to go with that gown, but first I've got a surprise booked for you."

"For me? What do you mean?"

But Cassie refused to say anything further. A few minutes later, we left the store with my new ballgown carefully wrapped in tissue paper and tucked into a large carrier bag. We joined the bustling throng milling down Cornmarket Street, the pedestrianised thoroughfare that was the main shopping strip in Oxford. Despite it being a week day, the city was heaving with people—from groups of Japanese tourists, excitedly photographing every gargoyle and lamp post, to college students sailing past on their second-hand bicycles and local residents walking briskly down the cobbled lanes, going about their business. And rising into the sky above us were the "dreaming spires" of Oxford—the Gothic towers, elegant turrets, and majestic battlements that made up the university city's famous skyline. That was the thing about Oxford: even taking a casual walk to buy a tube of toothpaste from the pharmacy felt like stepping back in time.

"This way," said Cassie, turning down a side lane and directing me towards a small shop tucked into the ground floor of an old Victorian building.

I was surprised to see that it was a modern nail salon, cleverly decorated to blend with its historic surroundings.

"I've booked you a manicure and a pedicure—my treat!" said Cassie with a smile.

"Oh, Cass! That's so sweet of you!" I cried, giving my friend a hug.

"Well, I figured that with the amount of abuse your hands get at the tearoom, it would be nice to pamper them a bit before the ball." Cassie gave me a wink. "It's a good excuse for me to have a pedicure too. This place has just opened and they're offering some fantastic deals at the moment."

We entered the salon, a tinkling bell announcing our presence, and a young Asian woman hurried over to greet us. She led the way to a row of leather recliners, each one with a foot spa fitted in front, and settled us into our seats. I sighed with pleasure as I slipped my weary feet into the warm, bubbling water. The therapist added a few drops of fragrant aromatherapy oil to our foot spas, then excused herself and retreated to the back of the salon to collect her other supplies.

I leaned back in the recliner and looked around. The place wasn't big but it had been cleverly decorated, with the use of pale wood, mirrors, and soft pastel colours to give a light and airy feel. Bamboo blinds shielded the front windows from the street and a water feature by the front door provided a soothing backdrop of trickling splashes.

The only thing that spoiled the peaceful ambience was the loud, brassy voice of the woman seated in the recliner next to us, talking on her iPhone. I glanced over curiously. She looked to be in her early thirties, with heavy make-up, dyed blonde hair, and gleaming red talons on her fingertips. Her legs were jutting out in front of her, propped on a cushioned bench, whilst a young Asian girl crouched in front of her and attempted to paint her toenails. It was no easy feat as the woman kept twitching while she spoke on the phone, jerking her toes in different directions.

"Oh!" cried the Asian girl as a sudden movement of one leg made her swipe nail polish across top of the woman's foot, leaving a bright red smear.

"Hey! Watch what you're doing!" snapped the woman, breaking off to glare at the girl.

"I... I am sorry!" squeaked the Asian girl.

She soaked a cotton ball with some acetone and carefully began wiping the offending smear away as the woman turned back to the phone. But a second later, the woman twitched her leg again, jolting the girl's elbow, which knocked against the bottle of acetone. It rolled over and spilled its contents onto the floor—and on the women's shoes nearby.

"AARGH!" snarled the woman. "You ham-fisted little cow!"

"I-I-I am... I am very s-sorry," cried the girl, looking on the verge of tears as she dabbed frantically at the shoes with some tissue paper.

The woman smacked the girl's hand violently away and snatched up the shoes. "These are a pair of Marc Jacobs! You've ruined them!" she yelled.

"Hey, it was an accident," Cassie spoke up. "There's no need to take your temper out on her like that. These things happen. If you hadn't kept moving around, she probably wouldn't have knocked the bottle over."

The woman rounded on Cassie, her face ugly. "Who the hell are you?" she demanded. "Why don't you mind your own sodding business?"

Cassie's eyes flashed. "Because I hate to see bullies throwing their weight around."

The woman sprang up from her recliner. "Who are you calling a bully?" she shouted, thrusting her face into Cassie's and waving a fist.

Cassie erupted from her seat too, and I started to say something, but at that moment, the other therapist came hurrying out from the back of the salon, her expression horrified as she took in the scene. She rushed towards the woman and said in a placating tone:

"I am so sorry, madam! Please accept my apologies. Please—we would like to give you this pedicure free of charge—and also a gift voucher for another visit?"

The woman calmed down slightly. "Yeah, that's more like it," she said.

She let the senior therapist finish her toes, then walked over to the counter to receive her free gift voucher. I noticed that she had left a plastic shopping bag behind, wedged into the side of her recliner seat, and I leant over to retrieve it. My eyes widened as I saw the boxes and boxes of paracetamol, ibuprofen, and aspirin tablets jammed inside, alongside a box of strong laxatives and a bottle of cough syrup.

"Hey! Give me that!" The woman rushed up to me and snatched the bag out of my hands. "What are you looking at?" she snarled.

"Nothing," I said, taken aback. "I was just picking it up so you wouldn't forget it."

"Yeah, right. You're just like your friend— sticking your nose where it don't belong!" She shot me a venomous look, then turned and flounced out of the salon, banging the door behind her.

There was an awkward pause, then the senior therapist gave us a strained smile and said:

"I am so sorry for any inconvenience! Please... excuse my little sister—this is her first day and she is still learning." She gestured to the young girl who stood trembling behind her.

"Oh, don't worry about us," said Cassie cheerfully as she settled back into her recliner and slipped her feet into her foot spa again. "We totally understand."

"I'd love your sister to do my toes for me," I added, smiling encouragingly at the young Asian girl, who gave me a tremulous smile back and came hesitantly forwards.

She showed me a chart of nail colours and, after Cassie and I had made our selections, hurried off to find the corresponding bottles. Meanwhile, her elder sister offered us refreshments, then retreated to make our cups of tea. As she disappeared into the back of the salon, Cassie wiggled her toes in the bubbling water and said:

"Thank God that woman left. She was spoiling the ambience even before she started yelling." She made a face. "Oxford's a small place. I hope we don't run into her again in the shops later."

"I don't think we will, not unless we're planning to shop at the pharmacy," I said with a wry chuckle.

"What do you mean?"

I told Cassie what I'd seen in the shopping bag. "She's either planning to start her own chain of chemists or she's planning to get a whopper of a headache."

"Or... she's planning to give someone an overdose."

"What?" I gave an incredulous laugh. "Where did you get that idea from?"

"I read this article about how dangerous it is to mix over-the-counter drugs like ibuprofen and aspirin. Even if you don't take any single one in a large dose, the combination can be lethal. So if you wanted to poison someone and didn't want to draw suspicion with a large overdose of a single drug, an easy way would be to mix them."

"Well... okay, but I don't understand why you think that woman—"

"Didn't you hear her on the phone?"

I shook my head. "I wasn't really paying attention."

"She was getting really nasty—complaining about her ex-boyfriend who'd dumped her or something." Cassie rolled her eyes. "Don't think I blame him."

"So? That doesn't mean she's planning to kill him with an overdose," I said, laughing.

Cassie's face remained serious. "Maybe. But I can tell you what she said before she hung up. She said: 'I'm going to murder him if it's the last thing I do!'"

CHAPTER TWO

My nails were so beautiful after the manicure that I found myself handling everything very gingerly as I strapped the cat carrier with my little tabby, Muesli, into the front basket and climbed on my bicycle the next morning to set off for work. I had overslept slightly so I cycled fast, anxious that I might not have enough time to check over the tearoom before we opened for the day. But as I pulled up in front of the Little Stables and jumped off my bike, I saw that I needn't have worried. Someone had already arrived. The drapes had been drawn back and the windows opened to let in the fresh air. Through the glass panes, I could see the Old Biddies toddling around in their sensible orthotics, straightening the chairs and rearranging napkins and cutlery on the tables.

I smiled as I watched them: Mabel Cooke, Glenda Bailey, Florence Doyle, and Ethel Webb— four nosy octogenarians who ruled the roost in the little Cotswolds village of Meadowford-on-Smythe, where my tearoom was situated. They might have looked the stereotype of sweet old grannies with their vintage handbags, woolly white hair, and tissues stuffed up the sleeves of their cardigans— but anyone who underestimated them did so at their peril. Meddling in other people's business was their speciality, especially if they thought a mystery might be involved. The only problem was, with their over-active imaginations and their love of Agatha Christie novels, the Old Biddies *always* thought that a mystery was involved! And they didn't hesitate to jump, sensible orthotics first, into any murder investigation... much to the frustration of the Oxfordshire police.

Still, on this lovely June morning, they seemed nothing more than sweet old ladies, fitting in perfectly with their quaint surroundings. Like many Cotswolds villages, Meadowford had the pretty thatched-roof cottages and winding cobbled lanes so beloved of tourists searching for authentic "Olde England". And my little tearoom, housed in an old Tudor inn, completed the experience—serving up traditional English afternoon tea in vintage porcelain teapots, accompanied by our signature scones with jam and clotted cream, as well as dainty finger sandwiches, cakes, and buns.

When I'd first had the wild idea of abandoning my executive career to open a tearoom on the outskirts of Oxford, I had no inkling if my dream could ever be turned into reality. It had been a huge gamble, leaving my high-flying job and sinking all my savings into this place, and the first few months had been nerve-wracking, especially when an American tourist was found murdered by one of my scones barely a month after we opened! But now, just eight months later, I couldn't believe how well things were going. Not only was the tearoom beginning to make a name for itself as having the best scones in Oxfordshire, but we were starting to get catering orders too, particularly from the prestigious Oxford University colleges and institutions.

I secured my bike then hurried into the tearoom, feeling a flash of pride as I always did every time I stepped into my little kingdom. I paused just inside the front door to let Muesli out of her carrier, then straightened and started to make my way to the kitchen.

Then I stopped short and stared.

Every. Inch. Of. The. Place. Was. Covered. In. Lace. Doilies.

From the white crocheted circles swarming over each table to the lace discs adorning the windowsills, from the scalloped doily covers over every sugar bowl and jam jar to the enormous knitted cobweb draped over the mantelpiece above the fireplace... the whole room was a sea of frothy vintage lace.

"Ah, Gemma, dear—we've been waiting for you to arrive," said Mabel in her booming voice. The most formidable of the Old Biddies, she had a bossy manner that belied her well-meaning intentions and kind heart. She waved an imperious hand around the room. "Glenda, Florence, Ethel, and I were chatting during bingo yesterday—very tedious game; that Mrs Curtis must have asked the caller to repeat every number four times! She really ought to take her hearing aid back for a refund—anyway, we all agreed that something seemed to be missing in the tearoom. And then we realised what this place desperately needed." She looked at me triumphantly. "Doilies!"

"D...Doilies?" I said faintly.

Glenda beamed. "And wasn't it lucky, dear, that we happened to have several spare doilies at home? Though, of course, we were concerned that we might not have enough for the whole tearoom, so we asked several of the other senior residents in Meadowford to donate their spare doilies."

"Uh... that was very kind of you."

"And Ethel even whipped up four extra doily coasters last night. She is such a whizz with the crochet needle," added Florence, smiling at her friend.

Ethel looked down and coughed modestly, her cheeks pink with pleasure.

"I always say there's nothing that can't be improved with a bit of crochet," declared Mabel. "And doilies are so versatile! I have even made my son-in-law in Melbourne a lace doily tire-cover for his Jeep."

I winced inwardly, wondering if the poor man was now the laughingstock of Australia. "Er... yes, they're lovely... but... um..." I looked weakly around the room. "Don't you think you can have too much of a good thing?"

"Nonsense!" said Mabel. "You can never have too many lace doilies."

"Now that we've done the tearoom, Gemma, how about making something for you?" asked Ethel. "Your T-shirt looks so bare. Wouldn't you like me to stitch a nice lace doily collar on to it for you?"

"Oh... no, no... I'm fine, thanks." I said hastily.

"How about a doily necklace then?" asked Ethel. "I've seen some featured in magazines. They're ever so easy to make. I could make you one tonight."

"No... no, thank you. I... um... don't wear necklaces much."

"Or earrings? I could do them in a chandelier style. Just think: lace doilies hanging from your earlobes! What could look more beautiful?"

"Er... um... I really don't need any lace doily accessories." I looked at Ethel in alarm. Where was all this doily-making fervour coming from? A petite spinster, Ethel was normally the gentlest and quietest of the Old Biddies... who knew that she had such an extreme lace doily fixation?

Desperate to change the subject, I made an exaggerated show of sniffing the air and said, "Mm... what's Dora baking this morning? It smells delicious!"

In fact, I realised—as I inhaled deeply and genuinely a second time—there really was a heavenly smell of fresh baking coming from the kitchen. I wondered if my baking chef, Dora, was making the tearoom's signature scones. But when I strolled into the kitchen, followed by the Old Biddies, I saw that Dora was bent over a large tray filled with little circles of crusty pastry tarts. She was carefully pouring a creamy yellow mixture into each tart case, then sprinkling the surface with freshly grated nutmeg.

"Ah... egg custard tarts!" said Mabel, rubbing her hands together. "A great British classic! There is no other pastry to match it."

"I think the *pastel de nata*—the Portuguese tarts—are delicious too," I protested. "It's quite similar to the English version, although they make it with puff pastry rather than shortcrust and cinnamon instead of nutmeg. I like the way they burn the tops slightly, so that the sugar is caramelised and—"

"*No* tart is superior to the English custard tart," said Mabel, glowering at me.

"Especially when they're made by Josh McDermitt!" gushed Glenda, clasping her hands to her chest. "Oh my, when he lays out the pastry dough and wields that rolling pin... I could be having hot flushes again." She fanned herself frantically.

I grinned to myself. Josh McDermitt was a celebrity TV chef who had suddenly risen to fame in the last few years. His blond good looks and blatant sex appeal had earned him the nickname of "Posh McDishy", but although his rivals sneered at the cosmetic reasons that made him such a hit with housewives and "ladies of a certain age", he *was*, in fact, a brilliant cook and pastry chef. His version of the English custard tart had taken the country by storm and was what had first made him a household name.

"I just found out that our custard tarts were featured on a 'food blog' last week," Dora spoke up, her usually stern face breaking into a proud smile. "My niece rang and told me, and she printed out the page from the interweb and sent it to me. The article even compared our tarts to Josh McDermitt's—and said that ours tasted so good, you could almost think that they were his famous recipe!"

"Really?" I said, delighted. "That must be why we had so many more customers than usual last weekend—and they were all asking for the tarts. In fact, the custard tarts actually outsold the scones!"

"It's a huge compliment to be compared to Josh McDermitt," said Florence, beaming. "You should be really chuffed, Dora."

"He's got such perfectly even white teeth," continued Glenda dreamily. "And that wonderful honey-blond hair..."

"Do you suppose he could be wearing a wig?" pondered Ethel. "When I used to work in the village library, there was a gentleman there with lovely blond hair like that and we all used to admire it—until one day, he tripped and fell, and his toupee came off. He was completely bald underneath!"

I laughed. "No, Josh's hair is real. He had that hair at uni. It used to be really long and wild, and people used to tease him about it."

The Old Biddies turned wide eyes on me. "Gemma! Do you know Josh McDermitt?"

"We're not close friends or anything," I said. "But yeah, I knew him from my time at Oxford. We weren't at the same college—he was at Boscobel, Cassie's college—but his room was in the staircase next to hers so I used to bump into him sometimes when I went over to see her."

Cassie arrived in the kitchen, catching the tail end of our conversation. "Who are you talking about?" she asked.

"Josh McDermitt," I told her.

She wrinkled her nose. "Oh. Him."

"Gemma says he was at your college. Did you know him well?" asked Glenda eagerly. "What is he like?"

"He's a bit of an arrogant git," said Cassie bluntly. "Don't let his charming TV image fool you. He's not as nice as he looks."

Glenda's expression was so crestfallen that I felt sorry for her. "Cassie never liked Josh much," I hastened to explain. "So she may be a bit biased."

"Biased?" Cassie snorted. "I just don't swoon at his feet like most girls do, so I can see the truth. Josh thinks he's God's gift to women—and everyone else too, probably. And I'll bet celebrity life has just made him worse. Well, I suppose we'll see for ourselves tomorrow."

I looked at her in surprise. "Tomorrow?"

"He's going to be at the ball, hadn't you heard? Special guest and all that. Coming to do a live cooking show in one of the pavilions."

"You're joking."

"No, I'm not. It's all part of this reality-TV thingamajig he's doing... life on the road with a celebrity chef or something like that. Anyway, they wanted to film him coming back to his old college and cooking up a storm here. Of course, the college ball committee was delighted; it's not the usual kind of 'entertainment' that you get at a ball—" Cassie gave me a wry smile, "—Josh is certainly not the latest hip band or comedy act, but he's such a star now that they thought it wouldn't matter. And they were right. I heard that all the remaining tickets for the ball sold out within minutes of the press release. And it's made our ball *the* event of the season. Normally, we'd never be able to compete with some of the larger colleges, like St John's and Christ Church, you know, with their deeper pockets and bigger guests, but this year, everyone's talking about the Boscobel College Ball."

"I don't suppose there *are* any tickets left?" asked Glenda.

Cassie shook her head. "Sorry."

"Not to worry," said Mabel briskly, patting Glenda on the shoulder. "We shall simply find out which hotel Josh McDermitt is staying at in Oxford." She waved a hand. "Come along—we've got some sleuthing to do!"

CHAPTER THREE

As the kitchen door swung shut behind the Old Biddies, a small furry shape slipped past their legs and into the kitchen, trotting up to join Dora, Cassie, and me at the wooden table.

"*Meorrw!*"

"Muesli!" I frowned at my little tabby cat and bent to scoop her up. "You know you're not allowed in the kitchen."

"That's exactly why she keeps trying to come in, of course," said Cassie with a grin. "Cats!"

"It might be my fault too," said Dora with a shamefaced smile. "I've been giving her some treats when she comes in here."

"Dora!" I looked at her in exasperation. "You mustn't encourage her! You know the food inspector said I can only have Muesli at the tearoom if she stays out of the food preparation areas. We have to stick to the rules."

"Yes, but the poor little mite always seems so hungry," protested Dora. "And when you see her wee face..."

I glanced at Muesli, who blinked back at me, looking undeniably cute with her big green eyes, ringed in black "eyeliner", and her dainty pink nose. She stretched a white paw towards me and said:

"*Meorrw?*"

"That's not going to work on me, you little minx," I said. "With all the trouble you get up to, I'm beginning to regret letting you come back to work with me."

"Oh, Gemma—you don't really mean that?" said Cassie with a laugh. "I have to admit—even though she can be a little monkey—it's been really nice having Muesli back in the tearoom."

"Well, it would be, if she would just do as she was told," I said with a scowl. "I mean, I made her a nice bed on the window seat behind the fireplace—I thought she could snooze up there and enjoy the view from the window, while keeping out of the way. And if customers want to pet her, they can go and sit on the window seat... but she just won't stay there! She keeps wandering around, going up to tables and getting under people's feet. I'm worried that someone might report her to the Food Standards Agency."

"Well, no one's complained so far," said Cassie. "In fact, all the customers love her—especially the seniors. They keep asking me if she needs a home. Seriously, I'd be more worried about one of the customers stealing Muesli than complaining about her. I think I saw old Mrs Purdey trying to stuff her into her canvas bag last week."

"Don't be ridiculous," I said, laughing as I carried Muesli back out to the dining room.

The first customers were already arriving, and soon neither Cassie nor I had time for chitchat as we flew around the tearoom, handing out menus, taking orders, and delivering trays of tea and platters of cakes and buns (whilst also surreptitiously trying to remove as many lace doilies as we could). Despite the hectic pace, I did try to pause and chat to customers. One of the pleasures of running a tearoom, I'd discovered, was the chance to meet all sorts of people from so many different countries and backgrounds, and I delighted in not only hearing their customs but also sharing many quaint English traditions.

"Well, we gotta have some scones," a smiling American man told me as I hovered by one table to take an order. "When our friends heard that we were coming over to England, they said: 'You gotta try the scones!'"

"We have scones in the U.S., of course," his wife hastened to add. "But I've heard that the English ones are very different."

"Yes, they are quite different from the triangular things you find in American coffee shops," I agreed. "English scones are round and usually plain or with a little bit of currants or raisins scattered through—they don't tend to have all the fruit and nut and chocolate add-ins like the American versions. They're also not made with as much butter or sugar—they're really more like what you'd call a 'biscuit', I think."

"Ah, so the English versions are healthier?" asked the wife.

I laughed. "Probably not. People just load the butter and sugar on afterwards! Scones in England are more like a base for you to slather on tons of butter and jam and clotted cream, and you always eat them accompanied by tea."

"Oh yeah, that 'clotted cream'... our friends were talking about that too," said the husband. "Some kinda fresh cream, isn't it?"

I nodded. "It's made from fresh milk—traditionally from Jersey cows—which is heated really slowly and then cooled over a long period. You get this lovely, silky, golden-yellow cream which rises to the top in little 'clots' and that's skimmed off and served with scones and other desserts. I've heard it described as like a cross between butter and whipped cream, but I don't think that quite does it justice. It's a very unique taste."

"I think I've tasted some. Back in the U.S., a friend of mine bought a jar of imported clotted cream from a gourmet market... but I'm sure it's nothing like the real thing made fresh," the wife said.

"Well, I'll bring some over now and you can have a taste and see," I said with a smile.

I hurried into the kitchen and returned a few minutes later with a tray laden with a pot of English breakfast tea, two teacups, and a plate of freshly baked scones, accompanied by little jars of home-made jam and clotted cream.

"You just cut the scones in half horizontally and then spread the cream and jam on top," I instructed them.

"Jam first or cream first?" asked the husband.

I giggled. "Uh-oh... now you're heading into dangerous territory! That's the subject of a heated national debate. Some say it should be jam first and then the clotted cream spread on top—that's how scones are eaten in Cornwall. Others say the cream should definitely be first, with a dollop of jam on top. That's the way they have it in Devon, also known as Devonshire cream tea." I leaned down and said in a mock whisper, "Whatever you do, don't ask a group of Brits that question—not unless you want to start a civil war!"

The husband chuckled. "We'll take your advice. And maybe we'll have some one way and some the other way, to compare."

I smiled and left them to their experimentation. The time flew by, and before I knew it, the "afternoon tea" crowds were thinning out and the day was drawing to a close. Finally, with just one customer left—an elderly lady sitting in the far corner—Cassie and I retreated behind the counter for a well-earned rest.

"What a day!" said Cassie, massaging her neck. "And it's only a Tuesday too—I can't imagine what's it going to be like by the weekend. Oh, speaking of the weekend, that new Bond film is out—fancy going to see it this Friday?"

"I'd love to but I can't; I'm having dinner with Devlin... and his mum. She's coming down to Oxford for the weekend."

"Ooh!" Cassie raised her eyebrows. "So is this the all-important 'meet the parents' meal?"

"Well, 'meet the mother', anyway," I said with a slight grimace.

"What's she like?"

I shrugged helplessly. "I have no idea! Devlin hardly ever talks about her and when I ask him, he just gives me vague responses. I don't understand why he's so reserved about it all."

"Well, your Detective Inspector Devlin O'Connor is a very enigmatic man," said Cassie teasingly. "Go on—admit it—it's part of his attraction. Devlin will always be a bit of a mystery to you and that's why you find him so attractive."

"Rubbish!" I paused, then gave her a sheepish grin. "Well, okay—maybe a bit."

"So what are you going to wear to this big

dinner?"

I sighed. "I don't know. It would help if I knew a bit more about his mum—like whether she's all prim and proper like *my* mother or more liberal and laid-back, like yours. I'd hate to be overdressed and have her think that I'm a vain bimbo... but on the other hand, I'd hate to dress down too much and have her think I'm a total slob. Oh, Cass—what should I do? I really want to make a good impression!"

"I wouldn't worry. You know no mother ever thinks any woman is good enough for her son. Devlin's mum will probably think you look hideous whatever you wear."

I gave Cassie a sour look. "Gee, thanks. That really makes me feel better."

Cassie grinned. "Well, it should. See, if she's going to disapprove of everything anyway, why even worry about it?"

"Huh. I'd like to see *you* act so brash and breezy when it's your turn to meet your future mother-in-law," I said. Then, realising what I'd said, I blushed and added hastily, "Not that Devlin has... I mean, I'm not expecting... we're haven't discussed..."

Cassie looked amused. "But you've been thinking about it."

I avoided Cassie's eyes. "Uh... no... I mean..."

She chuckled. "Hey, it's okay, Gemma—it's totally understandable if you have. Most girls think about it. And besides, Devlin did propose to you once—"

"Yes, but that was a long time ago," I said quickly. "He might feel completely differently now. I mean, he hasn't ever hinted that he's thinking about marriage..."

"Well, you guys have only been back together six months. And after the way you rejected him, you can't blame the poor chap if he doesn't rush to propose again."

I winced. "I know. I was an idiot. I was young and... well, just stupid."

"Who knows? Maybe it was meant to be. Maybe it's better that you and Devlin had some time apart. Anyway, you're back together now and that's all that matters." Cassie glanced at her watch. "I'd better go and shut up the kitchen. Dora's probably tidied everything before she left—but I'd better just check."

She disappeared into the kitchen and I turned as I heard the sound of footsteps. The last customer— the elderly lady—had finally finished her tea and was coming to the counter to pay. It was Mrs Purdey, who lived alone in a cottage just around the corner from the tearoom. She was one of the regulars, coming in for a "cuppa" most days, always accompanied by her umbrella (rain or shine) and her enormous canvas shopping bag. Now, she struggled to tuck the canvas bag under her arm as she paid her bill.

"That was lovely, dear," she said in a quavering

voice. "The egg custard tart was delicious."

"I'm glad you enjoyed it," I said, watching her struggle. "Would you like me to hold your bag for you while you get your purse?"

"No!" She jerked back. "Er... no, I can manage. Thank you, dear."

I gave her an odd look but took the cash she offered and rang up the till. However, as she began to turn away, I couldn't help noticing that the canvas bag seemed to be... *squirming.*

"Mrs Purdey... have you got something... er... alive in your bag?" I blurted out.

She started guiltily. "In my bag? No, dear, of course not." She pulled the bag tighter against her and began hurrying to the door.

I frowned. Was I imagining things? I stared at her retreating back and the bag clutched in her arms. No, I wasn't wrong—it was definitely squirming. And a second later, I heard a muffled: *"Meorrw!"*

"Muesli!" I gasped.

I ran after the elderly lady and caught her just as she was stepping out the door.

"Mrs Purdey..." I hesitated. How did you accuse a sweet old lady of stealing your cat? I cleared my throat. "Um... Mrs Purdey... have you seen Muesli anywhere? I can't find her... I think she might have... er... crawled into your bag by mistake."

"Certainly not!" cried Mrs Purdey, clutching the bag even tighter to her chest. "I told you, there's nothing in my bag."

I reached towards her bag. "Well, can I just take a look? Because you know, Muesli is so naughty—she might have just crawled in without you noticing—"

She twitched away from me. "No, no! She's not in my bag!" she gasped, struggling to contain the squirming.

The next moment, a little grey-striped head popped out of the gap at the top of the canvas bag.

"*Meorrw!*" said Muesli indignantly, the fur all ruffled around her ears and her whiskers bent crooked. She wriggled and heaved, and managed to pull herself out of the bag, then leapt for the floor. Giving herself a shake, she sat down and began to wash in a disgruntled fashion.

"Oh!" cried Mrs Purdey. She flushed. "Well, I... I... I thought Muesli might like to come and stay with me."

"Er... that's really sweet of you but—well, Muesli lives with me."

"She could live with me instead. I know she would love it. I would take very good care of her," she said earnestly.

I gave her a weak smile. "I'm sure you would but... you can't take Muesli home with you, Mrs Purdey."

The old lady looked sulky. "Why?"

"Because... well... she's my cat," I said helplessly.

"But she looks just like my Smudge! She could almost be him! She's got the same grey tabby fur, see? And the white fur on the chest... and the white paws. And Smudge had beautiful green eyes too... and a pink nose..." Her voice caught. "He... he died a few months ago and I've been all alone since then. I miss him so much..." She looked wistfully at Muesli. "She looks so much like him... Really, she could almost be him..."

"Yes, but she's not your Smudge," I said gently. "She's my cat and she has to stay with me. You can always see her when you come to the tearoom, though," I added with a smile. "You know you're welcome any time. Oh, except tomorrow—we're shut tomorrow as both Cassie and I will be attending a ball in the evening."

Mrs Purdey sighed, then with a last wistful look at Muesli, she turned and shuffled out the door. I watched her go with troubled eyes, wishing that there was something I could do, then went back to the counter. Muesli trotted after me and leapt up on a chair, sitting down again to continue her washing.

"*Meorrw!*" said Muesli, licking a paw and running it over her left ear, smoothing down the rumpled fur.

"Yes, well, you'd better behave yourself," I told my little cat. "Otherwise, the next time Mrs Purdey tries to take you home, I won't come to your rescue. I'll just—" I broke off as the front door of the tearoom opened. Glancing over, I started to say,

35

"Sorry, we're closed..." then paused as I saw a heavyset man with a rather bulbous nose storm in. He was followed by a harassed-looking woman with a clipboard and a man lugging an enormous video camera on his shoulder—the professional kind with microphone muffler, zoom lens, and dozens of buttons.

"You!" said the heavyset man, jabbing a finger at me. "You the owner of this place?"

I was taken aback by his manner. "Yes. Can I help you?"

"Yeah, you can explain how you stole Josh McDermitt's custard tart recipe!"

I stared at him, wondering if I'd heard right. "I'm sorry?"

The woman with the clipboard gave me an apologetic smile, looking very embarrassed. "Er... you have to excuse Jerry. He doesn't mean—"

"What's going on here?" Cassie demanded, coming back out of the kitchen to join me. She stared at the heavyset man. "Who are you?"

"I'm Jerry Wallis, Josh McDermitt's manager," he said, jutting his chin out. He turned back to me and wagged his finger. "And don't try to play the innocent with me, miss. I know what you've been doing: passing off your second-rate tarts as Josh's creations and using his name without his permission—"

"Now, wait a minute," I said, beginning to get angry. "I don't have a clue what you're talking about. I haven't tried to 'pass off' anything!"

"Oh yeah? Then how do you explain this?"

He thrust a piece of paper at me. It looked like a printout of a web page... a blog article, in fact. Then understanding dawned. It was the food blogger's feature about the Little Stables, raving about our egg custard tarts.

"Hey, we can't help it if some blogger compared our tarts to Josh McDermitt's," Cassie protested. "It's not as if we wrote this piece ourselves. And anyway, if she thinks our tarts are as good as Josh's... well, she's entitled to her opinion."

"Don't give me that! I know you put her up to it," growled Wallis. "What did you do? Give her a kickback? Pay her something on the side?"

"Jerry!" gasped the woman.

"No, we bloody well didn't!" said Cassie. "We didn't even know that she had visited the tearoom until someone told us about the blog."

"Bollocks to that! You probably arranged the whole thing! Thought you'd get a bit of free publicity for your place, didn't you? Cash in on Josh McDermitt's celebrity status and milk it for your fake pastries—"

"Our custard tarts are not fake anything!" I cried. "They're based on my chef Dora's own recipe, and if the general public thinks they taste good, who are you say to say no? It's not as if Josh McDermitt has a monopoly on all the custard tarts in Britain!"

"Don't get cocky with me, miss," Jerry Wallis

snarled, jabbing a finger at me again. "I've got friends in high places, me, and I can make your life pretty miserable if I—"

"Jerry!" The woman with the clipboard caught his arm, looking mortified. "You can't go around threatening people like that. These two young ladies have said that they knew nothing about the blog article—and I believe them. I think we should leave now."

He shook her arm off roughly and seemed about to retort, then changed his mind, swore viciously, and stormed out of the tearoom. The woman gave us a weak smile, mumbled an apology, then hurried after him, followed by the cameraman.

"Bloody hell... what was that all about?" said Cassie, staring after them.

I shook my head in bewilderment. "I have no idea."

"I told you Josh has got worse since he became a celebrity," said Cassie with a dour look. "I'll bet you anything you like that he was the one who got his manager to come and threaten us. His ego probably couldn't take it, having someone say that our tarts were as good as his." She wagged a finger at me. "You'll see—this won't be the last we hear of Josh McDermitt and his bloody custard tarts!"

CHAPTER FOUR

"Well, Muesli—do you think I'll do?"

I glanced at my little tabby cat, who was sitting on my bed, watching me as I pirouetted in front of the full-length mirror propped up in one corner of my bedroom. She tilted her head to one side, her green eyes serious, then gave an approving "*Meorrw!*"

I grinned, turning back at my reflection. The gown looked even more beautiful than it had done in the boutique, with the late afternoon sunshine from my bedroom windows catching the delicate silver threads in the embroidered bodice and shimmering through the layers of tulle that fell to my ankles. My hair had been styled so that the pixie crop curled fetchingly around my ears, emphasising the line of my neck and highlighting the smooth, creamy skin on my bare arms and shoulders. The rare luxury of a day off had given me hours to indulge in an orgy of waxing, scrubbing, and lathering, and now I felt almost like a butterfly newly emerged from a cocoon, ready to spread her wings.

And what spectacular wings, I thought with a smile, giving another twirl in front of the mirror and watching in delight as the full skirt billowed out in a cloud of soft pink silk. I couldn't wait to see what Devlin thought of my new dress.

As if on cue, I heard the sound of a throaty motor outside my cottage and I hurried to the window. A gleaming black Jaguar XK pulled up in front of the door and a dark-haired man stepped out. I felt my heart give a little skip, as it always did whenever I saw Devlin O'Connor. Tall, dark, and brooding, he was the epitome of the Byronic hero, with eyes of true Celtic blue and a lean physique shown to perfection in the tailored suits he usually wore.

Tonight, however, he looked even more breathtakingly handsome, dressed in classic "black tie" attire: black dinner jacket with silk lapels and matching trousers, crisp white dress shirt, black bow tie, and matching silk cummerbund. With a gun in his hand, he could easily have starred in the latest Bond movie that Cassie had been talking about. I grinned at my besotted thoughts, and then—pausing only long enough to grab my satin evening clutch and give Muesli a goodbye pat—I hurried downstairs to meet him.

Devlin's blue eyes darkened as I opened the door and he reached out to pull me to him. "You look beautiful," he said, his voice husky.

"Ooh... no, you'll ruin my lipstick!" I laughed as I ducked my head away from his kiss.

We were stopping at the Randolph Hotel first for a drink in the famous Morse Bar, named in honour of the legendary TV detective who had often pondered complex cases in the elegant, wood-panelled interior. It was situated just inside the entrance to the hotel, with a view back into the main foyer, and Cassie waved to us as soon as we entered. She looked ravishing herself, in a red silk gown that set off her gypsy colouring beautifully. She was already ordering drinks at the bar with her date for the evening: Seth Browning.

Seth was my other closest friend from college days, and he, Cassie, and I had formed an inseparable trio during our time at Oxford. Unlike Cassie and me, however, Seth had chosen to remain at Oxford after graduation and follow a life of academia—something which suited his shy, bookish personality perfectly. He was now a Senior Research Fellow in Chemistry and a tutor at one of the colleges, dividing his time between laboratory work and teaching. He smiled diffidently as he saw me and Devlin, and hurried to pull out stools for us.

"Wow, Gemma—you look gorgeous!" exclaimed Cassie, eyeing me up and down with approval. She elbowed Seth and grinned. "Doesn't she scrub up well?"

Seth nodded earnestly. "Yes, lovely—but not as well as you... I mean, not that you don't always look beautiful, Cassie... but tonight, you just... you're breath-taking... er, I mean..."

Cassie threw her head back and laughed. "Don't worry, Seth—I'm not expecting you to be a 'real date' so you don't have to ply me with compliments."

"No, I'm not... that is..." Seth floundered, an agonised look on his face.

I sighed inwardly, feeling sorry for him. The truth was, I knew Seth wished that Cassie *would* see him as a "real date" for the evening. He had carried a torch for her practically from the first time they met and was always secretly hoping that Cassie might return his feelings. But between his shyness and his fear of ruining their friendship, Seth never dared speak up and could only watch in frustration as a succession of other men moved in and captured Cassie's affections.

Now, I came to his rescue and said lightly, "You two chaps don't look half bad yourselves. We're almost—"

I broke off as my eyes suddenly focused on a group at a table on the other side of the bar. I did a double take, then hissed: "The Old Biddies! What are *they* doing here?"

The others turned to look, just as the four little old ladies made an exaggerated show of surprise at seeing us. They got up and immediately toddled over.

"Gemma, dear... fancy seeing you here!" Mabel boomed.

"Yes, what a coincidence," I said dryly.

"You look lovely, dear. I had a dress like that myself once, back in my heyday," said Glenda, giggling.

Despite her age, Glenda had kept the heart and soul of a teenage girl, and a keen interest in fashion and cosmetics. Tonight, however, I had a feeling that her flushed cheeks were due more to excitement than her usual heavy hand with the blusher, and I was proven right when she leaned over and whispered:

"We found out that Josh McDermitt is staying at this hotel! We've been waiting here all day, hoping for a glimpse of him. Mabel thinks... *oh my goodness, that's him now!*"

A commotion in the foyer made us turn our heads. Josh McDermitt strode into the lobby, accompanied by his manager and the lady with the clipboard that I'd met in the tearoom yesterday. He was also surrounded by a bevy of photographers and journalists, all calling his name and trying to get his attention.

"Mr McDermitt! Mr McDermitt, is it true that

you've replaced your rival, Antonio Casa, in the new season of *Superchef*?"

"Over here, Josh! Give us a smile!"

"What do you think of the critics calling you a 'vain peacock with no real cooking skills'?"

"Are you planning to open your own restaurant, Mr McDermitt?"

"Josh, did you have a one-night stand with the model Chloe Minx?"

"Is it true you're launching a men's skincare range?"

"This way, Mr McDermitt! A smile for the camera, please!"

The celebrity chef turned and posed for the flashing bulbs, offering his famous gleaming white smile and brushing off the questions with practised ease. Even from this distance, I could feel the force of his charisma and I wasn't surprised that half the nation was in love with Josh McDermitt. He hadn't changed much from our college days—he had filled out, perhaps, and added some fine lines around his dark brown eyes, but that only seemed to add to his sex appeal—and the self-assurance that he had always had in bucketloads seemed only to have multiplied.

"Still loves himself, I see," said Cassie, watching him askance.

Glenda sidled up to me and said breathlessly, "Oh Gemma—can you go and ask him for an autograph for me?" She reached into her handbag and pulled out one of Josh's cookbooks.

I looked at her in surprise. "Why don't you ask him yourself?"

"They'd never let me approach him! But you're an old college friend. I'm sure he'd recognise you and make an exception for you." Glenda clasped my hand. "It would be the best present anyone could give me!"

How could I say no after a comment like that? I hesitated, then took the cookbook and said, "All right. I'll try my best."

Feeling slightly self-conscious, I walked out of the bar and into the foyer. When I got there, however, I realised that the paparazzi had dispersed. Josh and his entourage were climbing the sweeping Gothic staircase that dominated the hotel foyer and provided an alternative way up to the guest rooms for those who didn't want to take the lifts. I hesitated again, wondering if I should abandon the attempt, but when I glanced back towards the bar, I saw Glenda waving her hand frantically in a "Go! Go!" motion.

Reluctantly, I turned, gathered up my full skirts with one hand, and started up the staircase. It was difficult going with my long gown—I was worried that I might tear the delicate tulle fabric with the heel of my shoes—so I took each step carefully. By the time I reached the first landing, Josh's group were almost out of sight on the next landing above. I hitched my skirts higher and quickened my pace, but when I arrived on the top landing, it was to find an empty corridor stretching away on either side of me.

Bugger. How was I supposed to find him now? I had no idea which room Josh McDermitt was staying in... But even as I had the thought, I saw two figures come out of a room halfway down the corridor on my right. It was Jerry Wallis and the harassed-looking woman with the clipboard. My heart sank as I wondered if the belligerent manager would recognise me, but thankfully he was too busy arguing with the woman and they passed me in the corridor with barely a glance.

I waited until they had descended the staircase and were safely out of sight before approaching Josh's room. As I neared the door, however, I was surprised to hear raised voices. It sounded like a vicious argument. I bit my lip. This definitely didn't seem like a good time to ask for an autograph! Turning, I was about to head back when a familiar brassy voice drifted out, loud and angry:

"...you heartless bastard! I stuck by you all those years when you were nobody and you dump me for that slut the minute you hit the big time!"

It was the woman that Cassie and I had met at the nail salon—I was sure of it.

Josh's voice cut in, calm and reasonable: "Leanne, I told you, it had nothing to do with my career taking off. Things weren't working between us anyway—"

"Things were fine between us! You even told me that you were going to marry me. And then you started going on TV and getting a big head... and suddenly, you were talking about needing 'space' and shagging models behind my back. I suppose I wasn't thin enough for you? My boobs weren't big enough?"

"You're being ridiculous." Josh's voice was contemptuous. "And I haven't got time for this. I've got to start getting ready—I'm leaving for Boscobel College in a minute."

"You can't just brush me off like that! I'm not going anywhere—"

"Oh yes, you are. If you don't leave of your own accord, I'm going to call hotel security and report you for harassment. The paparazzi are probably still hovering around outside. I'm sure they'd love to get some pictures of my old ex-girlfriend being kicked off the premises."

"You... you...!" Leanne spluttered in fury. "You're not going to get away with it! I'm not going to let you just push me aside again. You'll see, Josh McDermitt! You'll be sorry you ever abandoned me!"

The bedroom door was suddenly flung open and I jumped back guiltily just as the blonde woman stormed out. She pushed past me and rushed down the corridor, disappearing down the staircase in a clatter of high heels. I hovered uncertainly for a second, then scurried after her. I was too embarrassed to face Josh McDermitt. If I had

47

walked into the room then, he would have known that I had been eavesdropping at the door—and in any case, it didn't sound like he would have been in the mood to sign autographs. I returned to the bar and handed the cookbook back to Glenda.

"I'm sorry," I said. "I... It wasn't a good time. Believe me, I would have asked him if I had a chance but..." Seeing her dejected face, I said on an impulse, "I'll tell you what—I'll try again at the ball. I'll be going to watch his cooking demo anyway. If I manage to catch him for a moment afterwards, I'll ask him for his autograph."

"Oh, Gemma, dear—would you? Thank you so much!" cried Glenda, her face lighting up again.

"It'll have to be on a napkin or something, though," I said. "I can't lug that cookbook around all night."

"Oh, a napkin would fine," said Glenda. "Anything will do!"

When we finally entered Boscobel College half an hour later, however, all thoughts of Josh McDermitt left my mind as I stood in the main quadrangle and looked around in admiration. There were nearly forty colleges that made up the University of Oxford and, even as a student, you rarely got to know them all. Usually, you would hang out at the ones that your friends were from or where you attended university society events or had tutorials, and I was ashamed to say that there were many I had never even visited during my time at Oxford. However,

Boscobel College I knew well—this being Cassie's old college—and I had never thought it to be a particularly attractive or impressive institution. As one of the smaller Oxford colleges, it didn't have the grand quadrangles or majestic towers that characterised many of the larger establishments, nor the extensive parks and gardens, and magnificent views that many were famous for. It had always been a sort of nondescript "poor cousin" in the Oxford architectural hierarchy.

Tonight, however, it had been completely transformed into a magical wonderland, with fairy lights strung along the looming stone walls, clusters of ivory balloons tied to the wrought-iron lamp posts, and elegant marquees erected at the edges of the main quad. Live music could be heard playing in the adjoining Library Quad—a jazz band of some kind—and the wonderful smell of a sizzling barbeque drifted out from a nearby pavilion. A carnival atmosphere pervaded the place, with mock jousting competitions set up on the lawns and a small bumper car ring beside the main gate—and even a man on stilts who doffed his top hat to us as he lumbered past.

Devlin offered me his arm with a smile and we joined the crowds of people strolling around the quad, the men all looking suave in their black dinner jackets, the women dazzling in their shimmering gowns of silk and satin. I leaned into him, feeling a sense of déjà vu wash over me as I remembered another ball eight years ago when we had also strolled arm in arm like this, under a starlit sky.

"Hey, Gemma, look—they've got fortune tellers!" said Cassie from behind us, pointing at a booth nearby. She rushed over, dragging Seth with her.

"Oh, Cass, you know it's all rubbish," I protested as I followed good-naturedly. "They always say the same thing—like, you're coming in for good luck or due to receive a letter soon."

"That would be an email, nowadays," said Devlin with a chuckle. "And that's even more predictable—I mean, who isn't going to get an email soon?"

Cassie ignored us and sat down in front of the dark-skinned woman wearing a headscarf and the most enormous hoop earrings I'd ever seen. My friend held out her hand and waited eagerly as the woman peered at her palm.

"You're due to receive some good news..." the woman mumbled. "Your health has been good but your finances still need to be consolidated... You like to help people... and... you are creative! You dabble in the arts... perhaps you'll write a book some day?"

I rolled my eyes. Cassie grinned. She thanked the woman, then got up and waved me towards the seat.

"Go on, Gemma—let's hear your fortune."

I started to argue, then shrugged and decided to humour her. Sliding into the seat that Cassie had just vacated, I held out my palm. The woman picked up my hand in a bored fashion and glanced down at it—then jumped back with a shriek, dropping it like a hot coal. Everyone around us turned to stare. I looked at her dumbfounded. She was eyeing me with horror, her mouth opening and closing soundlessly.

"What is it?" asked Devlin, frowning. He stepped forwards and put a gentle hand on the woman's arm. "Is something wrong?"

She pointed a shaking finger at my open palm. "I... I saw death!"

CHAPTER FIVE

"Cheer up, Gemma—you've been looking glum the whole last hour!"

I gave my best friend a wry look. "You wouldn't be too cheerful either if a fortune teller just told you that you were going to die."

"She didn't say *you* were going to die," argued Cassie. "She just said that she saw death around you—that you were going to encounter it soon. It probably just means that you're going to get a very big catering order from a funeral home."

I laughed in spite of myself. "Well, if I come across a dead body, at least I'll have the best detective in the Oxfordshire CID with me," I said, giving Devlin a teasing look.

"No thanks," said Devlin with mock horror. "I'm

strictly off duty tonight. No murders allowed."

Seth, who had disappeared briefly, materialised out of the crowds next to us and walked up to Cassie, presenting her with a large stuffed toy bunny.

"This is for you," he said shyly.

"For me?"

"I won it in the casino tent," he explained, pointing over his shoulder.

"Aww... that's so sweet!" cried Cassie, reaching up to give him a peck on the cheek.

Seth went bright red and flailed his arms slightly, as if wanting to put them around Cassie but not daring. Then she stepped back and the moment was lost.

"I didn't realise there was a casino tent," said Devlin with relish. "Come on, I fancy a shot on the roulette wheel."

Seth led us to a small marquee which had been decorated to resemble a stylish casino, including uniformed croupiers presiding over green card tables. We drifted over to a table where several people were eagerly watching a spinning roulette wheel. The white ball circling the wheel rolled slower and slower, finally dropping into the centre and coming to rest on one of the numbers. Several groans went up from the table as the croupier leaned forwards and gathered all the losing chips.

"This game is rigged!" cried one man angrily as he turned away from the table in disgust. He looked vaguely familiar, although I couldn't work out where I had seen him before.

"Hey... that's Antonio Casa," Cassie whispered as he brushed past us and stormed out of the tent.

"Who?"

"He's a celebrity chef; haven't you seen him on TV? He stars in this programme called *Superchef*— oh, except that I heard they've kicked him off the show. He's got a foul temper and used to cause really ugly scenes."

"I would have thought that's almost a requirement if you want to be a TV chef these days," I said with a cynical laugh.

"Yeah, but Antonio didn't have the screen charisma to carry it off. I think people just found his temper tantrums annoying. Anyway, the rumour is they've replaced him with Josh McDermitt for the new season."

"You know, I remember now... one of the reporters at the hotel was asking Josh about that." I glanced towards the doorway of the tent, through which the swarthy chef had disappeared. "I wonder what Antonio Casa's doing here?"

Cassie shrugged. "Maybe he's come to boo at Josh's demo. I wouldn't be surprised. There have been lots of insults going back and forth on social media between those two; they really hate each other. The latest thing was Antonio Casa accusing Josh of sabotaging his new restaurant." She glanced at her watch. "Hey, speaking of Josh, his demo is going to begin soon. We should probably start making our way to the dining hall now. We want to make sure we get a spot at the front."

There was a cheer from the table and we turned back to see that Devlin had placed a winning bet on the roulette wheel. He turned away from the table, holding the prize: a huge stuffed toy bear.

"Here you go... wouldn't want you to miss out in the giant stuffed toys department," he said with a wink as he handed me the oversized teddy bear.

"Thanks," I said dryly.

"Listen, Gemma and I are going to head over to the dining hall. Why don't you chaps grab some drinks, then come and find us?" Cassie suggested.

When the men had departed for the cocktail booth, Cassie and I started making our way across the main quad and into the rear quad, where the college dining hall was situated. It was slow going, hampered as we were by our long dresses and the huge soft toys. When we got there, I saw that Cassie was right: people were already starting to form a long queue outside the building. We hurried to take our place in the line, apologising as the stuffed animals got in people's way.

I made an exclamation of annoyance. "We're not going to lug these things around all evening, are we?" I glanced towards the archway leading back to the main quad. Boscobel College was fairly small and it wouldn't take me long to walk to the Porter's Lodge and return. "Look, you keep our place in the queue. I'll take the toys over to the Porter's Lodge."

Clutching the stuffed toys in my arms, I hurried through the college towards the main gate and the Porter's Lodge housed in the building alongside. College porters, in their sombre black suits, were a charming quirk of Oxford University, providing twenty-four-hour concierge services to the students and tutors living in college, and maintaining the peace and security on site. They guarded the main gates against unauthorised visitors, shut down rowdy student parties after midnight, delivered mail to the individual student "pigeon holes", and were a friendly, dependable face to turn to, whether you needed a map of Oxford to guide you or had just locked yourself out of your room!

They often served in their positions for years and I still had fond recollections of the avuncular Head Porter at my old college. There were a few porters at Boscobel that I remembered too, from my visits to see Cassie, and I wondered if any of them might still be around. But as I entered the Lodge, I saw that the man behind the counter was unfamiliar. He was friendly enough, however, and took the two stuffed toys with old-fashioned courtesy, promising to keep them safe until they could be collected.

"The college looks so beautiful—they've done a wonderful job decorating it for the ball," I commented with a smile.

"Aye, the grounds are lookin' nice... but I'll be pleased when the night's over, mind."

I was surprised at his unenthusiastic attitude, then I remembered that for a college porter, the ball probably just meant more drunken students and ugly litter to worry about.

"I suppose it's a lot of extra work for you," I said sympathetically. "There are so many people this year."

He nodded. "And half of 'em probably shouldn't be in here."

"What do you mean?"

"Big problem with gate-crashers, we've been havin'. On account of that celebrity chef coming to the ball, I reckon. More people wanted to see him than could get tickets, so they're just findin' their way in."

"How are they doing that?"

"Some of them are bribin' students and gettin' them to pretend they're guests—others are just slipping past the security. We've been keepin' an eye on the main entrance, of course, but there's a smaller gate that leads in from a lane at the side of the college. That's normally locked and only the college residents have the key. But someone's jimmied the lock somehow, so the door won't latch properly. So people have been gettin' in that way." He gave an irritated sigh. "Anyway, Rodney—that's the other porter—he's gone down to fix it now, so hopefully that'll put a lid on things."

"Josh McDermitt's demo is due to start soon anyway," I consoled him. "Maybe a lot of the gate-crashers will leave once that's over."

Bidding the porter goodbye, I started making my way back to the dining hall. As I approached the archway leading into the rear quad, however, I was dismayed to see that my way was now blocked by a huge crowd, all jostling to join the earlier people who had arrived first to form the queue.

I hesitated, then turned and walked past the archway, farther down the side of the quad, until I came to a thick wooden door in the quad's wall. I remembered Cassie showing me how this door led to a passage which ran alongside the back of the building, past the Master's residence, and through the cloister, coming out at the rear of the dining hall. In fact, we had used this route a few times in our student days. No, it would provide me with an alternative way to get to the dining hall without having to fight through the mob.

Hoping that things hadn't changed, and that they still kept the door unlocked, I reached up and grasped the heavy brass ring. To my delight, it turned easily; I pushed the door open and stepped through. Inside was a small antechamber, lit by an ancient brass lamp, with a wooden staircase spiralling upwards on one side and a dim corridor on the other. I hurried down the corridor, stepping through at the end into a small, private courtyard. This adjoined the Master's residence and was surrounded by a stone cloister—a covered arcade with ornately carved pillars and arched ceilings. A middle-aged woman dressed in a dark evening gown was just stepping out of the cloister into the courtyard. She looked startled to see me, although her voice, when she spoke, was calm and pleasant.

"Are you lost, my dear?"

I flushed slightly, knowing that I was probably trespassing. "Er... no, I was just... um... trying to get to the dining hall. I remembered that there was... er... an alternative route this way."

The woman gave me an understanding look. "Yes, the other end of this cloister comes out by the rear of the hall. But you're not really supposed to be in this part of the college, you know—these are private quarters," she added gently.

"Yes, I know... I'm sorry." Her kind manner made me feel even worse. "It's just... I'm trying to get back to my friend in the queue and I couldn't get through from the main quad—there was such a mob of people."

"Yes, I don't think my husband quite realised how popular Josh McDermitt would be," she said with a little laugh. "Well, if you don't tell the porters..." She gave me a conspiratorial smile, stepping aside to let me pass.

"Thanks!" I gave her a grateful look, then picked up my skirts and started through the cloister.

Like most of the college, the cloister was lit by ancient lamps nailed into the stone walls and they cast an eerie light over the flagstones as I hurried along. My years as a student at Oxford had got me used to the creepy Gothic atmosphere of many of the colleges at night. Still, I was pleased to reach the other end of the long arcade and step out into a better lit square.

Looking around, I was relieved to see that I was at the back of the building which contained the college kitchen and the dining hall. A rear service door was standing open and, farther around the corner of the building, I could see chests of food supplies and other kitchen equipment, together with the paraphernalia of a TV production team. There was a hive of activity as cameramen, sound technicians, and other members of the crew rushed around, doing last-minute checks.

Two people were just coming out of the rear service door and I stopped short as I saw Jerry Wallis and the harassed-looking woman with the clipboard again. *Bugger!* Why did I have to keep running into them? I ducked hurriedly behind a bush, hoping that they hadn't seen me. The belligerent manager would probably accuse me of coming to spy on set and try to steal more of Josh McDermitt's culinary secrets!

"...how long does he want in there?" the woman was asking anxiously. "Because the crew have to do final sound checks, you know."

"He needs ten minutes alone before a demo. That's always been his routine. He likes to test the equipment himself and check over the ingredients, and psyche himself up for the audience," replied

Wallis. "Look, the crowd won't mind waiting—let Josh do his thing. You want a good show, don't you?"

Their voices faded away as they turned the corner and disappeared around the side of the building, joining the rest of the crew. I stepped out of my hiding place and started to follow, then paused as I drew near the rear entrance again. I thought suddenly of Glenda. I'd probably never get a better chance to ask Josh for his autograph. If I waited until after the show, I might miss him if he left quickly. And anyway, from the look of the mob waiting outside the hall, I'd probably have to fight off a hundred other women to get close enough to him.

Making a decision, I stepped through the rear entrance and hurried down the short hallway. It ended in a T, splitting into two corridors that ran in opposite directions. I saw a dark-haired man at the end of the corridor on my right, hurriedly pushing through a swinging door, and I caught a glimpse of gleaming steel benchtops and steam billowing from open pots before the door swung shut again. *That must be the kitchen... which means that the other corridor must lead to the dining hall.* I turned and followed that, stepping at last through a heavy baize door and into the beautiful old hall, covered in dark wood panels, with vaulted ceilings and stained-glass windows lining the upper walls. It had been lit with candles, as well as the vintage lamps along the long, wooden tables, and looked incredibly atmospheric: the perfect setting for "Posh McDishy".

But where was he?

I scanned the hall, looking for Josh, but the place was empty. I began walking across the hall, past the long wooden tables where students sat, to the heavy oak table placed on a raised dais at the other end of the room. This was the "High Table", where the dons and other senior members of the college faculty sat, and for the show tonight, it had been transformed into a makeshift "kitchen bench". My heels made a strange echoing sound on the wooden floorboards as I approached the dais and I felt slightly uneasy. Outside, I could hear the hubbub from the waiting crowd, but in here it was eerily quiet, with nothing but the occasional hiss of a burning candle breaking the silence.

"Josh?" I called.

No answer.

I frowned. Perhaps he wasn't here? But where would he have gone? I knew he couldn't have gone out the front of the dining hall—the crowd would have gone wild—and he definitely hadn't come out the rear entrance, because I would have passed him. Besides, from what Wallis had said, it sounded like they had just left him. So where was he?

Slowly, I stepped up on the dais and approached the solid oak table. It looked perfectly set up for the cameras, with spices and dry ingredients in matching glass jars, and fresh fruit and vegetables attractively arranged in wicker baskets. I saw a pile of napkins at the edge of the table and helped myself to one, as I hadn't brought anything else for Josh to sign.

Not that I'm going to get any autograph if I can't find the man, I thought wryly. I turned and scanned the hall again in frustration. Where was he?

Turning back to the table, I circled around it to the other side—then froze, the napkin falling from my nerveless fingers.

Josh McDermitt lay in a crumpled heap on the floor.

I stared at him, my heart pounding. I don't know if it was the stillness of the body or the pallor of his skin... but I knew that he was dead.

CHAPTER SIX

"Would you like a cup of tea?"

I looked up from where I was huddled on the sofa, in the middle of the Master's living room, and smiled wanly at the middle-aged woman leaning over me. It was the kindly lady I had met in the cloister earlier. Now that I could see her in better light, I realised that she wasn't as old as I had first thought. Somewhere in her late forties, perhaps. It was the lines on her face that made her look older. The skin was drawn tight across her cheekbones, giving her a tired, gaunt appearance, and there were deep lines etched on either side of her mouth.

She smiled at me gently and said: "I'm Irene Mansell—the Master's wife. Henry told me that you're the one who found Josh."

I nodded. "It was just after I saw you... I went into the dining hall to ask him for an autograph and I... I found him behind High Table."

Her face turned grave. "It must have been an awful shock for you, seeing a dead body."

I swallowed. "Actually, it's not the first time I've seen a dead bo—but you're right, it was a horrible shock. I think it was more disturbing in a way because I knew him, you see. I guess it's always different when it's someone you know personally."

"Oh, I'm sorry—was Josh a friend of yours?"

"Not a friend exactly, but... well, I knew him when I was here at Oxford. I used to see him around the college."

She looked at me in surprise. "Were you at Boscobel? You don't look familiar... and I'm usually very good with faces. I think I can remember all the students who have matriculated during my husband's time as Master of the college."

"No, Boscobel wasn't my college—but my best friend Cassie was here and so I used to come over a lot to visit her."

"Cassie?"

"Cassandra Jenkins."

"Oh! Yes, of course—I remember her. She was one of the first students I met, I think. Henry just accepted the Master's position, and we'd moved into college earlier that summer. She was very artistic, from what I remember—she painted some fabulous pictures for the college charity auction."

She looked at me in sudden concern as she saw me shiver. "Are you warm enough? Would you like me to bring you a blanket?"

"I'm okay," I said, rubbing my bare arms. "It's just the reaction, I think."

"A hot cup of tea," said Irene firmly. "And I'll fetch you a shawl to put around your shoulders. Did the police say how long you have to wait here for them?"

I shook my head. "I don't think it's going to be much longer. They just had to secure the area to make sure that it was safe, especially with so many ball guests milling around."

"Yes, we certainly don't want another accident," said Irene. "It's frightening to think how dangerous everyday kitchen appliances can be. In fact, you were lucky you weren't electrocuted as well when you found Josh's body."

I gave a shudder. "The plug was yanked out of the socket when Josh collapsed. Otherwise, he would have still been 'live', as he was still holding the whisk, and I would have been electrocuted too when I touched him."

She gave me a pat on the shoulder. "Well, don't think about it anymore. It's a terrible tragedy but thank goodness no one else was hurt. I know my husband is very grateful to your boyfriend—having a police officer take charge of the situation really helps."

I gave a dry smile. "Yes, it was lucky that Devlin

could be on the scene so quickly. Although I don't think he expected to be back in his official capacity so soon."

"Official capacity? What do you mean? I know your boyfriend is a CID detective—surely there isn't any suspicion of foul play?"

"Oh no, no, I just meant that when we arrived at the ball, Devlin was talking about enjoying a night off duty—"

We were interrupted by Devlin himself stepping through the living room doorway and clearing his throat politely. Irene Mansell hurried to fetch me a mug of hot, sweet tea and a woollen shawl, then left us alone to talk.

"You all right, Gemma?" asked Devlin, coming to sit next to me and putting a solicitous arm around me. "I'm sorry I had to leave you, but the lads from Uniform had just arrived and I had to brief them on the situation."

I waved a hand. "Don't worry—I'm fine. It was a bit of a shock, that's all."

"Feel up to a few questions?"

"Yes, sure." I looked at him, surprised by his tone. "Why—is something the matter?"

Devlin didn't answer me directly. Instead, he moved to a seat opposite me, so that he could see my face more easily, and placed a folder on the coffee table between us. Gone was my sexy boyfriend, replaced instead by a shrewd investigator, coolly analytical and focused on the case.

"Did you see anyone in the area just before you found McDermitt's body?"

"N-no... I mean, I saw his manager Jerry Wallis and a lady—I think she might be a member of the crew? Short woman with brown hair and glasses. She was carrying a clipboard. They were coming out of the rear entrance of the building. But they weren't in the dining hall."

"Ah, yes... Madeleine Gill—Maddie—she's the producer for this reality-TV show that Josh is filming. So she and Wallis were together?"

"Yes. And based on what they were saying, they had just been with Josh. He was obviously fine when they left him."

"You didn't see anybody else?"

"No, I... oh, wait! I did see a man in the corridor leading to the kitchen."

Devlin's gaze sharpened. "A man? What did he look like?"

"I didn't see his face," I said apologetically. "He was just going into the kitchen so I only got a back view. I could see that he had dark hair and was about medium height, but that was it, really."

"So you didn't recognise him?"

"Well, I..." I hesitated. "He did remind me of someone... the way he moved..." I shook my head. "But I'm probably wrong."

"No, tell me," urged Devlin. "Sometimes these unconscious associations are more accurate than we think."

"Well... I thought he looked like a guy I saw in the casino marquee. Cassie said it was Antonio Casa—another celebrity chef. In fact... she told me that Antonio and Josh were rivals, and that there was a lot of bad blood between them."

"Really? Hmm..." Devlin made a note of this information.

I was about to ask him again what this was all about but he reached into the folder and pulled out a photograph printed onto a sheet of A4 paper. He handed it to me and asked: "Did you happen to see this woman anywhere in the college this evening?"

My eyes widened as I stared at the familiar face with the heavy make-up and dyed blonde hair. It was the woman Cassie and I had met at the nail salon, the woman I had heard arguing with Josh in his hotel room.

"No, I didn't see her at the ball... but Cassie and I saw her in town two days ago. She was in a nail salon just off St Michel's Street. She was a real stroppy cow. She lost her temper at her therapist—when it was actually her own fault—and we had to step in to protect the girl."

"Yes, apparently she's renowned for having a nasty temper."

"Who is she?"

"Her name is Leanne Fitch. She's Josh McDermitt's ex-girlfriend."

"Oh, I guessed as much! Based on what she said

to him—"

"What she said?"

"Oh, sorry, I forgot—I actually did see her earlier this evening. Well, I heard her, really. This was when I went up to Josh's room at the Randolph Hotel to try and get his autograph for Glenda. There was a huge row going on—I could hear it through the bedroom door."

Devlin looked at me with interest. "They were arguing? What about?"

"Leanne sounded very bitter: she accused Josh of dumping her as soon as he got famous, even though she had supported him through the early years." I gave a rueful smile. "That was why I didn't get Glenda's autograph. Leanne stormed out of the room and nearly knocked me over—and then I felt too embarrassed to go in and see Josh. He would probably have known that I'd been eavesdropping and I didn't think he'd be in the mood for signing autographs anyway."

"Hmm..." Devlin looked thoughtful.

"But... I don't understand. Why do you have her photograph? Why are you asking about her?"

"The photo is from the internet. Leanne's a small-time actress."

I frowned. "I still don't understand... Devlin, what's going on? Why are you asking me all these questions?"

"I'm opening an investigation into what happened this evening."

"An investigation? Why?"

"It looks like there may be suspicious circumstances surrounding Josh McDermitt's death."

"What do you mean 'suspicious circumstances'? Are you saying he wasn't electrocuted by accident?"

"Oh, he was electrocuted all right, but it was no accident," said Devlin grimly. "I checked the cord on that electric whisk: it had been purposefully tampered with, so that the live wires were exposed. There were also traces of a conductive gel smeared onto the handle, so that anyone who held it would be even more likely to get a shock. In other words... Josh McDermitt was murdered."

CHAPTER SEVEN

I was still reeling from Devlin's announcement the next morning, and when I arrived at the Little Stables, it was to find half the village's senior residents camped outside the tearoom, gossiping about Josh McDermitt's murder and hoping that I could provide them with more gory details. I shook my head in bewilderment. I thought little old ladies were supposed to be interested in gardening and baking and knitting and grandchildren... where did they get such an appetite for mayhem and murder? Then I saw the Old Biddies standing in the centre of the group and wondered why I was even surprised.

I entered the tearoom through the back door leading into the kitchen, where I found Dora already busy with rolling pin and dough. I smiled a good-morning at her, thinking again how lucky I had been to find her to take on the position of baker.

With her living in the village, only a few minutes' walk from the tearoom, it meant that I had a few extra hours in the morning to catch up on chores—or even some sleep!—whilst Dora came in early to start the day's baking. In return, she usually left once all the fresh baking had been done and she then enjoyed the rest of her afternoons off. Since Dora was an early riser—whereas I struggled to even string a coherent sentence together first thing in the morning—it was the perfect arrangement.

In fact, in the eight months since my tearoom first opened, a lot of things seemed to have evolved into the ideal scenario. Cassie's years of waitressing experience had been invaluable for a first-time café owner like me, and my offer of flexible hours meant that she could continue to paint on the side, teach her dance classes at the local studio, or follow any of the other creative pursuits she enjoyed. And when things had got busy and we needed an extra pair of hands, I'd been pleasantly surprised to find the Old Biddies eagerly stepping in. They loved to serve customers at the tearoom—it gave them the perfect excuse to gossip and ask nosy questions—whilst the tourists loved the image of white-haired old English ladies serving tea.

Since they refused to accept payment, I'd invited the Old Biddies to treat the tearoom as their own—which meant that the Little Stables often looked like Seniors' HQ in Meadowford, as they drank tea and nibbled shortbread biscuits with their friends at their favourite table by the window. It also meant, unfortunately, that now they ignored the "CLOSED" sign on the front door and followed me into the tearoom, cornering me in the kitchen and demanding to know exactly what had happened at the ball.

"I really don't have much more information than what was released by the police," I protested. "Yes, I found Josh's body, but I didn't even realise it was murder until Devlin told me that the electric whisk had been tampered with."

"Who would want to murder Josh McDermitt?" wailed Glenda.

I gave her a wry look. "Well, quite a few people, it seems. Actually, the police are focused on two suspects in particular."

"They didn't mention that on the news." Mabel pounced on me. "Who are they?"

I hesitated for a fraction of a second. If the police hadn't released this information to the public, then I wasn't sure I should have been sharing it either. But with the Old Biddies staring at me avidly, like starving dogs hoping for a bone, I didn't have the heart to deny them. "One of them is an old ex-girlfriend Josh had: Leanne Fitch. Apparently she'd been sending threatening letters to him, saying that she was going to 'get even' with him for abandoning her. Devlin found out about this from Maddie Gill, Josh's TV producer, who'd intercepted some of the letters." I glanced at Glenda. "I heard them fighting myself, actually, when I went up to Josh's room to get his autograph for you. Leanne was really laying into Josh, saying that he left her for another woman once he got famous—"

"Did she threaten to make him pay?" asked Cassie, entering the kitchen and catching the tail end of our conversation.

"She did actually say: 'you're going to be sorry'... or something like that."

"A jealous ex-lover!" exclaimed Ethel in her soft, breathless voice. "Ooh, just like in Agatha Christie's *Death on the Nile!*"

"But people say things like that all the time when they're angry. You don't expect them to mean it," I protested. "Besides, Leanne seems like the type to flip out over any small thing. You know, Cassie and I saw her in a nail salon in Oxford a couple of days ago, and she lost her temper and got really abusive over something silly—"

"Yes, and I told you she was planning to kill someone, remember?" said Cassie. "All those drugs and pills she had..."

"Except that Josh McDermitt didn't die from poisoning," I pointed out. "He was electrocuted."

"Well, maybe she changed her mind about how to do it," said Cassie. "Maybe she decided poisoning wouldn't be harsh enough and she wanted him fried instead."

I laughed. "You really have it in for her, don't you?"

Cassie scowled. "She was a total bitc—" She broke off, glancing at the Old Biddies, and hastily amended her words. "She was really unpleasant. I just wouldn't be surprised, especially with that temper. She looks just like the kind of person who could snap and kill someone in a murderous rage."

"Yes, but this murder seems premeditated, rather than a crime of passion," I pointed out.

"What about the other suspect, dear?" asked Florence. "You said the police were focused on two people."

"Oh, yes, a rival TV chef called Antonio Casa—"

"I know him," said Glenda, wrinkling her nose in disapproval. "Oh my goodness, someone needs to wash his mouth out with soap! He's got the most frightful temper. And he's always saying terrible things about Josh."

I raised my eyebrows. "Really? Cassie did tell me that there's some sort of a feud between the two chefs."

Glenda nodded earnestly. "Antonio claimed that Josh tried to sabotage his new restaurant on its opening night. He said that Josh made several fake bookings... as if Josh would ever do anything like that!" she said indignantly.

"Well, it would be a pretty clever prank," said Cassie. "I heard that lots of people didn't turn up, so Antonio's new restaurant was full of empty tables on the opening night and it was a huge embarrassment. It would have been the perfect way to sabotage him."

"But Josh completely denied it in his interview," protested Glenda.

"What interview?" I asked.

"There was a special feature about Josh on Breakfast TV last week," Glenda explained. "He looked ever so handsome. Such wonderful teeth," she sighed.

"Oh, yes, I saw that programme," Dora spoke up from the other end of the table, where she was rolling out dough for scones. "It was quite titillating. They were talking about his rise to fame and all the secrets and scandals—"

"Maybe he revealed something in his interview that got him killed," said Cassie jokingly. "Some deep, dark secret that somebody else wanted to keep hidden."

"No, no, I'm sure it was Antonio Casa who killed him out of jealousy and revenge," insisted Glenda. "He has always hated Josh because the latter is younger and more handsome and charming—and much more popular on TV."

"Yes, everybody wants Josh instead on *Superchef*," Florence agreed with a nod.

"Aha!" said Mabel, her eyes gleaming. "That gives Antonio Casa a perfect motive for murder. Not only would he be getting revenge, but he would also be removing a rival—and with Josh gone, they might consider taking him back on the show." She rubbed her hands together. "Yes, it all fits!"

"The only thing is, Antonio would have to have been at the ball to fiddle with the electric whisk," Ethel reminded us in her soft voice.

"Oh, he *was* at the ball!" exclaimed Cassie. "Gemma and I saw him—didn't we?" She elbowed me. "He walked past us when we were in the casino marquee. We were wondering what he was doing at the ball."

"Actually, I saw him again later—at least, I think I did." Quickly, I described the man I saw entering the kitchen at Boscobel College. "It was a back view, though, and it was dim in the corridor, so I can't be sure. But... well, the man really did remind me of Antonio Casa, especially because I just saw him earlier, from a similar back view..."

Glenda gasped. "It must have been him! He must have just been in the dining hall, tampering with the wires, and was just making his escape when you saw him! Oh, he needs to be reported—"

"Don't worry, I've told Devlin all of this and the police are investigating."

"Humph! The police!" Mabel waved a dismissive hand. "What would they know? A case like this requires professionals."

I gave her an exasperated look. "Er... that's what the police are."

"*Real* professionals." Mabel glowered at me. "Individuals like Glenda and Florence and Ethel and myself, who have spent a lifetime studying the art of murder—"

"In novels," I muttered.

"—and who possess a keen instinct for crime. Coupled, of course, with the wisdom of age and experience." She smiled complacently and clasped her hands in front of her.

"Er..." I was just wondering how to answer when the kitchen door opened and my mother sailed inside. She was perfectly groomed as usual, in a cream linen dress and matching shoes, not a hair out of place in her elegant coiffure. And, also as usual, she instantly made me feel unkempt and slovenly in my old cotton blouse and faded jeans.

"Darling! What is that *dreadful* thing you're wearing? I hope you're not planning to wear that to the cookery workshop tonight. Remember, one has only a few seconds to make an impression, and first impressions are *so* very important."

"What?" I stared at her in confusion.

"Don't say 'what', darling—say 'pardon'."

I gritted my teeth. "Pardon, Mother? I don't know what you're talking about."

"The Josh McDermitt cookery workshop, darling! It's on tonight, at the Oxford University Fine Dining Society—we were lucky that your father's position on the board meant that we were eligible for tickets. Oh, Dorothy Clarke will be coming too, although she did say she might be late because she has to stop in Marks & Spencer's to pick up a new mesh laundry bag—would you like one, darling? They've got them in three sizes... or you can get a set of four... oh, and there's a padded version for your silk and lace undies, as well as a specially domed one for your bras, up to size GG, I think—or was it DD?"

I blinked, my head swimming at the sudden onslaught of laundry bag options.

"Of course, one really ought to hand-wash the delicates," my mother continued, undeterred by my stupefied silence. "That is the *proper* way to do them, but I have to admit, it's very convenient when one is strapped for time to just pop them in a mesh bag and drop them in the washing machine... although, of course, still washed separately on a 'delicate' cycle—"

"Mother," I interrupted her desperately. "Thanks, but I don't need a mesh laundry bag. I'm fine—"

"But you do wash your bras and knickers separately, Gemma?" My mother looked at me severely.

I thought guiltily of the haphazard bundle of dirty clothes—whites, colours, underwear and all— that I had piled into the washing machine that morning.

"Er... yes, of course... Look, anyway, you were telling me about this cookery workshop—I don't understand, Mother, I thought you said you wanted me to keep tonight free for a dinner at home with Dad?"

"Ah, well, it was to be a surprise!" said my mother, beaming. "I thought it would be a marvellous opportunity to learn from a master chef—especially for you, Gemma." Her face changed to a frown. "Since you refused to attend the Cordon Bleu cooking course I wanted to send you on after school, your culinary skills must be very sadly lacking."

I sighed. My mother never let me forget that. "I manage okay, Mother—I'm just not very interested in cooking and it seems silly to spend the money—"

"Really, darling! How can you expect any man to want you as his wife when you can't even cook a proper three-course meal?"

"Well, nowadays men marry women for things other than their skill in the kitchen," I retorted. "Anyway, I don't understand—how can you still go to a Josh McDermitt workshop when he's dead?"

"Oh, isn't that an awful tragedy, darling? Well, I rang up the Society secretary this morning when I heard the news and they've asked Antonio Casa to fill in for him," my mother explained. "The tickets were quite pricey and the Society didn't want to have to refund everyone, so they thought this would be a good way to salvage the workshop. And what a lucky coincidence that Antonio Casa should happen to be in Oxford too."

"Yeah, very lucky coincidence," I said dryly.

"Are there any tickets left?" Mabel spoke up.

"Well, they were all sold out initially, but since the news of Josh McDermitt's death, several people have cancelled and asked for a refund—so there are some spaces now. And I've heard that they've marked them down to half price." My mother fished in her handbag for her phone. "I can give the Society secretary a ring, if you like, and see if there are any available?"

"That would be lovely, dear—we would like four tickets," said Mabel.

I gave her a suspicious look. "You're coming to the cookery workshop?"

"I think it's a good time to brush up on our cooking skills," said Mabel airily, fluffing her white hair.

"You mean your snooping skills," I said in an accusing tone. "You're just coming because you heard that Antonio Casa will be there. What are you planning to do? You know you shouldn't meddle in a murder investigation."

"We do not 'meddle'," said Mabel indignantly, making it sound like some kind of sexual perversion. "And you would think that the police would be grateful for our efforts. After all, with our special talents in the mystery department, we're bound to notice something that the police wouldn't think of."

I gave up. When Mabel set her mind like this, it was impossible to argue with her. Anyway, since I'd be at the workshop too, I would hopefully be able to keep an eye on the Old Biddies and make sure they didn't get into any trouble. Still, as I left the kitchen to go out and open the tearoom, I couldn't help thinking of the phrase: *"Famous last words..."*

CHAPTER EIGHT

"Oh, I don't believe it..." muttered Cassie, her eyes fixed on the other side of the tearoom.

"What?" I followed her gaze and saw an elderly lady sitting alone at a table, with a pot of tea and a slice of Victoria sponge cake, bulging with strawberries and fresh whipped cream, in front of her. This wasn't so unexpected; what was unexpected was the sight of the little grey tabby cat sitting on the chair next to her, reaching out every few moments to dip a paw in the whipped cream and lick it clean with smug satisfaction.

I rushed across and glared at my cat. "Muesli! What on earth are you doing?"

I bent to pick her up but the old lady—who turned out to be Mrs Purdey—put out a hand to stop me.

"Oh no! Let her have it," she pleaded. "She's really enjoying that. Just like my Smudge! He loved whipped cream, and whenever I did any baking, I always gave him some as a special treat—"

"Mrs Purdey, you can't let Muesli eat from your plate like that. It's... it's not hygienic."

"I don't mind," she said, giving me a bright smile. "I ordered the cake especially for her."

"Yes, but... Muesli can't eat from the table like that. I'd lose my Food Hygiene Certificate."

I bent again to pick up Muesli but Mrs Purdey grabbed her and pulled her close. "Oh, let her stay with me. I won't let her eat from my plate anymore—I promise."

I hesitated, looking down at my little tabby cat, who had her eyes half-closed with pleasure as the old lady scratched her chin. "All right. But please try to keep her off the table."

As I left them, I could hear Mrs Purdey cooing: "Never mind, I'll bring a tin of sardines for you next time! Smudge used to love sardines—they were his favourite, although he liked tuna as well. And he always enjoyed a bit of smoked salmon on Sundays..."

"If anyone was going to get top prize as 'Crazy Cat Lady', Mrs Purdey would be it," said Cassie as I re-joined her at the counter.

I sighed and looked back across the tearoom to where the old lady was still cuddling Muesli in her lap.

"I do feel sorry for her, though. She lives alone and she's just lost her old cat; I think she misses him terribly. Anyway, listen..." I glanced at my watch. "Can you hold the fort for a bit? I need to pop back to Oxford to drop off a catering order."

"Sure. The lunchtime rush is over and things will be quiet now until tea-time."

Half an hour later, as I was coming out of the faculty building where I had dropped off an order of finger sandwiches and scones, I spied the tall steeple of Boscobel College chapel in the distance. It made me remember that I'd never picked up the stuffed toy animals from the Porter's Lodge. In all the excitement following the discovery of Josh McDermitt's body, I had completely forgotten. For a moment, I was tempted to leave them, but I felt a bit guilty about dumping the toys in the Porter's Lodge. It seemed very rude and inconsiderate. Besides, if Cassie and I didn't want to keep them, I could donate them to the local children's hospital.

I looked at my watch again. There was easily an hour still before things would get busy at the tearoom—I had plenty of time to walk across to Boscobel and retrieve the toys. Okay, so part of me might have been hoping to meet that friendly porter again and maybe get some gossip on Josh McDermitt's murder—but hey, that was natural. Anyone in my situation would have been interested to get more news, especially since I'd discovered the body. *This is nothing like the Old Biddies' snooping*, I told myself firmly. *Not at all.*

When I entered Boscobel College, instead of heading straight into the Porter's Lodge, I paused in the main quad and surveyed the college grounds, marvelling at how different they looked in the broad light of day. Then, on an impulse, I began walking across the main quad, towards the archway that led to the college dining hall. I don't know what it was— maybe a sense of morbid curiosity—but I felt an urge to see the scene of the crime again. When I reached the rear quad, though, I was disappointed to find that the hall had been closed off to visitors. There was crime scene tape across the huge wooden door, and a sign advising all students that meals were now being served in the Junior Common Room.

Turning away, I hesitated before following the path beside the building. It took me to the rear of the quad, curving around the back of the dining hall—past where the TV crew and their equipment had been stationed last night—to the rear entrance where I had gone in to look for Josh. This was now also firmly locked. Beyond it, the path widened into a little square. On one side was the entrance to the cloister—I certainly didn't want to go that way; it would have been embarrassing if Irene Mansell, the Master's wife, caught me trespassing again—and the other side of the square opened out into a small garden.

I wandered into this, drawn by the sight of dozens of butterflies flitting amongst the shrubbery. Like all Oxford colleges, Boscobel had a full-time gardener, and boasted manicured lawns and beautifully tended flowerbeds. This rear section of the college, however, adjoined a wild meadow, and the back of this garden had been left to a more natural look, with a hedge of prickly holly bushes that encircled the garden mingling with the natural shrubs and grasses.

Thinking of my recent encounters with an adorable little hedgehog named Pricklebum, I was pleased that there wasn't a solid wall surrounding this garden. It meant that wildlife could pass in and out easily while looking for food. In fact, it sounded like something was busily foraging at the moment, as I heard a loud rustling coming from the bushes on my right. Curious, I went towards the sound, then jerked to a stop as I saw a flash of grey tabby fur.

Wait... is that...? I rubbed my eyes, sure that I was seeing things. *Muesli can't be here in the middle of Boscobel College!* And yet I was sure I had caught a glimpse of grey tabby fur and a white chest and paws. I had even seen a pair of big green eyes, encircled by exotic black "eyeliner".

"Muesli?" I called, feeling a bit stupid.

There was a moment's silence, then there came a deep "*Miaowww...*"

I crept closer and crouched down, peering

through the undergrowth. There was another rustle, and then suddenly a cat stepped out of the bushes and stared at me. I caught my breath. For a moment, I thought it *was* Muesli—then I realised that this cat was much larger. A tomcat, in fact. He had exactly the same markings as my cat, except for her pink nose—his was dark brown instead—and upon closer inspection, I could see that he was a bit of a battle veteran, with a ragged ear and scars across his face.

"Hullo! What's your name?" I asked softly.

He eyed me with suspicion, then gave another imperious "*Miaowww...*"

"You're a very handsome boy," I said, putting out a hand towards him. "Though you're a bit thin, aren't you? I bet you'd love a nice meal of chicken and tuna—that's one of Muesli's favourite combos." Then I caught myself as I realised what I'd just said. *Sheesh, I'm beginning to sound like Mrs Purdey*, I thought with a rueful smile. I was turning into a Crazy Cat Lady myself!

I was rewarded, however, by the tomcat walking slowly up to me and stretching his neck out for a careful sniff. I held very still as he came even closer, until he was almost touching me. He sniffed my shoes, then my ankles, working his way up to my knees, then turned and rubbed himself against my legs. Slowly, I put out a cautious hand and touched him lightly on the head. He stiffened but didn't pull away. I began to pat him very gently, stroking the fur between his ears, then moving my hand down to rub the side of his jaw. To my surprise and delight, I heard a low rumbling emanating from him... he was purring!

"You're a bit of a charming rogue, aren't you?" I said with a laugh, as he butted his head against me when I stopped the chin-scratching. I reached out again but a noise behind us made the cat suddenly jerk away from me, his fur standing on end. He hissed and spat, then turned and darted into the undergrowth. In a flash, he was gone from sight. I turned around to find Irene Mansell, the Master's wife, standing behind me with a look of disbelief.

"Were you stroking the cat?" she asked.

"Yes..." I straightened, feeling slightly embarrassed and hoping that she hadn't heard me talking to him too. "Does he belong to the college?"

"Heavens, no!" she laughed. "He's a feral cat—he lives in the meadow behind the property, I think, although he often comes into the college grounds." She made a face. "He causes no end of trouble, digging in the flowerbeds and scavenging food around the kitchen. He's even attacked a couple of the students—although to be fair, I think they were teasing him... Still, we just can't allow it, especially in this day and age, with the risks of litigation and all that... If a student were to get a scratch which developed into a bad infection, the college would be liable."

"Have you tried to catch him?"

"Yes, but he's extremely wily and has avoided all the traps so far. And he won't let anyone near him—he can get quite vicious, you know. It's why I was so surprised to see you stroking him just now. You're the first person I've seen who's been able to approach him, let alone touch him." She gave me an admiring smile. "You must be quite a cat wrangler."

"Actually..." I gave a sheepish laugh. "I've always been more of a dog person. But I do have a cat of my own. She was a... er... an unexpected adoption, and I have to admit: since I got her, I've developed an appreciation for cats. They're quite fascinating creatures."

"I'll take your word for it. I've never really cared for them much—and Henry positively hates them. He doesn't like dogs either, or any animal, really."

"Oh? That must have been hard when your kids pestered you for a family pet," I said with a chuckle.

A shadow crossed her face. "We don't have any children."

"Oh." An awkward silence fell between us. I felt like kicking myself for not thinking before I opened my mouth. "Um... so if you can't trap the cat, what else can you do?"

"Henry has been talking about calling in a pest control company to remove it. The college gardener is all for it too—he's furious at the cat ruining all his flowerbeds and digging up his seedlings."

I gave her a wary look. "How would the pest control company deal with the cat?"

"Well..." She shifted uncomfortably. "I suppose if they can't catch it, they would have to shoot it."

"*Shoot it?*" I stared at her, aghast.

"They're trained, licensed operatives—it would be a humane killing," she said quickly.

"Yes, but still..." I swallowed, my horror warring with my social instinct to be polite. I knew it was really none of my business how the college managed their property.

"I hope you've recovered from last night?" asked Irene Mansell, changing the subject.

"Oh... yeah. I mean, it's still a horrible memory but the shock is wearing off. I actually came by today because I felt the need to see the dining hall again... maybe I'm trying to lay the ghosts..." I gave an embarrassed laugh.

"That's understandable. I'm afraid no one is allowed in the dining hall, though."

"Yes, I saw the sign and the crime scene tape... That must make it very inconvenient for the college, with all the student meals?"

"Well, actually, most of the students have gone home now. The ball officially marked the end of term. There are always a few that stay on in the holidays, of course, but they can easily be accommodated in the J.C.R." She paused, then looked at me curiously. "I understand that the police are treating Josh's death as suspicious now? Has your boyfriend told you anything? My husband is very worried about the impact of a prolonged investigation on the college."

I gave her an apologetic smile. "I probably don't know very much more than you do, Mrs Mansell. Yes, it appears that Josh McDermitt was murdered—the electric whisk had been purposefully tampered with. And I know the police have a few suspects... but I don't think they'll be making any arrests quickly."

She sighed. "Well, at least it's the end of term. I suppose we ought to be thankful for small mercies. The college will be quiet now with the summer holidays, and hopefully the investigation will be wrapped up before the start of the new year. And naturally, we all want to find Josh's killer," she hastened to add. She gave me a small smile. "I didn't mean to sound heartless, focusing on the college instead of on Josh. I suppose one leads such a sheltered life in an Oxford college, with such peaceful routines and simple academic pursuits— somehow, you resent any kind of interruption or invasion in your world. You just want everything to go back to the way it was."

"I can understand that," I assured her.

And as I walked slowly back through the college to the Porter's Lodge, I could see exactly what Irene Mansell meant. There was a good reason why people often referred to Oxford's "dreaming spires": there *was* an otherworldly feeling when you walked around an Oxford college, through the majestic quadrangles and ancient cloisters, overlooked by the soaring towers and carved stone gargoyles... it was like being somewhere frozen in time and removed from the real world, a place found within the pages of a fairy tale or a beautiful historical novel...

Perhaps it was why coming across a murder seemed even more shocking and unbelievable, like a black spot on a dreamy, pastel landscape. When I arrived in the Porter's Lodge, I found the same porter I'd met on duty and he seemed to be struggling with the same sense of unreality as well.

"Jus' can't believe it... jus' can't believe it..." he kept saying, shaking his head. "Was only talkin' to Mr McDermitt a few hours earlier. Seemed like a really nice chap. The missus loves him, you know. Always watches him on telly. Can't believe that I was jus' sittin' here and he was bein' murdered on the other side of the college!"

"Have the police said anything to you?" I asked.

He shrugged. "They've been goin' around questionin' everyone, of course. Askin' if me and Rodney—that's the other porter—if we saw any suspicious strangers last night. How are we supposed to answer that, I tell you? It was the bloomin' college ball... place was full o' strangers! And that's not countin' all the gate-crashers... we're college porters, not professional security men. We try to keep the college safe, of course, but we can't really keep out criminals from the streets."

"I don't think it was a random killing by some

street thug anyway," I said. "It sounds like it was a carefully planned murder."

The porter shuddered. "Yes, he was electrocuted, I heard. Who would do that? Must be sick in the mind! I tell you, the press are lovin' it, though. Have been kickin' reporters out of the college all morning! And I heard there's been all sorts of rumours goin' around... It's the students, you know, always puttin' stuff online on that Facebook place. I saw a bunch o' them outside the dinin' hall this morning, takin' pictures o' themselves with it... Ghoulish, if you ask me... Poor Prof Mansell—I wouldn't want to be Master o' Bocobel now, I can tell you—he must have his hands full dealin' with the media... and this always bein' a bad time o' year for Mrs Mansell... It's the anniversary o' when they lost their baby," he explained at my blank look.

"Oh..." I winced as I thought of my tactless remark to Irene Mansell. "I didn't know..."

He shrugged. "Well, you wouldn't, would you? And it's a while back now, of course, but I suppose you never get over these things... Still, maybe this murder will be a blessin' in disguise, help take her mind off things... not that you'd want such a reason, of course... Terrible business... terrible business..." He shook his head again. "In all my years at the college... never seen anythin' like this. And that young Mr McDermitt was such a nice chap too! Did I tell you my wife loves him? Never misses him when he comes on the telly."

"Uh... yes, you did," I said with a smile. "I have an elderly friend who loves him too and she's devastated. She'd been hoping that I could get his autograph at the ball."

"The missus wanted me to ask too. I'd been plannin' to catch Mr McDermitt on his way out last night..." He sighed and got up to retrieve the stuffed toys from the rear of the porter's office. "Here you go..."

I eyed the large, unwieldy toys with reluctance. "I don't suppose you know of anywhere I could donate these to? My friend and I won these at the ball last night but we don't really need them."

"The children's hospital would probably be glad to have them. My wife volunteers there. I can take them home and get her to take them to the hospital, if you like."

"Oh, that would great! Thank you—if you don't mind doing that."

"Don't mind at all." The porter gave me a sad smile. "It would be nice if something good came out of last night after all."

CHAPTER NINE

The encounter with the feral cat followed by the chat with Boscobel's porter had delayed me and, by the time I got back to the tearoom, the afternoon rush was over and it was almost closing time.

"Sorry, Cass!" I gasped as I rushed in. "I didn't mean to be so long but I got held up at Boscobel—" I broke off as I saw her face. "Is something wrong?"

"I can't find Muesli!" she said. "I've looked everywhere for her—under the tables, in the kitchen, in the shop, outside in the courtyard, even out on the street... she's just disappeared!"

My heart gave a lurch. Exasperating as she was, I loved my little cat and couldn't bear the thought of losing her.

"Are you sure you looked in all the potential

hiding places? You know how naughty she can be sometimes... Remember that time she climbed into the wall cavity at my parent's place and I had to call the fire brigade to cut holes in the walls?"

"I tell you, Gemma—I've looked everywhere."

"Come on, I'll help you look again."

But twenty minutes later, after we had scoured every nook and cranny around the tearoom, looking and calling for the little cat, I had to admit defeat.

"Do you think she could have wandered off into the village?" asked Cassie. "I mean, she's never done it before—but I suppose there's nothing stopping her from slipping out the front door and walking down the high street... in which case, she could be anywhere!"

I snapped my fingers. "No, not 'anywhere'... I think I know where she might be."

I checked the dining room. There were still two tables with customers, but the table I was interested in—the one in the far corner where an elderly lady had been sitting previously, feeding whipped cream to my cat—was empty.

"I'll be right back," I said to Cassie.

I stepped onto the street and turned right, following the pavement down the road for a few yards, then turned right again and walked down a cobbled lane which led to a row of cottages situated behind the tearoom. The first cottage in the row belonged to Mrs Purdey. I made my way to the door and rang the bell, hoping that my hunch was right.

I had my answer a few minutes later when Mrs Purdey opened the door, looking like a guilty child who had been caught with her hand in the sweets jar.

"Mrs Purdey... is Muesli here with you?"

For a moment, I thought she was going to deny it, then she sighed and held the door open. "I was going to bring her back to the tearoom tomorrow! I just thought she would like staying with me for a night. I've even made some beef rissoles. They were always Smudge's favourite."

I followed her into the house—a tiny little cottage filled with floral upholstery and dark wood furniture, and crotcheted white lace on every available surface (no doubt Mrs Purdey was one of those who had contributed to the lace doily makeover of my tearoom). We found Muesli sitting on the sofa in the living room. She had an enormous pink bow tied around her neck and seemed to be wearing some kind of strange woolly garment.

"I thought she might be cold, you see," Mrs Purdey explained. "I knit these baby jumpers to donate to International Aid Trust and I thought they would fit her perfectly. Doesn't she look adorable?"

"Adorable" wasn't quite the word. "Incredibly grumpy" was more like it. Muesli gave me a long-suffering look and let out a loud "*Meeeeeeorrw!*" which plainly said: *"What took you so long?"* Then she hopped off the sofa and trotted towards me.

Or *tried* to trot towards me, rather, as the woolly jumper hampered her movements, making her hobble and hump along like a three-legged toad.

"Oh dear..." said Mrs Purdey, hurrying to pick her up. "Well, perhaps the jumper is a wee bit small..."

Five minutes later, Muesli was naked again and looking more cheerful as she sat on my lap while I sipped a cup of tea. I hadn't really wanted to accept Mrs Purdey's invitation but the elderly lady was obviously so lonely and desperate for company that I didn't have the heart to say no. So I sat and listened while she told me about Smudge's favourite toys and Smudge's naughty antics, Smudge's sleeping positions and Smudge's missing teeth... When we got onto Smudge's bowel habits, however, I hastily decided to change the subject.

"Do you watch *Superchef?*" I asked, spying a copy of the latest TV guide, which sported a picture of Antonio Casa on the cover. He was obviously trying his best to look the heartthrob, standing with his arms folded and one eyebrow raised as he attempted to smoulder into the camera. Somehow, though, all he managed to do was look slightly constipated.

"Oh yes!" cried Mrs Purdey. "I never miss a show. I'm quite upset, really, that they're replacing Antonio with someone else."

"Really?" I looked at her in surprise. I guess the swarthy, bad-tempered chef did have some fans after all. "Do you like him? I got the impression that he wasn't very popular."

"Oh, well... I suppose he's a bit prickly on the outside, and he does have an awful temper sometimes. The language he uses would make you blush! But he doesn't mean any harm, you know—it's all just hot air. I'm sure that underneath it all, he's a total lamb."

"Er... right," I said, thinking that Mrs Purdey obviously watched *Superchef* with rose-tinted binoculars.

"And I do think it's admirable the way he's come up from nothing like that. He didn't start out as a chef, you know—he came from a poor immigrant family and he didn't go to any cooking schools or get any formal culinary training. He was working a day job while he taught himself to cook at night; he was an apprentice electrician, in fact."

I sat up straight. "He was an electrician?"

Mrs Purdey nodded. "He said once in an interview that it still comes really handy as he can always fix any broken kitchen gadgets or appliances easily."

Or tamper with them easily, I thought, wondering if Devlin knew about Antonio Casa's previous job. I was sure the police would have run a complete background check on the rival chef—still, I would make sure that I mentioned it to Devlin the next time I saw him.

Thoughts of Devlin reminded me of the Old

Biddies' interest in Josh McDermitt's murder and I hoped they wouldn't do anything too outrageous. Devlin generally suffered their meddling with weary resignation and I knew that he had let them off several times in the past, but I had a feeling that his patience was wearing thin and the last thing I wanted was for the Old Biddies to get in trouble with the police. If I could just keep them out of trouble tonight...

Tonight... I gasped as I suddenly remembered the cookery workshop and glanced at my watch. *Yikes!*

"I'm sorry, Mrs Purdey, I've got to go!" I cried, springing up with Muesli in my arms.

Before she could react, I bid her a hasty goodbye, rushed Muesli out of the house and back to the tearoom, where I bundled her into her carrier, and then jumped on my bike and pedalled furiously back to Oxford. By the time I dropped off (a very windswept) Muesli at my cottage, wriggled into a change of clothing, and raced to the local cooking school where the workshop was to be held, I was more than a little late. I tiptoed into the large converted barn, bracing myself as I joined my mother at the workbench. In Evelyn Rose's book, Being Late was one of the seven deadly sins.

"Gemma!" my mother hissed, glowering at me. "Where have you been?"

"Sorry, Mother, sorry!" I said breathlessly. "I... er... had to sort out something at the tearoom. Anyway," I looked around brightly, "what did I miss?"

"Just the introduction, dear," said Mabel from the adjoining bench, where she and the other Old Biddies were looking slightly ridiculous, each wearing a large white chef's hat. I turned around and realised belatedly that my mother was also wearing an enormous chef's hat and, before I could react, she reached out and plonked a similar hat on my head.

"I'm not wearing this—I'll look ridiculous!" I cried, trying to yank it off. I could see a few other workshop attendees glancing over their shoulders and sniggering.

"Oh, nonsense, darling—I think you look marvellous," my mother said, slapping my hand away. "Oh, and remind me later to give you the mesh laundry bags I picked up this afternoon. I bought two for Devlin too, in different sizes, and I can also get the padded one if you think you might like that..."

"*Ahem!* IF YOU WILL PAY ATTENTION PLEASE..."

I glanced to the front of the classroom where Antonio Casa stood behind a display bench, holding a spatula in one hand and a bowl in the other. He was wearing a pristine white chef's double-breasted jacket and a *toque blanche*—the traditional chef's hat—and from the scowl on his face, he was not pleased with the turnout that evening. It *was* a bit embarrassing, I thought, glancing around the room.

Over half the workbenches were empty. It seemed that "cooking with Antonio Casa" just wasn't as big a draw as an evening with Josh McDermitt.

Still, once the teaching began, everyone seemed to give the swarthy chef their full attention... well, everyone except the Old Biddies, that is. I looked up from trying to create a "Hand-Made Linguine with Seared Tuna, Fresh Pesto, and Green Olives" to find the bench next to mine empty.

Huh? Where are they?

I straightened and scanned the kitchen classroom. Heads were bent over workbenches all around me and Antonio Casa himself was standing next to one of the attendees—a young Asian guy— passionately discussing the merits of pasta versus noodles. The Old Biddies, though, were nowhere to be seen.

No, wait...

I squinted across the room. Four white chef's hats bobbed into view. They wobbled along behind an open shelving unit stacked with sun-dried tomatoes, pesto sauce, and tinned olives, disappeared from sight, then reappeared again next to an industrial-size refrigerator, where they congregated in a huddle.

What are those nosy old coots doing? I wondered in annoyance. Then I caught myself. *Perhaps I should give them the benefit of the doubt. Perhaps they're simply retrieving some ingredients from the shelves or looking for fresh supplies in that giant fridge...*

The next moment, I saw a door behind the fridge open furtively and four white chef's hats whisk inside, then the door shut quickly again.

Uh-oh. I had a bad feeling about this. I put my wooden spatula down and was about to head across the classroom when a voice spoke next to me:

"And where are the four little old ladies?"

CHAPTER TEN

I spun around to see Antonio Casa looking quizzically at the empty bench next to us. My mother straightened from her pan of simmering pasta and looked across in surprise.

"Oh! How strange! Mabel and the others were here a moment ago. Perhaps we ought to go look for—"

"More herbs to put in our linguine!" I gabbled. "I think it needs more basil and... um... mint... and chives... and... er... nutmeg—"

"Chives? Nutmeg? What rubbish are you talking about?" Antonio scowled at me. "You must follow my recipe! The one I have created, with my superior skill and expertise—you do not add random herbs to my masterpiece!"

"Oh no, we have followed your instructions to the letter, Mr Casa," my mother assured him, proudly showing him the pot of bubbling sauce.

He leaned over the pot and sniffed critically. "Hmm... good, good..." Straightening, he glanced over at the Old Biddies' empty bench again and frowned. "But the old ladies—"

"Uh... they've probably gone to the bathroom," I said quickly.

"All of them?"

"Yes, er... well, they like to keep each other company..."

He stared at their bench where a half-chopped tomato lay on the cutting board and a pan of pasta simmered in a sludge of cloudy water, and said, "But they have left their pasta boiling—it is turning to mush!"

He switched off the cooker and removed the pan from the heat, then looked angrily around.

"Where are they, these old ladies? I must speak to them! A good cook never leaves his pots unattended. They are being disrespectful in my kitchen and I will not allow that." He started towards the other side of the classroom. "I will go look for them—"

"Ahh—Antonio!" I cried, jumping in front of him and blocking his path. "Er... um... I just wanted to tell you how much I... er... admire you."

He stopped in surprise, then a smug look crossed his face. He gave me a slow smile and raised an eyebrow in a suggestive way.

"I mean... admire your career!" I amended hastily. "The way you... um... rose up from such humble beginnings and... um... your dedication in—"

"But you admire me as a man too, don't you?" he said, coming closer. "It's okay, you can admit it. I know the effect I have on women."

I blinked. *Did I hear him right?*

Antonio Casa grinned at me and said in a sexy growl, "I'm not the kind of man to boast, but you know, there's a reason I'm known as the 'Italian Stallion' of British cooking... and it isn't because of the size of my... ladle." He waggled his eyebrows.

Ugh. I didn't know whether to recoil or laugh. He leaned towards me and I hastily backed away.

"Um... you know what? I think someone had better go look for the old ladies after all... I'll... er... I'll just check the bathroom."

I bolted across the room. When I was safely behind the open shelving unit with the dry ingredients and supplies, I paused and glanced over my shoulder. To my relief, Antonio Casa had been distracted by another workshop attendee and was now busily arguing with a middle-aged woman whose linguine had turned a strange shade of green. I breathed a sigh of relief and then, instead of turning towards the toilets, I headed for the door behind the big industrial fridge. Throwing another glance over my shoulder to make sure that Antonio wasn't watching, I turned the doorknob, opened the door, and slipped inside.

It was some kind of office, I realised—probably for the cooking school staff. There were two large desks and an assortment of computers, printers, and filing cabinets, as well as a shabby old sofa in the far corner. It was by this that the Old Biddies were standing. They had been bending over something on the sofa but jumped guiltily as I stepped into the room. They whirled around, their expressions defensive.

"Mabel! Florence! Glenda! Ethel! What are you doing?" I hissed, rushing over to them. "Do you know what I've had to go through to stop Antonio Casa coming to look for you? And you left all your cooking—"

I broke off as I saw what they had been bending over. A small overnight case was lying open on the sofa, the contents rumpled and pushed aside, as if someone had been hastily searching for something.

I drew a sharp breath. "What are you doing?" I asked again. "Whose case is that?"

"It's Antonio Casa's," said Mabel with a triumphant note in her voice. "His name is on the label... and look what we found inside!"

She held up a small plastic bottle. I stared at it uncomprehendingly.

"It's conductive gel, dear," she explained. "The kind that helps to transmit electrical activity across surfaces."

Glenda caught my arm, her eyes sparkling with excitement. "It's proof that Antonio Casa is the murderer!"

I reached out and took the bottle from Mabel, frowning as I turned it around to read the label on the back: "*Hypoallergenic, salt-free and chloride-free conductive gel, ideal for making good electrical contact. Particularly suitable for long-term applications.*"

I looked back up to see the Old Biddies watching me, their expressions expectant.

"This isn't really proof that Antonio Casa is the murderer," I protested.

"Of course, it's proof!" said Mabel. "It shows that he tampered with the electric whisk that killed Josh McDermitt. Why else would anyone carry conductive gel in their case?"

I had to admit, she had a point. And coupled with what I had just found out at Mrs Purdey's place—about Antonio Casa's electrician background—it did look very suspicious.

"We've got to tell the police!" cried Glenda. "You must call your young man, Gemma, and tell him that we found conductive gel in Antonio Casa's bag—"

"Whoa...!" I said, holding my hands up. "I can't tell Devlin about this!"

"Why not?"

"Because... because he'll be furious, that's why! Do you realise you've just illegally searched another person's private belongings? Even the police would have to get a search warrant if they wanted to go through Antonio's things. Devlin will do his nut if he finds out that you've been meddling in the investigation again."

"We're *helping* the investigation," said Mabel tartly. "This is a vital piece of evidence that—"

She broke off as we heard a footstep outside the door. Ethel squeaked and Glenda clutched Florence's arm. I shoved the bottle back into the case and tried to pull other things over it to cover it. I was still madly piling clothes on top of the bottle when the door opened and Antonio Casa entered the room. I jerked back from the case, trying my best to look nonchalant.

"What are you doing?" he demanded, coming towards us.

Ethel let out another squeak and Glenda clutched Florence even harder, but Mabel, as usual, was unfazed. She smiled brightly and said in an airy voice:

"Ah, Mr Casa—we were just leaving. I'm sure you can help Gemma find what she's looking for better than we can. We must get back to our linguine now. See you later!"

I stared in disbelief as she and the other Old Biddies sailed out of the room, leaving me alone with the chef. They were doing it again! Getting me in trouble and then leaving me alone to deal with the consequences. *Oooh, I'm going to kill them!*

Turning nervously back to Antonio Casa, I gave him a weak smile and racked my brains for some kind of plausible reason as to why I was standing here with his case open next to me. But before I could speak, he said:

"Why did you open my case? What are you looking for?" Then his eyes dropped to my hands and a slow smile spread across his face. "Ah... I should have guessed..."

I looked down and saw to my horror that I was clutching a pair of his underpants. I must have grabbed it, along with other items of clothing, when I was trying to cover the bottle of conductive gel. I hadn't realised that I was still holding it in my hands when I'd jerked away from the case.

"Eeuughh!" I flung the pair of white briefs away from me. "I... that... that was a mistake... I didn't mean to take—"

"Ah, no need to be shy," said Antonio, grinning and coming closer. "I like a woman who isn't afraid to go after what she wants. But you should have just told me, you know—I would have been happy to give you a pair. Any pair you like. I can even spritz them with my special cologne..."

Oh God. I was either going to die of mortification or shrivel up in disgust. A few minutes later, I left the office very red in the face, with a pair of Antonio Casa's underpants stuffed in my pocket. *I'm going to burn them as soon as I get home... after I strangle the Old Biddies, that is,* I thought as I stomped back to the workbench I was sharing with my mother. Mabel and the others were industriously stirring pasta sauce and slicing herbs at the adjoining bench, and ignored the dirty look I shot them.

"Darling, where have you been?" asked my mother. "I've done the Linguine now and the Asparagus-Prosciutto Bruschetta too—and I've started on the Amaretto Biscotti." She grated parmesan cheese enthusiastically onto the bruschetta and beamed at me. "I must say, this workshop is much more enjoyable than I expected. Aren't you having a lovely evening?"

Across the room, Antonio Casa caught my eye and gave me a lecherous wink.

I sighed. "Oh... yeah, I'm having a *wonderful* evening."

CHAPTER ELEVEN

The duty sergeant at the police station gave me a cheery nod as I walked past him the next morning. Being Inspector Devlin O'Connor's girlfriend would have already made me familiar to many of the officers, but I knew that it was my own part in helping to solve several murder cases lately that had earned their respect. I returned the sergeant's greeting and negotiated the corridors until I reached the double doors which led into the Criminal Investigation Department offices. Here I paused, wondering again if I was doing the right thing.

Okay, so I was still furious with them, but in the end, the Old Biddies had managed to persuade me to come and tell Devlin about the conductive gel we'd found in Antonio Casa's case. I knew they were right: it was too much of a strange coincidence to ignore and could have been an important lead in the case. In fact, it might've very incriminating evidence against Josh's arch-rival. Still, now that I was here, I wondered uneasily how I was going to tell Devlin about the gel but not reveal how we'd got the information.

I shifted from foot to foot. *Maybe this isn't such a good idea after all. Maybe I should just write Devlin an anonymous note—like a "tip off".* That way he could still get the lead, without ever having to find out about the Old Biddies' shenanigans...

"Gemma?"

I turned around and found Devlin standing behind me, a Styrofoam cup of coffee in one hand. He was looking at me with a mixture of surprise and pleasure.

Leaning close, he gave me a kiss and said, "Nice to see you. You didn't say you were dropping by... Is everything okay?"

"Er, yes... fine..." I hesitated, then plunged on. "Um... Devlin, can I talk to you for a minute?"

"Sure." He gave me a curious look but said nothing further as he led me to an empty interview room, where we could have some privacy. Pulling out one of the chairs for me, he perched one hip on the edge of the table and said, "What's up?"

"It's about Josh McDermitt's murder..." I licked my lips. "Um... so have you had any more leads on the suspects, like... um... Antonio Casa?"

"We're still working on it. I questioned both Casa and Leanne Fitch yesterday. The latter has an alibi—she says she was in her room at the time of the murder."

"Did you check that?"

Devlin nodded. "My sergeant spoke to the hotel maid who delivered some laundry to her last night. So that looks like it rules Leanne out. But I may question her again. Anyway, I've told both her and Casa that they can't leave Oxford for a few days yet, while the investigation is still ongoing."

"And what about Antonio Casa—does *he* have an alibi?"

"No. He admitted that he was at the ball but he flatly denies that he was anywhere near the dining hall. He said he wasn't interested in—I quote—*'seeing that puffed-up tosser try to boil an egg'.*"

"So why did he go to the ball then?"

"Apparently he was meeting some woman there, although he wouldn't give me her name. That may be true or it may be wishful thinking." Devlin chuckled. "I get the impression that Casa rates himself as a bit of a Lothario: seems to think every woman is swooning for him, if they so much as look at him—"

"You can say that again," I muttered under my breath.

"—so it might just be his ego talking. In any case, he hasn't denied that he was at the ball, so he could have had the opportunity to commit the murder."

"He might have had the means too," I said.

Devlin raised an eyebrow.

"He was an electrician before he became a chef—did you know that?"

"Yes, we looked into his background. It's certainly suggestive—but it's not enough to identify him as the murderer. Just because he was once an electrician does not point to him using his knowledge in this instance."

"What about if he's found with something that improved electrical conductivity?"

"What do you mean?" Devlin looked at me sharply.

I hesitated, then blurted: "Antonio Casa has a bottle of electro-conductive gel in his travel case."

Devlin looked at me sharply. "How do you know this?"

I tried to channel Mabel and waved a hand, saying airily, "Never mind how I know—the important thing is that it's the kind of thing you would use if you were trying to electrocute someone, right? Which means Antonio could have been the one who tampered with the wiring. You should get a warrant and search his things—and confront him about the gel, before he has a chance to get rid of it."

"Gemma." Devlin gave me a look. He was no fool and he knew I was evading his question. "I need to know how you found out about Casa and the conductive gel. I can't just take your word for it—I need a good reason to apply for a search warrant."

I swallowed. "Er... well, you see... I was at a cookery workshop last night where Antonio was filling in for Josh McDermitt... and the Old Biddies were there too. And... um... well, during the class, they happened to... er... look in Antonio's overnight case and saw the conductive gel."

Devlin's brows drew together. "*Happened* to look in his case? You mean, they searched it without his permission!"

I winced. "They... they meant well! They're just trying to help the investigation—and you have to admit that this time, they've unearthed a really good lead. This conductive gel could tie Antonio Casa to the murder."

"The CID does not need 'help' in the investigation!" Devlin growled. "Especially when it involves illegal invasion of personal property. That would simply give the defence attorneys more ammunition to get Casa off the hook, if he really is the killer. We don't follow rules for the fun of it, you know! Things have to be done by the book otherwise the evidence may not be admissible in court. I presume that both you and the Old Biddies handled the bottle?"

I nodded sheepishly.

Devlin bit off a curse. "So your prints are all over the bottle's surface? Aside from the fact that they could be obscuring Casa's own prints, you do realise that this means a defence lawyer could claim that one of you planted the bottle to incriminate Casa? If there are other prints alongside his, there is no proof that the bottle belonged to him. We could be losing our best evidence against him."

I stared at Devlin, horrified. "Oh God... I hadn't thought of that... I'm sorry..."

Devlin looked as if he was going to say something else but thought better of it. Instead, he got up from the table and stalked to the window. I sat and stared at my hands, feeling like a schoolgirl being chastised in the principal's office. Finally, Devlin returned to the table and sat down opposite me with a sigh. I peeked at him from beneath my eyelashes, relieved to see that he seemed to have calmed down a bit.

"I'm sorry, Devlin," I said in a small voice. "I did try to stop them but you know what Mabel is like when she gets an idea in her head... They just disappeared suddenly in the middle of the workshop and by the time I went to look for them and found them in the back office, rifling through Antonio Casa's things, it was too late."

Devlin sighed. "I know. I'm sorry to have taken my temper out on you. Look, just... try to keep the Old Biddies out of trouble from now on, okay? And I'll get a search warrant for Casa. I just hope that the extra fingerprints won't be an issue. At least he didn't see you searching his things—"

"Er... about that..."

Devlin groaned. "Don't tell me he caught you in the act?"

"It's okay, he didn't realise we found the gel. In fact, he doesn't suspect anything at all."

"What do you mean, he doesn't suspect anything? If he caught you searching his case—"

"Well, you know Antonio Casa's big ego. He just thought we were searching for some... um... fan souvenirs."

"Fan souvenirs?" Devlin looked puzzled.

There was no way I was going to tell him about Antonio's underpants! Quickly, I changed the subject.

"So...have you got any other leads on McDermitt's murder?"

"As I said, we're still gathering information at this stage. It may sound boring, but sometimes slowly assembling evidence is the key to successfully solving a case. Oh—one interesting thing that did come up was that McDermitt had a life insurance policy."

"Oh?" I looked at Devlin with interest. "Who was the beneficiary?"

"His manager, Jerry Wallis. I gather it was set up to protect the business, should anything happen to Josh."

"Do you think that's a motive for murder?"

Devlin shrugged. "Anything's possible. It's a decent payout but not a crazy sum of money. I'm not sure it's worth committing murder for—not unless you're desperate for cash. And it doesn't look like his manager is short of funds."

"No, not if he's managing Josh's career."

"In any case, Wallis has an alibi. I questioned Maddie Gill, the TV producer, yesterday as well, and she confirms that she was with Wallis the whole time they were in the dining hall. So it's unlikely there was any opportunity for Wallis to tamper with the equipment."

I glanced at my watch and sprang up from the chair. "Oh! I've got to go, otherwise I'm going to be late opening the tearoom."

"How's business going?" asked Devlin with a smile. I was pleased to see that his bad mood seemed to be lifting.

"Great! Dora's egg custard tarts are a big hit— they even got featured by a food blogger and we've had tons of customers asking for them."

"Mmm... maybe I'll pop by on Sunday and have a taste. By the way, you haven't forgotten about dinner with my mum tonight?"

I actually had temporarily forgotten about it, what with all the excitement from the murder. Now my previous anxiety came back to me.

"Devlin, what should I wear? I mean, what's your mum like? Is she quite conservative? Do you think if I wear that new denim shirt dress, she'll think it's too short?"

"Don't worry about it, Gemma—whatever you wear will be fine."

I rolled my eyes. "Men always say that. You just don't understand how important it is to get the dress code right, especially for an important meeting."

"It really doesn't matter... I told you, it'll be fine whatever you wear. My mum won't mind."

"Yes, but if I know what she's like, I can dress more to her taste—you know, make a good first impression," I said with a shy smile. "It would really help to get some idea of what she's like before I meet her. I mean, is she quite casual and laid-back or is she more formal and proper like my mother—"

"She's nothing like your mother," said Devlin quickly. He cleared his throat. "My mum isn't... uh... like most mothers."

"What do you mean?"

"I just... I don't want you to have the wrong expectations, that's all. Honestly, Gemma, I'm sure Mum will love you whatever you wear."

"Aw, come on! That's not helping me! Why can't you tell me more? Why are you always so secretive about your mother?"

"I'm not secretive!" Devlin said hotly. "I just... Look, my mum had me when she was very young, okay?"

"Oh." I hesitated. "Well, teenage pregnancies aren't that uncommon. It's not... I mean, it's nothing to be ashamed of."

Devlin said nothing.

"Um... so was your father quite young too? I

know you said he left when you were still a baby...?"

"Actually, I never knew my father," said Devlin bluntly. "I have no idea who he is. I don't think my mother does either. She was... well, she was a bit of a party girl and she liked the boys."

"Oh." I didn't know what to say.

Devlin cleared his throat again. "When my mum found out that she was pregnant with me, her parents were horrified. They were devout Catholics. They didn't exactly disown her but it amounted to the same thing. So... after I was born, my mum ran away from home... and she took me with her."

I stared. Devlin had never opened up to me about his family before. Now I realised why he had always been reluctant to talk about his background. It was worlds apart from my own very "proper", respectable, upper-middle-class upbringing with my Oxbridge-educated parents in their elegant Victorian townhouse...

"I... I'm sorry... I didn't know... It must have been really tough for your mum, bringing you up as a single mother..."

Devlin looked uncomfortable. "Well, she was never single for very long. As I said, my mother... er... enjoys the company of men." He gave a humourless laugh. "I got pretty used to the succession of 'boyfriends' that kept coming and going in our household."

There was an awkward silence as I struggled to

think of something to say that wouldn't be either pitying or judgemental. "Um... so... she never married?"

"No."

The silence stretched between us again. Just as I was opening my mouth to say something—anything—Devlin heaved a sigh and said, "I probably should have told you all this earlier, Gemma... I didn't mean to keep you in the dark, but every time I started to tell you, I'd think of your family and your home life and how different it was from mine... And I knew that *your* mother already disapproved of me—"

"That's all changed now, remember?" I said quickly. I gave him a teasing smile. "You know you've become her blue-eyed boy—literally!—ever since you found her missing iPad."

Devlin chuckled. "Yes, I know... She's been dropping things off at the station for me every week. It's very sweet of her. Last week it was some freshly baked shortbread. Yesterday, she left two mesh laundry bags and some strict instructions on how to wash my socks and boxers."

I groaned. "Not the bloody mesh laundry bags again..." I glanced at my watch and gave a shriek. "Yikes! I really have to go!"

Devlin caught my arm. "For dinner tonight, why don't you wear that light blue knitted top you've got? I always love you in that—and I'm sure my mum will too."

I gave him a grateful smile, then rushed out of the station to get my bike and start the ride out to Meadowford-on-Smythe.

CHAPTER TWELVE

"Where's Muesli?" asked Mrs Purdey, standing anxiously at the counter.

"I didn't bring her today, Mrs Purdey. I had to stop off at the police station this morning on my way in to work and I didn't think it was fair to keep her waiting in the carrier. She's probably snoozing in her favourite spot on the sofa back home," I said with a smile.

"But I made her some Catnip Crumbles!" the old lady cried, looking distressed. "How is she going to eat them now?"

"Well, if you'd like to give them to me, I can take them home and give them to Muesli tonight. Or if they'll keep, then maybe you can give them to her yourself tomorrow? I promise Muesli will be here tomorrow."

Mrs Purdey looked mollified. "I'll give you a bit now so Muesli can have some sprinkled on her dinner tonight—and I'll keep the rest for her tomorrow."

I dutifully took the little Tupperware container she handed me and promised to sprinkle the treats on Muesli's dinner that evening.

"Blimey!" said Cassie when the old lady had left the tearoom. She came over to join me, followed by Seth, who had popped into the tearoom to say hello. "I'm almost beginning to wish I was a cat, so that Mrs Purdey would spoil me like that too!"

I made a face. "I feel a bit bad though. Here's Muesli being spoilt rotten with Catnip Crumbles on her dinner—and there are all these poor, homeless cats out there, desperate for a meal... or even just struggling to find a safe place to live! I met this really handsome tomcat yesterday in Boscobel College; he had the same markings as Muesli and he was a real charmer. I really fell for him. And I was horrified when Irene Mansell, the Master's wife, told me that he's feral and has become such a nuisance that they're planning to get the pest control company to come in and shoot him."

"That's such a stupid way to deal with a feral cat problem!" cried Seth. "Aside from it being completely inhumane, it only makes things worse because more feral cats will simply move into the area, as long as there's a source of food there."

I glanced at Seth, surprised to hear him sound so heated. He was normally such a mild, shy sort of person. Then I thought of the work he did with the Domnus Trust, a charitable organisation that helped the homeless in Oxford, and remembered that championing the underprivileged was something Seth felt very passionately about. Back in our college days, seeing someone vulnerable get bullied was the only time Seth could be roused to anger and aggression.

Now his face was flushed and earnest as he said to me: "You can't let them shoot that tomcat! You need to speak to them and persuade them to use TNR methods instead."

"TNR?"

"Trap-Neuter-Release. It's the best way of dealing with a feral cat problem. The cats are caught using humane traps, neutered and marked, and then either released back in the original location or—if that's not suitable—then a new home is found for them."

"The problem is, they've tried traps already. That's what Irene told me. But the tomcat is too clever for them."

"They need to keep trying," insisted Seth. "Maybe feed him in the trap for a few days, without setting it, so that they can gain his trust."

"I don't see them doing that. Henry Mansell, the Master of the college, hates cats, and I think they've reached the stage where they just want to see him gone. In any case, Irene said the cat doesn't trust anybody—won't let anybody near him and gets quite aggressive... which is a bit weird because he seemed fine when I saw him. He even let me stroke him."

"Then you should do it, Gemma!" said Seth. "You should set the trap and coax him in. I'll speak to one of my contacts. I know someone at one of the local animal welfare groups—they've been helping me with veterinary care for dogs belonging to those living on the streets—and I'm sure I can get you a cat trap. Maybe even tomorrow."

"We-ell... okay, but I'll need to ring Irene Mansell and check with her first. After all, I need the college's permission to go on site and trap the cat."

Seth nodded, then he cast a furtive glance at Cassie, who had gone to serve a table on the other side of the room, and said in an undertone:

"Um... Gemma, can I ask you a favour?"

"Sure."

"I was going to ask both of you to go watch the new Bond movie together but... can you... do you mind if you say no?" He blushed. "I mean, so then it would be just Cassie and me."

I looked at him in surprise. "I don't mind at all but... I don't understand. Why don't you just ask her? I mean, without asking me as well."

Seth flushed. "I can't! It would... it would look too much like I'm asking her out on a date."

"So?" I smiled at him. "Is that so terrible?"

He looked down and shifted uncomfortably. "I don't want to ruin our friendship—"

"Seth, you can't keep hanging in limbo like this either. You need to tell Cassie how you feel about her."

"But what if she doesn't feel the same way? Once I tell her, I can't take it back. It will be something hanging between us. Things will never be the same again... She'd look at me differently and if she doesn't... um... doesn't return my feelings... then it would make everything incredibly awkward." He adjusted his glasses. "You know, research shows that most cases of romantic confessions between friends have a high rejection rate. More than fifty percent of respondents in one study said they regretted—"

"Seth!" I said with an exasperated laugh. "This isn't one of your lab experiments or scientific papers! Yes, I know in a lot of cases, people who fall in love with their best friends don't have their feelings returned and it can spoil the friendship... but there are also a lot of cases of couples who are really happy and they're glad that they took the risk."

He looked at me, his face sombre. "Don't you agree that sometimes, living in hope is better than the hurt of outright rejection... and knowing that you've lost your friend too?"

I bit my lip, not knowing what to say. I could relate to what he said, having just spent a cowardly few weeks myself agonising over whether Devlin was having an affair and being too scared to challenge him about it. It *had* seemed easier to live in uncertainty than to find out the truth. And selfishly, I didn't want the status quo to change between my two best friends. If things got awkward between them, I'd be stuck in the middle. But at the same time, I'd seen how much Seth yearned and suffered, and I wanted him to have a chance at happiness.

"Look, you're assuming Cassie won't feel the same way, but what if she does? What if she does return your feelings and has just been waiting for you to say something?" I gave him an encouraging smile. "This might sound like a line from a cheesy Hollywood movie but you know... sometimes the really precious things are the ones worth taking risks for."

He started to reply, then broke off as Cassie rejoined us.

"That's the third order of scones and cakes from that table of Japanese tourists. Look at them— they're all so tiny! Where are they putting all that food?" asked Cassie, shaking her head.

I elbowed Seth and gave him a meaningful look. He swallowed, opened his mouth, hesitated, then took a deep breath and said nervously:

"Er... Cassie? Do you... are you free next Saturday? Because... I mean, I'd completely understand if you said no... and of course, this doesn't necessarily have any special signifi... I mean, it's just a friendly thing to do... but... um... I was wondering if you'd be interested in seeing the new Bond mov—"

The door to the tearoom swung open and a tall, good-looking young man dressed all in denim stepped in.

"Scott!" cried Cassie, a smile lighting up her face. "You're back!"

The big Canadian grinned. "Did you miss me?" He strolled over to the counter and included us all in his friendly smile. "I had to come back to England for business sooner than I expected, and I thought, I've got to visit my favourite tearoom." He winked at Cassie. "And maybe pick up another painting. The landscape of yours looks awesome over my mantelpiece back home. I get so many compliments when people come over—everyone's just wowed by your use of colour and light."

"Oh!" Cassie flushed with delight. "Thanks. And I can't thank you enough for bringing your friend here last time. I can't believe that he's decided to include some of my paintings in his autumn exhibition—his gallery is one of the most respected in London!"

"Ah, Brett just recognises talent when he sees it," said Scott with a smile. "I'm sure he's glad to snap you up before someone else discovers you." He leaned across the counter towards Cassie. "Hey, listen, the other reason I came in was 'cos I wanted to catch the new Bond movie. Want to come with me? We'll have dinner first—make it a date."

"I'd love to!" said Cassie, beaming. She glanced at Seth. "You don't mind, right? I know you were just asking us, but I'm sure you and Gemma will be fine without me."

I winced. Seth looked like someone had punched him in the stomach.

"Uh... no... that's fine... of course..." he stammered.

Cassie grabbed a menu and turned to Scott. "So... where would you like to sit?"

The Canadian indicated a nearby table. "How about over there? And are you on a break?" He smiled at her. "Come and sit down and have something with me."

"I can look after things for a while," I offered.

"Great!" Cassie glanced at Seth. "Would you like to join us, Seth?"

"Er... no... no, thanks. I've... er... got to be going now. See you later!"

Cassie watched in bewilderment as Seth practically ran out the door. "What on earth's got into him?" she asked.

I wished I could tell her. Instead, I left her talking and laughing with Scott and retreated behind the counter, where I put the call through to Boscobel College and asked for the Master's wife. Irene Mansell sounded doubtful at first when I suggested the TNR method to catch the feral tomcat, but finally she agreed to let me try.

"I probably won't be able to get the trap and come to the college until late Sunday, though," I said.

"That's quite all right. I'll let the porters know and you can come on site whenever it suits you," Irene replied. "I'll be in church on Sunday morning but I should be around later in the day. You're familiar with the college, anyway, so you won't need me to give you directions. In fact, feel free to use the private route through the Master's courtyard and the cloister, if you like, since you already know the way."

I gave a cough of embarrassment. "I'm sorry again about trespassing the night of the ball—"

Irene laughed. "Don't let it worry you. You're not the only one who tries to use that route. Students often try to come that way and, in fact, there was another lady wandering around the cloister the night of the ball. She must have thought I was going to reprimand her, because she ran away as soon as she saw me."

I felt a prickle of interest. "Was she going to the dining hall?"

"No, I think she was just coming back—she was walking from that direction."

"When was this?"

"Oh... it was just a few minutes before I saw you, I think."

"Was she a student?"

Irene thought for a moment. "No-o, she was older. Somewhere in her early thirties, I think— although it was hard to tell because the light was fading by then and she had so much make-up on... You know how people always look older with heavy make-up."

"Heavy make-up?" I said sharply. "Was she blonde?"

"Yes, I think so... her hair looked quite yellow, even in the dim light. Quite unnaturally yellow, in fact. I suppose it must have been dyed."

Heavy make-up, dyed blonde hair... I knew someone who matched that description: Josh's ex-girlfriend, Leanne Fitch. Did this mean that she had been at Boscobel College on the night of the ball after all? But what about the alibi she had given to the police? Had she lied about that? Devlin had said that his sergeant checked it out, and the maid had confirmed that Leanne had been in her hotel room on the night of the ball...

So who was the woman that Irene Mansell had seen in the cloister?

CHAPTER THIRTEEN

After I hung up, I mused on what Irene Mansell had said all afternoon. I was tempted to ring Devlin but I hesitated, wondering if I might have been jumping to conclusions. After all, Leanne wasn't the only blonde woman in the world who favoured heavy make-up, and in fact, with it being the night of the ball, most of the women there had probably worn more make-up than usual. Nevertheless, the thought bothered me for the rest of the day. I was still wondering if I should call Devlin when the door to the tearoom opened late that afternoon and a swarthy man stepped in.

I sprang up in surprise. It was Antonio Casa. I saw the Old Biddies sit upright at their table by the window and start whispering urgently amongst themselves, their eyes following the chef as he approached the counter.

"He-llo, Gemma..." he drawled.

"Er, hi, Antonio," I said, giving him a perfunctory smile. "How nice of you to drop by. Were you thinking of having some tea and scones?"

"No, I came to see you," he said, waggling his eyebrows. "I have been thinking about you, ever since our meeting last night in the workshop..." He gave me a complacent smile. "I know you must have been thinking about me too."

"Oh... er... well, actually..." I groped for an honest but polite response. "I think you misunderstood my—"

"So... you'll be ready at eight tomorrow night? I don't like to eat too early."

I gaped at him. "I'm... I'm sorry?"

"And wear something sexy. I like to look at my women while I eat." He waggled his eyebrows again.

I spluttered with a mixture of outrage and disbelief. The man was unreal! "Look, Antonio, I think there's been a misunderstanding. I'm flattered, of course, by your invitation, but I'm sorry, I'm afraid I can't—"

"—wait to see you tomorrow evening!" came Mabel's voice.

Huh? I turned to see that the Old Biddies had scurried over and were now hovering next to us, their faces alight with glee.

"Oh, Gemma is just delighted," gushed Mabel.

"She's been talking about you ever since we left the workshop."

I gasped. "I have not—"

"You're such a handsome man, Mr Casa— Gemma's a very lucky girl," said Florence, beaming.

Glenda clasped her hands and fluttered her eyelashes at him. "Ah, if I was fifty years younger..."

"Gemma said she thought you were wonderful on *Superchef*, Mr Casa!" Ethel piped up.

I stared at the Old Biddies incredulously. What on earth was going on? I raised my hands, palms outwards, and said hastily:

"Wait—hang on—you're all putting words in my mouth! I never said—*OWW!*" I broke off and glared at Mabel, who had just stepped on my toe.

She grabbed my arm and pulled me aside, leaning close and hissing in my ear: "Say yes, dear! It's a chance to get close to him and question him about the murder!"

"But—"

"This is a golden opportunity to get close to a suspect! You can't pass it up!" Mabel put her face close to mine. "If you won't go to dinner with him, then we'll have to find another way to investigate him. Maybe we can sneak into his hotel room—"

"Uh—no, no! Don't even think about that!" I glanced at the smug man behind us and recoiled at the thought of spending an evening with him. On the other hand, it would keep the Old Biddies out of trouble...

"Mabel, I really can't face the thought of a whole evening with him," I pleaded.

"Well, do lunch tomorrow then."

"I can't do lunch! That's one of the busiest times in the tearoom—"

"Glenda, Florence, Ethel, and I can give Cassie a hand," Mabel declared. "We've managed without you before."

"I..." I glanced at Antonio again, then capitulated. "Oh, all right. I'll do it—but just a very quick lunch! And if he starts to grope me, I'm leaving—suspect or no suspect."

Turning back to the chef, I managed to conjure up a sickly smile and thank him for his invitation. "I'm afraid I can't do dinner, Antonio—but how about a quick lunch tomorrow? Have you been to the White Horse? It's one of the most well-known pubs in Oxford. We could meet there at say... twelve-thirty?"

To my relief, Antonio readily accepted and, a few minutes later, swaggered out of the tearoom. I watched him go, wondering how I'd let myself be talked into a date with such a repulsive man.

***

"Darling, I did press the record button! At least, I *think* it was the record button... or was it the pause button?" My mother frowned, staring at the digital recorder under her TV. "Anyway, I told you on the phone—it's just not working. I'm not sure now if I've recorded the programme after all... oh dear, and I promised Helen that I'd watch it... Do you think it might still be on there if we just pressed Play? But I tried that this morning... and there was a menu... and something called 'On Demand' came on the screen... but I'm sure Helen said the programme was called *'Diana: A Modern Princess'*, not *'On Demand'*... Oh! I just remembered—the instructions said there's supposed to be a little red light... or was it a green light?"

I stifled the urge to grind my teeth. After a busy day at the tearoom, I had been pleased to leave slightly early and have enough time to get ready for the big dinner date with Devlin and his mother tonight. But as I was locking up, my mother had rung in a state of panic, babbling about her TV recorder. So I had taken a detour on my way home and stopped off in North Oxford where my parents lived.

"Did you put the recorder on, Mother?" I asked, indicating a switch at the side of the box. "See this button? It's the power switch. Did you press this before you pushed the record button?"

"Now, let me see..." My mother pondered this for a long moment. "I'm sure I did... but of course, Eliza Whitfield rang while I was in the middle of trying to figure it out—you know, her daughter has just had a baby, a little girl, and they're thinking of naming her Zuki, which is the most ridiculous name. Why, it makes her sound like a vegetable! And can you believe it, the parents took the baby out to dinner with them barely two days after she came home from the hospital—really, the way children are brought up nowadays!—I told Eliza she ought to say something—"

"Mother!"

"Oh... oh yes, the switch... well, I'm not sure, darling..."

"Well, if you didn't turn it on, Mother, then it wouldn't have recorded anything. I can check to see if the programme is saved in your archives but I don't think—ah, wait... here's something..."

I pressed the buttons on the remote, navigating swiftly through the menu until an image flickered onto the screen. I sat up in surprise to see Josh McDermitt's handsome face. He was sitting in a studio, facing the two hosts of a popular breakfast show.

"Oh, that's the Josh McDermitt interview," said my mother brightly. "I'd forgotten that I recorded that. I think that was from last week, when I was testing the recorder... your father was here and he helped me set things up. But you can get rid of that now, darling—I've watched it already—"

"No, wait," I said. "Can I watch it for a moment? I never saw it when it aired... There might be something relevant to his murder."

"Well, I'll go and make us both a nice cup of tea, then. Would you like English breakfast or Earl

Grey? Or perhaps a herbal? I bought a lovely new box of Twining's Forest Fruits at the supermarket..."

Her voice faded away as she retreated to the kitchen but I was barely listening anyway, all my attention riveted on the screen in front of me. Josh looked tanned and handsome, lounging casually against the sofa cushions, his brilliant white teeth gleaming in his famous smile as he answered questions from the show hosts.

"...*can't deny that my looks do help,*" *he was saying with a chuckle. "But I'd like to think that it's my culinary skills that have really shot me to fame. Especially my willingness to challenge convention and try new ways of doing things.*"

"*Ah, yes... and some of your recipes have been quite controversial, haven't they?*" *said one of the hosts. "Like using white wine instead of red in your spaghetti bolognese sauce, or boiling your pasta in milk instead of water—*"

"*Ah, people complain until they taste the results,*" *said Josh. "Then they love it! You know, the thing is—cooking is art. And like all great art, sometimes you just have to throw out the rulebook and do something daring, even if it goes against popular practice. For example..." He leaned closer to the hosts and lowered his voice conspiratorially. "I'll tell you a few secrets... things I've never revealed before..."*

"Yes?" The two hosts looked at him breathlessly.

"The reason my potato mash tastes so divine is because I add a dash of maple syrup in with the butter and nutmeg. Yes, maple syrup. Not Golden Syrup—it has to be the real Canadian deal. And my famous egg custard tarts? Well, the key is unpasteurised cream. It just gives an extra dimension and richness to the flavour, something I discovered quite by accident the first time I cooked it for a big event. I didn't tell anyone, but people were raving about the tarts—said it was the best egg tart they ever tasted. I use pasteurised cream now in public because... well, litigation, but nothing beats the raw stuff. I also use a bit of monosodium glutamate in my sausage recipes. Yes, I know, I know—MSG is a bad word in cooking these days— but in fact, glutamates naturally occur in lots of foods, such as meat, fish, and mushrooms... even breast milk contains glutamate! Cheeses like parmesan contain tons of the stuff. So let's not get neurotic about it. The problem with the world nowadays is that people are so sensitive about everything—"

"But Josh, you have to admit, some people really do have a problem with MSG. There's even a name for it, isn't there? 'Chinese restaurant syndrome', I think it's called. People were complaining of headaches and skin flushing and sweating after a Chinese meal and they thought it was due to the MSG added in the cooking—"

"There's actually very little scientific evidence linking those symptoms to MSG," declared Josh. "It's a myth. The FDA in the United States has approved it as a safe ingredient, as have similar governing bodies in the UK and the EU... It's fine if used in small doses."

"But surely having such controversial cooking practices makes it easier for your rivals to attack you," said the other host. "Are you not worried, Josh?"

The handsome young chef shrugged. "There's always going to be envy and jealousy—I can't do anything about that. In any case, I think a lot of the rivalry is exaggerated by the media."

"Ah... but you can't deny that there has been a bitter feud between you and Antonio Casa for many years now? In fact, only a few weeks ago, he publicly accused you of trying to sabotage the opening night at his new restaurant."

Josh laughed. "I didn't even know it was his opening night! That's a ridiculous suggestion."

"So you deny it?"

"Of course I deny it! Antonio is just too embarrassed to admit that his restaurant didn't generate enough interest and bookings. He needed an excuse so he made up this story—to blame me and save face. But the truth of the matter is, he's a crap chef and everyone is beginning to realise it. That's why they've kicked him off the next season of Superchef."

"And is it true that you will be replacing him?"

Josh gave a coy smile. "Ah... you'll have to wait and see, won't you?"

"Well, thank you so much for coming into the studio, Josh. It's been an absolute pleasure—"

The screen went blank, then reverted to the main menu. The recording was over. I switched off the machine and sat back, mentally going over the interview again. If I'd been hoping for some obvious clue to help solve the case, I was disappointed. Still, I couldn't help feeling there was something in that interview—something that I had missed—that was relevant to the murder...

"Now, would you like to have your tea in here, darling, or in the kitchen?" My mother sat down on the couch next to me and placed a tray laden with teacups and biscuits on the coffee table.

I glanced at my watch and sprang up. "I'm sorry, Mother—I just realised the time! I can't stay for tea. I've got to get back—"

"Darling, I'm sure Muesli won't mind if her dinner is a bit late—"

"It's not that. I'm going out to dinner tonight with Devlin and his mum, and I've got to get ready."

"Oh? Devlin's mother is in town?" My mother looked up with interest. "Why didn't you tell me? I would love to meet her. I think—"

"Sorry, Mother, I've really got to go!"

I pecked her cheek, then dashed from the house.

CHAPTER FOURTEEN

Halfway home, one of my bike tyres got a puncture and I was forced to wheel it the rest of the way. I *had* been tempted to return to my parents' house and ask to borrow my mother's car, but I decided that involving my mother would probably just delay me even more and I kept walking. By the time I got home, I was really running late. I hurried into the cottage, intent on heading upstairs and straight into the shower, but I was met by loud, plaintive meows as soon as I stepped in the front door. Muesli was *not* pleased at having been left alone all day and she let me know in no uncertain terms, adding with a reproachful twitch of her tail that, as if that wasn't bad enough, I was also home late and she was starving to death!

"All right, all right, it's coming!" I said with a sigh, dumping my bag on the sofa and hurrying into the kitchen to get her dinner.

A few minutes later, the petulant meowing was replaced by a loud, contented purring which filled the kitchen. I paused for a moment and smiled in spite of myself as I leaned against the counter and watched Muesli eat. There was something so nice about seeing my little cat enjoy her food. Then I remembered guiltily that I had forgotten to sprinkle the Catnip Crumbles from Mrs Purdey onto Muesli's dinner. Oh well, no time now, I decided as I headed upstairs for a quick shower. Towelling my hair dry several minutes later, I recalled Devlin's special request and started hunting for the baby blue knitted top he liked.

"Come on, come on... where is it?" I muttered as I rummaged frantically in my chest of drawers.

Then I stopped and smacked my head. *Of course! Idiot...* I'd put it in the wash last night. I ran downstairs in my bra and jeans and eagerly pulled the pile of fluffy, dry clothes out of my washer-dryer. *Uh-oh...* I realised belatedly that the knitted top probably shouldn't have been tumble-dried after the wash. It wasn't wool or silk, thank goodness, but the synthetic knit fabric was still very delicate... To my relief, I remembered that I'd decided to put it in one of my mother's new mesh laundry bags and now, as I pulled the bag out of the pile, I was delighted to see that the top looked undamaged.

Quickly, I unzipped the mesh bag, but when I tried to pull the top out, something caught and held fast.

I frowned and tugged. Then tugged again. No, it was stuck fast. I turned the top over, my eyes widening with horror as I saw that the mesh bag's zipper had somehow snagged the fabric.

"Oh, bugger...!" I twisted and turned the folds of the fabric, trying to unhook it from the zipper. The more I pulled, though, the tighter it seemed to catch, and the rest of the mesh bag twisted on itself, so that it formed a giant, monster knot.

Arrghh. I gritted my teeth, bent my head, and tried again to loosen the top, all the while conscious of the ticking clock on the kitchen wall. *Grrr...* Suddenly, my previous delight evaporated and I couldn't help thinking resentfully that if it wasn't for my mother and her blasted mesh laundry bags, I'd be leaving the house already!

After several minutes of frustrated wriggling and tugging, I managed to work the zipper loose and detach my top from the mesh bag. I slipped it on, then hurried back upstairs and applied make-up with a hurried hand, chagrined that I couldn't take my time like I'd planned. I had wanted to attempt some fancy eye make-up and maybe even put on some nail polish, but there was simply no time. I resorted to sweeping on some shimmery eyeshadow and running a brown eyeliner along my lids as fast as I could, my flustered hands struggling to keep the lines straight. Forget "cat's eyes" or "smoky eyes"... at this point, I'd settle for matching eyes!

Finally, I dragged a comb through my hair, then ran out of the house and into the waiting taxi, flushed and breathless. Devlin would normally have picked me up, but as he was fetching his mother from the train station, I'd offered to meet them at the restaurant. Now I hoped that the train might have been delayed or Devlin had got stuck in traffic or something. When I alighted outside the restaurant and walked in, however, I was dismayed to see that Devlin and his mother were already there.

Great. What a good way to make a first impression: be late and keep them waiting!

I approached the table nervously, eyeing the tall blonde woman sitting opposite Devlin with interest. She was very attractive—the kind of woman who would turn heads when she walked into a room— with Devlin's vivid blue eyes and the same thin, sensual lips. She looked younger than I'd expected, although that may have been partly because of the way she was dressed: in a denim jacket over a hot pink Lycra top and short skirt, paired with black leather ankle boots. It was the kind of thing that you might see on a teenager going to the Glastonbury music festival, rather than a woman who was the mother of your boyfriend. I tried not to stare; after Devlin's comments this morning, I had been expecting his mother to be a bit different, but I hadn't expected her to be quite so... well, *rock chick*.

She was just raising a wine glass and saying something laughingly to him when she looked up and saw me. "Gemma!" She sprang up and gave me an air kiss on each cheek. "Great to meet you, luv. I've heard loads about you from Dev here..."

"It's so nice to meet you too, Mrs O'Connor."

She giggled. "Oh, please—call me Keeley. Mrs O'Connor sounds so *old*! Besides, it's not really 'Mrs', you know."

I gulped, wanting to kick myself for the faux pas. "Oh, yes, of course. Devlin told me that you were... er... I mean..."

She laughed again, a loud, throaty sound that made people at tables nearby turn to look at us, but Keeley O'Connor didn't seem to mind. "Ah, so Dev's told you my dark, dirty secret?" She gave me a wink. "It's okay. I use 'Mrs O'Connor' most of the time. Pretending you're 'respectable' often makes things easier."

I smiled apologetically. "I'm so sorry I'm late. I was delayed getting home from work and then I had... er... a bit of a laundry mishap."

She waved a hand, obviously not sharing my mother's disapproval of tardiness at all. "Oh, don't worry—we've been enjoying a drink... haven't we, Dev?"

She giggled again and took a large gulp from her glass. She was slurring her words slightly and I realised suddenly that she was a bit tipsy. It seemed that Devlin's mum had been enjoying quite a few drinks already. Maybe it explained why Devlin himself looked so grim. There was an awkward silence as I slid into the seat next to him and pretended to look around the restaurant and admire the décor.

Brown's Brasserie was one of the most popular restaurants in Oxford, situated just north of the main city, opposite the picturesque St Giles church and a beautiful terrace of eighteenth-century townhouses. It had a warm, bustling atmosphere and an extensive menu full of local favourites like British mussels with white wine sauce, garlic, parsley, and warm toasted bread, or steak and Guinness pie accompanied by crisp prosciutto ham, and the quaint traditional English dish called "bubble and squeak"—a delicious mash of "leftover" potato and vegetables. My favourite had always been the signature Brown's Burger and I was pleased to see that they still had it on the menu: a juicy beef patty in a brioche bun, packed with Irish Cheddar, smoked bacon, tomato, crisp gem lettuce, pickles, and English mustard mayonnaise, and served with chunky, golden fries.

The place was heaving with the usual Saturday night crowds but service was still prompt and a waiter was soon standing by our table to take our order. We decided on the large sharing plate of breads and dips for starters, then I asked for the burger, Devlin ordered the fish and chips, and his mother settled on the smoked haddock fishcakes.

"Oh, and another bottle of wine, please," Keeley O'Connor added with a flirtatious smile at the waiter, holding up her empty glass.

"Mum... don't you think you've had enough to drink...?" Devlin asked quietly when the waiter had gone.

"Oh, rubbish—I've only had a few glasses."

"It's been more than a few glasses."

"Well, it's the weekend! Honestly, luv, you're such a stick-in-the-mud." Keeley O'Connor pouted prettily, then turned to me and said: "Is Dev like this with you? He's always so responsible and so... so principled, my son!" She giggled again. "Sometimes I wonder how I gave birth to him."

I saw a flash of hurt in Devlin's blue eyes, but he said nothing, just looking away with a resigned sigh.

Keeley O'Connor sat back and regarded me curiously. "So, Gemma—Dev told me you run a teashop?"

"Yes, a traditional English tearoom, out in a little village on the outskirts of Oxford."

"Ooh, that sounds adorable. So you serve scones and finger sandwiches and all those cute little afternoon tea treats?"

I smiled. "Yes, all the classics in British baking, although scones are what we're famous for. Recently a lot of customers have been asking for our egg custard tarts as well—"

"Custard tarts!" Keeley gasped and opened her

blue eyes very wide. "Shit, did you hear what happened to Josh McDermitt?"

I was startled to hear the oath coming from her mouth and, for a moment, I wondered if I'd heard wrong. *My* mother would rather have been boiled alive than be caught uttering the S-word in polite company.

"Um... yes, I was the one who found the body, actually."

"Bloody hell." She smirked and leaned close to me, asking in a mock whisper, "Was he just wearing his boxers? There's a rumour going around that Josh McDermitt was wearing nothing but his boxer shorts when he was found. It was in all the tabloids this morning."

I shook my head in disbelief. "Where on earth did they hear that from? No, he was fully clothed."

"Shame..." Keeley smiled suggestively. "I'd kill to see Josh McDermitt in nothing but his boxers... and a chef's hat," she added with a giggle. "Can you imagine what he'd look like in bed? I bet he would have been a great lover though. Good with his hands, you know—"

"Mum!" Devlin shifted uneasily in his seat.

Keeley laughed. "Oh, come on, Dev! You're a big boy now. Don't tell me you think I live like a nun? I'm single and I'm only forty-five; there's nothing wrong with a woman who knows how to enjoy herself. And you know, a lot of men like an older, more experienced woman in the bedro—"

"Mum, please." Devlin looked desperate now.

Keeley giggled and gave me another wink. I felt my lips tugging into a smile, in spite of myself. She was outrageous and yet I found myself liking her. There was something very appealing about her irreverent attitude and unapologetic confidence. Keeley O'Connor was an attractive woman in the true sense of the word—not just in her looks but in the warm charisma she radiated. Still, I felt sorry for Devlin. Nobody wants to *think* about their parents having sex, never mind hearing them talk about it. Hurriedly, I tried to change the subject.

"Mrs O'Connor—I mean, Keeley—I love your boots."

"Thanks! I got them on sale, actually. They're gorgeous, aren't they?"

She beamed, raising her foot and sticking it straight out from the table to show me the boot better. Her skirt was so short, though, that she also revealed a long length of shapely thigh and calf, and I saw several men at nearby tables ogling discreetly.

Keeley seemed unconscious of the attention she was drawing. She turned to me and said, "I was actually thinking that I'd love to look around the shops in Oxford this weekend, especially the second-hand clothes shops. You always get great bargains in those—"

She broke off as the waiter approached our table again, this time bearing a large bottle of champagne.

"We didn't order champagne," said Devlin, frowning.

The waiter cleared his throat and looked at Keeley. "This is for madam, from the gentlemen over there..."

He nodded towards a table several feet from us, where two young men were sitting together. They were dressed in smart suits and looked like they worked in the City or had other equally high-flying corporate jobs. Now one of them caught Keeley's eye and grinned, then raised his glass to her. Devlin's mother flushed with pleasure and returned his grin with a coy look. Then she turned back to the bottle of champagne.

"Oh, how sweet! Look, there's a note..."

She unravelled the piece of notepaper twined around the cork. I caught a glimpse of some scribbled words and what looked like a phone number. Keeley's smile widened and she threw the men another coy glance. Then she fluffed her hair, smoothed down her skirt, and said airily:

"I think I'd better go over and thank them..."

Devlin opened his mouth but, before he could say anything, his mother had got up and sashayed over to the other table.

CHAPTER FIFTEEN

Devlin and I sat in silence as he watched Keeley lean flirtatiously against the other table, talking and laughing with the two men.

I cleared my throat, feeling the need to break the strained silence. "Um... your mum seems really nice," I said with a tentative smile.

Devlin glanced at me, then flicked his eyes back to the blonde woman on the other side of the restaurant. "You don't have to pretend, Gemma."

"I'm not! I really like her. I mean, you're right— she isn't like my mother. Or most mothers," I admitted with a laugh. "But she's... well, she's fun."

"I don't want my mother to be *fun*," said Devlin through clenched teeth. "I want my mother to act her age and dress properly and talk about things normal mothers talk about and... and... and just act like my mother!"

I stared at him, suddenly hearing in his voice all the pent-up frustration and humiliation he must have suffered growing up. I'd always thought that no one could have as frustrating a relationship as I did with my mother and her upper-middle class snobbery, with her fussy concern for respectability and proper etiquette... but for the first time, I began to realise that there were other types of maternal crosses to bear.

Before I could reply, Keeley came back and sat down again opposite us, looking very much like the cat who had not only got the cream but two fat canaries too.

"Such sweet blokes! They're in Oxford on business but they're staying till Sunday and they told me that they know this great wine bar up in Jericho. They've invited me to go with them tomorrow night—"

"You didn't accept, did you?" asked Devlin, frowning.

"Why not? It sounds like a cool place to check out—"

"*Mum!* You don't know anything about these two men! You can't just go around accepting invites from random strangers—"

"But they're not strangers!" said Keeley with a coquettish smile. "Not anymore, anyway. I was getting to know them pretty well just now..." She gave her son a playful slap. "Oh, stop worrying, luv! You're always so suspicious. It's that job of yours, dealing with murderers and rapists all day... Honestly, most men aren't criminals, you know."

Devlin looked as if he might explode but he bit off what he was going to say as the waiter arrived with our food. He spent the rest of the meal in a fuming silence—I could practically see smoke coming out of his ears—while his mother talked and laughed, and I tried to respond appropriately. It was a relief when the waiter came to clear our plates away.

"Oh—*oops!* Excuse me," the waiter said as he tried to lift a stack of plates by my elbow and something caught in his fingers.

I looked down and saw a length of blue yarn dangling from under my arm. "Oh, that must be from my top..." I twisted, trying to catch hold of the yarn, but it was such an awkward angle that I couldn't reach properly.

"If you'll allow me..." said the waiter, bending and catching hold of the yarn.

He gave it a sharp tug, obviously hoping to snap the thread and break the piece off, but instead it just got longer and longer, until he stood looking bewildered with a spool of blue yarn in his hands. I felt cold air against my skin. Looking down, I saw that the knitted pattern had unravelled and there was now a gaping hole in my side.

"Oh my God! I'm so sorry! I... I don't know what

happened—" The waiter covered his mouth, his eyes wide with dismay.

"It's all right—it's not you," I assured him. "I snagged my top earlier this evening. I thought it was okay but it must have caused a bigger hole than I realised."

Still apologising, the waiter left while I examined the hole ruefully. The good news was it was almost right under my armpit so as long as I didn't raise my arm in the air, no one should have been able to see it. But I had to do something about the unravelling yarn.

"If you pull the yarn back inside your top and tie a knot, that should fix it temporarily," Keeley said.

"Thanks, I'll try that." I stood up. "Excuse me while I pop to the Ladies."

I hurried across the restaurant towards the ladies' toilets, passing a large group on the way. I did a slight double take as I recognised the heavyset man with the bulbous nose sitting at the table. It was Jerry Wallis, Josh McDermitt's manager. Sitting next to him was the producer, Maddie Gills, and what looked like several other members of the crew—I recognised the man who had been carrying the video camera on the day they came into my tearoom. From his flushed face and overly loud voice, it was obvious that Jerry Wallis had had a bit too much to drink, and the rest of the group had long-suffering expressions on their faces. I passed by them swiftly, wondering what would happen to filming now that the show's star was dead.

Once in the toilets, I was pleased to find a cubicle empty. I had barely locked myself in and taken my top off when I heard the outside door open again and female voices talking.

"Bloody hell—that Jerry never shuts up! I reckon he's been banging on about the BAFTAs for the last twenty minutes."

"He's an obnoxious git." I recognised Maddie Gill's voice. "If I had been Josh, I would have fired him long ago. I almost didn't take on this job when I heard that Jerry would be involved. Do you know, he told me that he wants to keep filming and turn the murder investigation into part of the show... I mean, poor Josh hasn't even been buried and Jerry's already exploiting the whole thing for publicity! And he was just laying into some poor girl up at that tearoom in Meadowford a few days ago, accusing her of cashing in on Josh's name for her custard tarts—"

"No, really?"

"Yeah, I was with him and it was so embarrassing! I tell you, if it wasn't for the money being so good, I would have walked out then and there."

There was the sound of water running, followed by the hand dryer. Then the click of a lipstick being capped. Then the other woman spoke absentmindedly:

"He was probably pushing because he needs the

dosh. Rick told me Jerry has the sharks after him."

"Mm... wouldn't be surprised... Still, I'm only doing this for the dosh too, and so are you and the rest of the crew, but you know, there's a thing called sensitivity and decency... Do you think these jeans make my bum look big?"

"Naw... what are you talking about? They really suit you."

"You reckon? Thanks. They're new."

"You seem to have got a lot of new clothes lately. You seeing someone?"

Maddie's voice was coy. "Maybe... You're looking good too. You've lost weight. Is it true that you're dating Garret from Post-Production?"

"Garret? You've got to be joking!"

Maddie laughed. "I guess the rumour's wrong, then. Anyway, listen, you should go check out this shop where I got the jeans from, next time you're back in London. It's down by Piccadilly Circus. They've got a great selection of..."

I heard the door open and their voices fade away. Hurriedly, I finished knotting the loose yarn, then slipped my top back on and came out of the cubicle. As I washed my hands, I thought about the conversation I had just overheard. It sounded like there was no love lost between Maddie and Jerry Wallis—which was no surprise. I remembered her pained expression and apologetic embarrassment the day he had stormed into the tearoom.

My lips tightened as I thought of what she had

said Jerry was suggesting... What a bloody cheek! Him accusing me of exploiting Josh's name when he was happy to do it himself before the man was even in his grave!

CHAPTER SIXTEEN

I was woken up the next morning by the insistent ringing of my mobile phone and I sat up blearily in bed to answer it.

"Hello...?" I mumbled,

"Darling, do you think Mrs O'Connor would like Madeira cake?"

"Huh? Sorry...?" The cogs in my brain struggled to turn. I rubbed my eyes and glanced at my bedside clock. It was barely seven o'clock.

"Well, I thought I'd bake some scones and perhaps a lemon drizzle cake. And muffins are always welcome, of course. But Dorothy gave me a new recipe for a Madeira cake the other day and I thought this would be a marvellous chance to try—"

"Mother, what are you talking about?"

"Oh, didn't I say? Well, since Devlin's mother is visiting Oxford, I thought it would be a lovely opportunity to meet her! So I'm inviting her round for Sunday morning tea—"

"*What?* No, Mother, no," I said, suddenly wide awake.

"Why ever not, darling? I'm sure Helen and the others would love to meet her."

Oh God. I shuddered. I couldn't think of anything worse than turning Keeley O'Connor loose amongst my mother's friends from the cashmere twinset and pearls brigade. Especially Helen Green, who was an even bigger snob than my mother and already viewed Devlin with contempt and resentment, since I had chosen him over her son.

"Um, Mother... I really don't think it's a good idea. Mrs O'Connor is... well, she's very different from your friends."

"Oh, nonsense, darling—that should make it all the more interesting. I shall ring Devlin now and tell him. Make sure you're here at eleven o'clock. And do try to wear a nice dress, darling, instead of those horrid jeans you always wear."

"Mother, wait—"

It was too late. She'd hung up. I lowered the phone and stared at it for a moment in frustration, whilst Muesli stirred in the blankets at the foot of my bed. The little tabby cat stood up and arched her back in a perfect cat stretch, then sat down and yawned widely, showing her pink tongue and tiny white teeth.

"*Meorrw*?" she said, eyeing me curiously.

"Muesli, this is going to be a total disaster," I groaned, flopping backwards on the pillows. Then I thought of something and sat up quickly again. I dialled Devlin's number. It was engaged. I tried again, my attempts getting more and more frantic until he finally answered five minutes later.

"Devlin! Listen—my mother's going to call you... you have to say no! Say you're busy... say you're taking your mother for a drive in the country and will be out of Oxford all day... just don't say yes!"

"Er... it's a bit late, Gemma," he said dryly. "I just got off the phone with her. We'll be at your parent's house at eleven tomorrow morning."

"Why did you agree? You know what your mum's like—" I gulped. "I mean, she's lovely and I really like her but... well, my mother's friends are quite different from her and—"

"I tried to say no," said Devlin. "But... I don't know what happened—your mother was talking... and I couldn't really get a word in edgeways... and then the next thing I knew, she was telling me what time to arrive... and then she'd hung up."

I couldn't really blame him. I knew better than most what my mother was like when she had her mind set on something. It was like dealing with a force of nature—you didn't have much choice but be swept along in her wake.

Devlin's voice changed, becoming serious and

professional. "Listen, sweetheart—since you rang I wanted to tell you that we managed to get an expedited search warrant for Antonio Casa's things and we found the conductive gel—"

"Yes, and?" I asked eagerly.

"Casa claims it's for an EMS machine he'd bought, to help him with his workouts."

"And you believe him?"

"Well, we did find a portable EMS machine in the case too. And he was very relaxed about us searching the case and finding the gel. So either he's supremely confident or a very good bluffer... or he's telling the truth and the gel has an innocent purpose."

"Hmm..."

"But the boys in Forensics are testing the gel this morning to see if it's a match for the traces found on the whisk handle, so it'll be interesting to hear what they say. I have a meeting with them in a minute."

"I'm surprised you're at work," I said. "I thought you were taking the weekend off to be with your mother."

"That was before Josh McDermitt got murdered," said Devlin sardonically. "When an investigation is ongoing, detectives don't get weekends off. I was hoping I might be able to finish by lunchtime and spend this afternoon with her... but it doesn't look promising at the moment." He sighed. "I suppose she'll be all right on her own, wandering around the shops in town, although I feel a bit bad since she did make the trip down especially—"

"I'll meet up with her," I said impulsively. "I'd be happy to mooch around the shops with her."

"What about the tearoom?"

"Cassie should be able to look after things. And anyway, I'll be in town already since I'm meeting—" I broke off as I realised belatedly that I didn't want Devlin to know about my "date" with Antonio Casa. "Um... meeting someone about a possible catering job," I finished lamely.

"Oh? One of the colleges?" asked Devlin with a smile in his voice. "It's great you're getting so much catering business, Gemma."

"Er... yes." I hated lying to him but there was no way I could explain how the Old Biddies had bulldozed me into having lunch with the most repulsive man in Oxford.

"Well, if you don't mind, Gemma... that would be great," said Devlin, sounding touched and grateful. "I'm sure Mum would love your company."

I arranged to meet Keeley O'Connor by Carfax, the main intersection in the centre of town, at two o'clock. Hopefully that would give me enough time with Antonio Casa... not that I was planning to linger at lunch. I made a face again as I thought of my date with the amorous chef. I couldn't wait to get it over with.

***

The White Horse was one of Oxford's famous historic pubs, housed in a Grade II listed building hailing from the sixteenth century and often used in the filming of the TV detective series *Inspector Morse*, as well as the subsequent *Lewis* and *Endeavour*. But even before it gained "TV fame", it had been popular with the locals for its real ales and traditional home-cooked food. I remembered often popping in as a student for their chunky steak pie, made with rich shortcrust pastry, whilst Cassie's favourite was the classic "toad in the hole": a giant Yorkshire pudding filled with two fat and juicy pork and leek sausages, mashed potatoes, vegetables, and homemade onion gravy.

I had picked the pub partly because of its central location—sandwiched next to the iconic Blackwells Bookstore and opposite the even more iconic Sheldonian Theatre, right in the heart of the city—but also because I knew that it would probably be heaving with tourists and students from the nearby colleges on a Saturday lunchtime. I wanted to make sure that I had plenty of people around me, should Antonio Casa decide to get too "friendly".

He was already at the bar when I stepped into the cosy, wood-panelled interior and I plastered a smile on my face as I made my way over to him. Thankfully, the pub was as busy as I'd expected and the raucous din from all the talking, laughing students and tourists made conversation quite difficult as we put in our orders. But when we'd carried our drinks over to a more secluded table under a sloping wooden ceiling beam in the corner, I found myself racking my brains for something to say. We sat down—me surreptitiously pulling my chair out so that I was sitting at an angle away from him. I didn't think the chef would go so far as to grope me under the table but I was taking no chances.

"Um... so, Antonio... you must be busy with your new restaurant?"

As he started talking, I realised that I had been worrying for nothing. Antonio Casa loved to talk about himself. All I had to do was nod and smile and look interested, and he rambled on, talking non-stop about his childhood, his training, his recipes, his TV career... He was the perfect candidate to pump for information. The only thing was, the longer he talked, the more I began to feel that he couldn't be the murderer. As Poirot would say: the psychology was all wrong. I could see Antonio Casa killing someone in a murderous rage, especially if they'd insulted his ego, but I just couldn't see him carefully planning a cold-blooded murder. And whoever had killed Josh McDermitt had planned the murder meticulously, with cool, scientific precision.

"...of course, there are other male chefs in the UK, but I told them they'd never find someone with my unique combination of skills and sexual charisma. If they didn't appreciate that, then it's their loss, really. Anyway, I was thinking of leaving *Superchef*—the show was getting boring and there are other shows that deserve my talents. My manager's been in talks with some American networks—I'm sure they'd love to have me over in the States... don't you think?"

"Er... yes, I'm sure you're right," I said, coming out of my own thoughts and hastily focusing on the man opposite me. Reminding myself of the reason I had agreed to meet him, I leaned across the table and gave him a winsome smile. "Antonio... I've been hearing all these rumours about you and Josh McDermitt's murder. Is it true that you were at the Boscobel College ball the night he was killed?"

He hesitated for a split second. "Yeah, I was there. I went to meet a lady friend."

"So you didn't see Josh at all?"

"No," he said quickly. *Maybe too quickly?*

I pretended to fiddle with a beer coaster on the table and said casually, "Oh... that's funny... because you see, I was at the ball too and I thought I saw you near the dining hall. Just by the college kitchen. I thought maybe you'd gone to speak to Josh—"

"That wasn't me!" he snapped. "I was never anywhere near the dining hall or the kitchen."

"I guess I must have been mistaken. It was quite dark and men often look alike in black tie."

He calmed down slightly, then smirked. "So you

were at the ball too, huh? Ah, if only I'd known, I would have—"

He broke off as his phone rang shrilly. Frowning, he picked it up and stabbed a button, but he must have hit the Speaker mode by mistake because, the next moment, a distorted female voice crackled from the phone.

"Antonio? Antonio? Where are you? We were going to have lunch together, remember?"

The chef swore. "I… uh… I'm tied up with something."

"Where are you? I'll come and meet you."

"No, no… I'm busy, okay? I can't see you today."

The voice turned shrill and accusatory. *"You're with some woman, aren't you? I knew it! Who is she?"*

"N-no… I'm not. I told you, I'm busy—"

"Who is she, you bastard? Where did you meet her?" The voice turned tearful. *"How could you do this to me, Antonio? I thought you loved me but you just treated me like a piece of toilet paper to use and toss aside. You said I was special… and I believed you! But you didn't mean a thing you said, did you? You lying son-of-a—"*

"Hey… there's no need to get excited," growled Antonio.

"Excited? EXCITED?" The voice became even shriller and I winced as everyone in the pub turned to look at us. *"YOU'RE CHEATING ON ME WITH SOME WOMAN AND YOU'RE TELLING ME NOT TO*

GET EXCITED?"

I tried to shrink down in my seat as I saw everyone swivel their gazes to me. *Great.* Now I was going to look like "the other woman" in some sordid cliché drama. I wondered if there was any way I could sneak out while Antonio was still arguing. Then he saved me the trouble by swearing at the phone and storming out of the pub, still shouting into the mouthpiece. I hunched my shoulders as all eyes followed him out, then turned back towards me. Trying to appear nonchalant, I gathered my things and got up, hoping to scurry out of the pub as fast as I could.

But as I passed a table near the door, I heard a familiar voice call my name. I faltered to a stop as I recognised the tall, good-looking man. It was Lincoln Green. The son of my mother's closest friend, Helen Green—and an eminent doctor to boot—Lincoln was the man my mother had always hoped I'd marry. For a while, after I'd returned to Oxford, she'd driven me crazy with her embarrassing matchmaking schemes, trying to throw us together. Thankfully, though, it looked like my mother was finally accepting that Lincoln and I would never be more than good friends, and that Devlin was a permanent part of my life now.

"Gemma, how nice to see you," said Lincoln, his brown eyes warm as he smiled at me.

"Er... hi, Lincoln," I said, shifting uncomfortably.

I glanced at his companion and recognised the

Chinese girl as Dr Josephine Ling. Petite and pretty, Jo looked nothing like the skilful forensic pathologist that she was, equally at home dissecting dead bodies as analysing DNA and blood splatters. I wondered if they were on a date—I was very fond of Lincoln and liked Jo a lot too—and I thought they'd make a great couple.

"I'm sorry, but was that... Antonio Casa?" asked Jo in her soft, melodious voice. "I recognise him from the show *Superchef*."

"Yeah, I was having drinks with him—It's not what you think," I added hastily as their expressions flickered. "I only agreed to meet him because I thought it would give me an opportunity to question him about Josh McDermitt's murder."

"Oh... I see." Jo grinned at me. "So you're helping the Oxfordshire CID on a murder investigation again."

"Well, not officially. Devlin doesn't know that I'm here today. I'd... er... appreciate it if you didn't mention it to him."

"Mum's the word," said Jo, giving me a wink. "So did you pick up any leads?"

"No, not really. I only just started questioning him and then his phone rang."

"Is Antonio Casa a suspect in the murder?" asked Lincoln.

I nodded. "He was at the ball—and I actually think I saw him near the dining hall, where Josh was killed, although he denied it just now when I

172

asked him about it. Also, there was some conductive gel found in his overnight case. The kind used to improve electrical contact. And the electric whisk which electrocuted Josh had conductive gel smeared on the handle."

"Mmm... yes, I saw that when I was doing the autopsy..." said Jo.

"What's Casa's motive, though?" asked Lincoln, frowning.

I shrugged. "Revenge, I guess. He was very jealous and resentful that he was going to be replaced by Josh in the next season of *Superchef*. Also, he claims that Josh sabotaged the opening night at his new restaurant and a man with an ego like Antonio Casa's wouldn't take that lying down."

"Yes, but still... revenge?" Lincoln looked sceptical. "People don't murder each other for revenge."

"You obviously don't know anything about women," said Jo with a laugh. "We can bottle things up and stew on something for decades! I know of several cases where a woman tried to kill her boyfriend or husband, in revenge for him cheating on her."

"Funny you should say that, because the other suspect is Josh's ex-girlfriend," I commented. "And revenge would be her motive too. She's very bitter that Josh dumped her when he rose to fame. She blames him for abandoning her and she's been threatening to make him pay. I have to say...

personally, she's the one I'd go for. Antonio Casa is just too... I don't know... Having talked to him today, he just feels like the wrong type of person to plan a cold-blooded murder."

"Yes, murder by electrocution is a pretty elaborate plan," Jo agreed. "Most people wouldn't bother to go to all that trouble—they'd just use poison... or bash the person over the head."

"I don't suppose there was anything interesting in the autopsy?" I asked her.

"It was pretty boring, really. There were the expected burn marks on his hand, where he held the whisk, and a matching one on his left foot, where the current exited his body. And of course, there were the internal physiological changes consistent with electrocution... but nothing else really. No special fibres found on him or a convenient piece of broken nail with distinctive nail polish..." She grinned at me. "What a shame real life can't be like crime novels, eh?"

CHAPTER SEVENTEEN

With Antonio storming off like that, I was finished with lunch much earlier than I'd anticipated and I arrived half an hour early at Carfax to meet Keeley O'Connor. I found a spot at the base of the twelfth-century St Martin's Tower—known more popularly as "Carfax Tower"—which dominated the junction and provided great views across the famous skyline of Oxford, and settled down to wait for her.

The medieval tower played a special role in the university city—all students were required to live within a certain distance of the tower and no building in central Oxford was allowed to be built higher than it. For me, it was one of the landmarks that I'd always taken for granted in my university days, and there was a strange sense of déjà vu standing beneath it now and listening to the tower clock chime the quarter hour on its six bells.

I didn't have long to wait—within a few minutes, I spotted Keeley looking at window displays as she wandered down the other side of the street. I hurried across and tapped her gently on the shoulder.

"Gemma, luv! Am I late?" she asked as she swung around and saw me.

"No, no... I was early." I looked down at the shopping bags she was clutching and grinned. "It looks like you've been busy."

"They've got summer sales starting already in a lot of stores!" she said, beaming. "I picked up some gorgeous pieces. Oh, I got something for you..."

"For me?" I said, surprised.

"It's just a small thing... nothing much..." She looked around. "Is there somewhere we can sit down? I'm dying for a cuppa."

"Why don't we find somewhere in the Covered Market? Come on—I'll help you carry that."

I took some bags from her and showed her the way to the historic indoor market hidden behind the buildings of the main shopping strip. Dating back to the 1770s, the Covered Market was one of the top tourist attractions in Oxford and a warren of winding lanes filled with stores showcasing local crafts, food, and drink, as well as some services going back several generations, like the traditional cobbler and a quaint hat shop. We found seats at one of the cafés and Keeley sat down with a gusty sigh.

"Ahhh... my feet are killing me." She stretched her long legs out in front of her and leaned back in the chair, tossing her blonde hair over her shoulder. Reaching into one of the shopping bags, she withdrew a small pile of fabric, handing it to me. "Here you go. I saw this and thought you might like it—in case your top from last night was ruined. This one looks quite similar."

"Oh! Thank you." I was touched at her thoughtfulness. Carefully, I shook out the folded fabric to find that it was actually a delicate knit top in a pale lilac colour, very similar in style to the blue one I had been wearing last night. "It's beautiful! Thanks so much."

Keeley O'Connor smiled at me. "I'm glad you like it. The store had great stuff. I even picked up something that I might wear to the wine bar in Jericho tonight."

I sobered. "Oh. Um... so you're still going?"

She threw me a defiant look. "Yes. You're not going to start lecturing me like Dev, are you?"

"No, of course not... that is, I..." I swallowed. I didn't feel that it was in my place to chastise her. On the other hand, some lingering sense of loyalty to Devlin made me feel like I ought to say something. "It's just... well, Devlin is right in a way. It *is* a bit risky to... um... meet up with strange men... and... er, I know Oxford looks all pretty and genteel and historic, but underneath the 'dreaming spires', it's still a bustling city with crime and... and darkness..."

Keeley chuckled. "Well, it would have to be, otherwise my son would be out of a job!"

"Look, here's my number. If you need help or... or anything while you're out tonight, just send me a text or give me a ring. I stay up quite late."

She smiled. "Thanks. That's really sweet of you." She reached across and patted my hand. "But stop worrying, luv—I'll be fine. I've been taking care of myself for forty odd years and I can manage perfectly well... even though Devlin won't believe me," she added with a touch of asperity.

"Devlin just cares about you," I said gently.

She sighed. "Yes, I know. And I know it's frustrating for him..." She gave me a rueful smile. "As a mother, I'm a real disappointment to him, aren't I?"

"Er..." I floundered for a way to answer that.

Keeley's smile turned sad. "You know, I was too bloody young when I had him. Barely fifteen. A little more than a baby myself. I was never ready to be a mother... and I still don't feel ready." She shrugged helplessly. "I guess some of us just aren't maternal types. Oh, don't get me wrong—I adore Dev and I'm not sorry that I had him. But... " She sighed again. "It just feels like he always wants me to be something I'm not... something I can never be."

I bit my lip, wondering what to say. "Keeley, I'm sure Devlin doesn't—"

"Oh, you don't have to protect my feelings," she said with another sad smile. "I know Dev resents me for not acting like a 'proper' mother... and I tried—I really tried when he was younger..." She shook her head. "But... this is me. I can't change who I am, just to make him happy."

I squirmed in my seat, feeling a mixture of compassion and embarrassment. As if reading my thoughts, Keeley O'Connor gave a laugh and said:

"I'm probably making you feel uncomfortable with all this breast-baring! It's funny, you know— I've never talked about Devlin like this to anyone else before. But it's so easy talking to you... even though we only met yesterday." She patted my hand again. "But then, I could always tell from the way Dev talks about you that you're special... I'm really glad that he has you."

I squirmed even more. *Oh God. This is really embarrassing now.*

Keeley leaned back and tilted her head to one side. "You're the girl who broke Dev's heart eight years ago, aren't you? He never talked about it much—he doesn't confide in me anyway—but I can hear the same tone in his voice when he mentions your name..." She gave me a glare and wagged a finger in my face. "I may not be very maternal, but I warn you, you'd better not break my boy's heart again or you'll have me to answer to."

Then she burst out laughing at the expression on my face and said, "Come on, let's order some tea and cake."

I started to answer, then paused as I noticed a woman sitting alone on the other side of the café.

"Is something the matter, luv?" asked Keeley.

"N-no..." I tore my gaze away. "I just saw someone I recognised. That woman sitting in the corner—the one with the brown hair and glasses—she's the producer for Josh McDermitt's reality TV show. Her name's Maddie."

Keeley turned her head and glanced across the room. "Looks a bit weepy, doesn't she?"

I nodded. It had been the producer's red, swollen eyes that caught my attention.

"Yes... I wonder if she's just heard that they're scrapping the whole show. She'd be out of a job and probably a very good income too—"

"No," said Keeley, looking at the other woman with a practised eye. "She's crying over a man."

I smiled to myself. With Keeley O'Connor, it was *always* a man. "How could you know that?" I asked with a laugh.

"I know the signs," said Devlin's mother sagely.

Before we could speculate further, Maddie Gill got up from her table, paid her bill, and left the café. I watched her go thoughtfully, wondering if Keeley could be right.

CHAPTER EIGHTEEN

I'd planned on staying with Keeley all afternoon but she shooed me off after our tea together, declaring that she was fine shopping on her own and insisting that I return to the tearoom. So I found myself back in Meadowford just before four o'clock and slipped into my apron in time to help Cassie deal with the teatime rush.

The Old Biddies had pounced on me as soon as I arrived, eager to hear the details of my lunch with Antonio Casa, but they were forced to wait until the rush had died down and the tearoom had emptied. Their faces fell in disappointment, though, when I told them what had happened at the pub and how little I'd learned.

"Anyway, I don't think Antonio killed Josh," I said as I finished. "He just doesn't seem like the type. And even if he really was capable of a premeditated murder, I can't see him saying nothing about it. Antonio Casa is a megalomaniac. He needs to be adored and applauded. He would *have* to let people know how he pulled off such a great crime—he'd never be able to keep quiet about it."

"But what about the gel we found in his case?" Glenda asked.

"Well... I spoke to Devlin briefly this morning. The police got a search warrant and they went through Antonio's things. They did find the gel but Antonio claimed that it was for use with an EMS machine that he'd bought."

"An EMS machine? What's that?" Florence frowned.

"It stands for Electronic-Muscle Stimulation. It's basically a machine with little pads that attach to you and it sends tiny electrical impulses which contracts your muscles. It's sort of the lazy way to build biceps and get flat abs." I grinned. "I'm not sure it works but I think a lot of men get taken in by late-night infomercials on TV and buy one of these. Given how vain Antonio Casa is, I'm not surprised that he has one."

"But we only have his word that that's what the gel is for," Glenda pointed out. "He could be lying."

"Yes, I suppose he could. The police did find a portable EMS machine, though, in his case."

"Bloody hell, have you seen this?" Cassie spoke up from the other side of the room, where she had been clearing a table. A customer had left a copy of the local tabloid on a chair and Cassie was tilting her head, peering at the headline, which was half hidden under Muesli's furry bum. For some reason, the little tabby cat loved to sit on pieces of paper lying around, and now she hunched happily on top of the folded newspaper, her front paws tucked into her chest and her green eyes narrowed into sleepy slits.

"Come on, Muesli... get up..." muttered Cassie, tugging at the edge of the newspaper and trying to pull it out from underneath the cat.

"*Meorrw!*" cried Muesli indignantly as the paper shifted underneath her.

Cassie wrestled with her a moment longer, then finally extricated the newspaper. Muesli jumped down from the chair and stalked off in a huff as Cassie came across the tearoom to join us. She held it up for us to see as she approached. The front page showed a soft-focus photograph of Leanne Fitch in a very revealing outfit, with the headline: "MCDERMITT'S EX-LOVER TELLS HOW SHE FEARED FOR HIS LIFE!"

Cassie put on a falsetto voice and read from the article:

"*'Josh and I shared something special. I was there for him before he became famous and I knew the real man beneath the chef's hat'... 'I've always been a very sensitive person—I believe I may even be a little psychic—and I knew something was wrong the night of the ball'... 'I feared for his life. That's why I went to see Josh at his hotel, even though he'd hurt me terribly. It was like a stab in my heart every time I saw him! But I put my own pain aside; I've always put others' needs first, I'm a very nurturing person'...* Oh, pul-lease!" Cassie tossed the paper aside in disgust. "I can't believe how she's milking the publicity from his murder!"

I laughed. "Well, you have to admire her initiative. She probably got paid a very nice packet for that piece and those pictures."

"If Leanne didn't murder Josh herself, I'll eat my favourite paintbrush!" Cassie declared.

"Cassie, she's got an alibi too. Remember? The hotel maid said she saw Leanne in her room at the time of the murder."

"*Pfft!* Alibis can be faked," said Cassie, waving a hand.

"Well, I have to admit, I did wonder... I mean, that description that Irene Mansell gave of the blonde woman she saw skulking in the cloister sounded a lot like Leanne. And she said the woman ran away as soon as she saw her."

"I'll bet it was Leanne!" exclaimed Cassie. "When did Irene Mansell see this woman?"

"About ten, fifteen minutes before she saw me, she said."

"Well, then, the timing is perfect!" Cassie declared. "I'm sure it was Leanne: she'd sneaked into the dining hall before Josh and his entourage arrived, and tampered with the wiring, then sneaked out again. Since she used the private route through the cloister, nobody saw her... except the Master's wife, of course. That's why she ran: Irene Mansell spotted her. If that's not an indication of guilt, I don't know what is!"

"But how would she know how to tamper with the wiring?" Mabel spoke up. "She hasn't got an electrician background, like Antonio Casa does. No, dear... I think you're barking up the wrong tree. It's Antonio Casa. He has the skills to fiddle with the wires—"

"The tampering part is easy!" said Cassie impatiently. "You can find anything on the internet these days. Leanne probably just googled it and found detailed instructions online on how to electrocute someone with faulty wiring."

"But what about the electro-conductive gel?" Mabel insisted. "You can't deny that it's a strange coincidence that Antonio Casa should be carrying that in his case. I know Gemma says it was for his electric muscle machine but I don't believe it."

Cassie shrugged. "Well, maybe we'd find some gel in Leanne's travel bag too, if we searched—"

"Uh... let's not get any ideas," I said hastily.

"You haven't met Leanne in person," Cassie told Mabel. "If you did, you'd agree with me. She's just the kind of woman to murder her ex-boyfriend."

"No, dear, you're wrong," Mabel said with calm superiority. "The murderer is Antonio Casa."

"No, it's not! I'm telling you, Leanne did it."

"Definitely not."

"Yes, she did!"

My head swivelled left and right between Cassie and Mabel, like someone watching a tennis game. I had never seen either of them clash like this before. This wasn't about Josh McDermitt's murder anymore—this was about being proven right and getting the last word.

"You forget, young lady, that Leanne Fitch has an alibi," said Mabel triumphantly. "That makes it impossible for her to have committed the murder."

"And I told you, alibis can be faked!" Cassie growled. "All right—you know what? I'm going to prove it to you. I'm going to show you that Leanne faked her alibi." She turned and stormed into the kitchen.

"Cass—" I started to follow her but, at that moment, someone opened the front door of the tearoom and stuck their head in. I glanced up and realised that it was Seth.

He gave me an uncertain smile and said, "Have I come at a bad time? I've got the cat trap on my bike outside. Wasn't sure if I should bring it in the tearoom."

"Oh, Seth—that's great! I'll come out and get it."

I followed him out to the little courtyard—which used to be the stables of the old inn and which gave the tearoom its name—and surveyed the long, rectangular cage strapped to the back of Seth's bicycle. It looked slightly scary, all gleaming steel and wire mechanisms, but when Seth took it off the bike and showed me how to work it, I felt less daunted.

"You'll be fine, Gemma," Seth assured me. "Test it on Muesli, if you're really worried."

I bit off a laugh. "Are you joking? She'd never forgive me! Anyway, thanks for bringing it. I'll take it to Boscobel tomorrow and give it a whirl."

"Let me know how you go... Oh, and I can organise for an animal welfare vets to neuter the tom," Seth offered.

I waved a hand. "That's okay—I don't mind paying for my own vet to do that. Save the resources for the charity. The bigger problem is going to be where to release him."

"I'll speak to my contact and see if she has any suggestions. The best place is a rural home or a farm or stables—somewhere the feral cat can roam safely, have regular food and water, and a warm place to shelter, like a barn or an outbuilding. Of course, if the cat is tame enough, we can try to place it in a pet home... but most ferals are too wild for that."

"Hmm... this tom is pretty friendly. At least, he was to me. In fact, I wondered if he used to be someone's pet once. Anyway," I gave Seth a cynical smile, "better not get ahead of ourselves... let's catch him first!"

CHAPTER NINETEEN

Dora normally left the tearoom early afternoon, once her baking for the day had been done, so I was surprised to see her pop her head out of the kitchen as Cassie and I were closing up for the day.

"Is everything all right?" I asked.

She nodded and beckoned me and Cassie towards her. "I've got a bit of time today. I want to give you girls a baking lesson."

Cassie and I looked at each other uneasily. We both knew that when it came to delicious baking, we were much better at eating it than making it. It was why finding Dora had been so key to the success of the tearoom. In fact, the one time that Cassie had tried to don the chef's hat and take over, the baking had been a total disaster, with burnt scones and imploded sponge cakes littering the tearoom kitchen.

"Baking lesson?" Cassie said. "But why do we need to bake when you're doing it much better than us anyway?"

"You should know what you're serving," said Dora tartly. "And those egg custard tarts are so popular right now—"

"Probably because everyone thinks the bloke who made them was murdered," Cassie muttered under her breath.

"—you ought to at least try your hand at making some yourselves. Come on: finish closing up the tearoom, then come into the kitchen. And don't forget to wash your hands."

We did as she bid, then rolled up our sleeves and approached the large wooden table in the centre of the kitchen. Dora was already mixing little cubes of butter into a bowl of flour, rubbing it with her fingers until the mixture looked like breadcrumbs, before adding a small bowl of caster sugar and some ground almonds.

"That isn't in the traditional egg custard tart recipe," she said, indicating the ground almonds. "But I think it gives the pastry a lovely, nutty flavour."

We watched as she added an egg to the mixture and gently folded it in until the dough was formed. She shaped this into a flat oblong and wrapped it in cling film.

"Put that in the fridge—it needs to chill for thirty minutes," she instructed Cassie. "In the meantime, we can make the custard filling. Here, Gemma—grab the whisk."

I couldn't help thinking of Josh McDermitt as I picked up the old-fashioned hand whisk. He might have still been alive if he hadn't been so reliant on electrical appliances. Then Dora was barking instructions at me and all thoughts of the murder left my mind as I started whisking eggs and sugar together in a large bowl, whilst Cassie followed instructions for heating milk and fresh cream on the stove. I whisked even harder as my best friend brought the warm milk over and poured it into my bowl. I was worried that the eggs would scramble if I didn't whisk fast enough and my fervour had the creamy yellow liquid frothing all over.

"Easy now—you're not making a bubble bath," Dora grumbled, taking the bowl out of my hands.

She added a few drops of vanilla essence into the custard mixture, then set it aside while she got the chilled dough out of the fridge. Separating it into two large pieces, she handed me and Cassie each a rolling pin and gave instructions for rolling our pastry dough out into a thin layer.

When Dora popped out of the kitchen briefly, Cassie paused in her rolling and leaned close to me.

"Listen, Gemma, can you do me a favour? Can you ring Devlin's sergeant and ask him the name of this maid he spoke to—the one who confirmed

Leanne Fitch's alibi?"

I gave her a curious look. "Sure. But why do you want to know?"

"Just... humour me, okay? I've got an idea."

I wiped my hands on my apron and fished out my phone. A few minutes later, I hung up again and turned back to my best friend.

"Her name is Marta Jasiewicz. She doesn't actually work for the hotel where Leanne's staying. The hotel outsources all room cleaning to a company that supplies maids for hotel chains and Marta is one of their employees."

"Jasiewicz—that's a Polish name, isn't it?" said Cassie thoughtfully. "I'll bet she's an immigrant worker being abused and paid less than the minimum wage..."

I was puzzled. "Well, that would be terrible... but I don't understand how that's relevant—"

"Well, girls? How are you getting on?"

Dora came back into the kitchen and walked up to the table to inspect our handiwork. Cassie and I hastily began pushing our rolling pins again.

"Good, good..." said Dora, leaning over us to look. "Now, cut out little discs to form the tart cases—you can place them in each of the moulds there." She pointed to a metal muffin tray next to us.

We did as she instructed and soon had twelve little circles of pastry arranged across the muffin tray. Carefully, we pressed each pastry circle down into the edges of each mould, so that they formed little tart cases, and then poured the custard mixture into each, filling it to the brim. A generous helping of freshly grated nutmeg across the top of each tart and they were good to go.

I walk slowly to the oven, carrying the muffin tray with agonising care. Somehow, I managed not to spill any of the custard mixture out of the cases and I slid the tray into the pre-heated interior with a sigh of relief. All the preparation had really whetted my appetite and I could barely wait the twenty-five minutes it took for the tarts to bake.

"Are they ready yet?" Cassie asked fifteen minutes later, sounding like a whiny toddler on a car trip.

"Almost," said Dora placidly. "You have to wait until the custard sets—it needs to form a little dome on top, but still have a slight wobble."

Finally, they were ready, and my mouth watered as Dora slid the muffin tray out of the oven. She removed each tart and placed them on a rack to cool. They looked delicious, each little shell of golden crust surrounding a creamy yellow custard filling, lightly speckled with nutmeg.

"Ooh... That smells heavenly!" Cassie said, inhaling deeply. She helped herself to a tart, holding the still-warm pastry by the edges as she took a big bite. "Mmmm... ohhhh... amaaaaazing..."

I picked up a tart and took a bite as well. Cassie was right. It *was* heavenly: the biscuity, crumbly shell of the tart contrasting beautifully with soft and silky custard filling.

"Mm... I've got to have another," said Cassie, grabbing another tart and cramming it into her mouth.

"You'll get a stomach ache if you eat so quickly," said Dora with mock severity, but I could see from her twinkling eyes that she enjoyed our reactions.

We had one more tart each, then reluctantly saved the rest and helped Dora clear up. Muesli had somehow sneaked into the kitchen again while none of us were looking and was now curled up asleep on one of the chairs by the large wooden table. I shook my head with a smile and picked her up, cuddling her soft, warm body close to me.

"*Meorrw?*" she said sleepily.

"Come on, Muesli—time to go home."

Then I paused, eyeing the little tabby speculatively. I glanced at the cat trap in the corner of the kitchen and remembered what Seth had suggested.

"Coming, Gemma?" asked Cassie from the kitchen doorway.

"Actually, Cass—can you help me with something? It won't take a moment."

"Sure." She gave me a quizzical look.

I pointed to the cat trap and asked her to bring it with her, then led the way out to the tearoom courtyard.

"Here, you hold Muesli," I said, thrusting my cat

at Cassie.

I took the cage from her and carried it over to the far wall. Putting it down on the ground, I tried to remember Seth's instructions on how to set the trap. Carefully, I raised the door and latched it, then I placed a few of Mrs Purdey's Catnip Crumbles on a piece of napkin at the back of the cage, behind the trigger plate.

"Okay. Put Muesli down," I called, backing away.

I retreated to where Cassie was standing and watched as my little cat strolled over to inspect the new item in the courtyard. She approached the cage slowly, pausing every few steps to sniff the ground. When she finally reached the entrance to the trap, she spent several minutes sniffing the steel frame intently. Then she hesitated, threw a glance back at us, and took a step into the cage. Her whiskers quivered as she spied the Catnip Crumbles. I held my breath and crossed my fingers. Muesli hesitated again, then walked forwards, deeper into the cage, towards the bait behind the trigger plate...

BANG!

The door to the cage slammed shut with a rattle and Muesli jumped in fright. Her fur puffed up into little spikes all over her body and she began throwing herself against the sides of the cage.

"*Meeeorrw! Meeeorrw! MEEEEORRW!*" she wailed.

"Sorry, Muesli, sorry!" I cried, hurrying towards the cage.

I was beginning to feel a bit bad for using her as a guinea pig. I fumbled with the cage, struggling to release the door mechanism, and I'd barely lifted the flap when Muesli shot out. She streaked past me and up the whitewashed brick wall surrounding the courtyard.

"Muesli—"

I started after her but she had already reached the top of the wall. She balanced for a second on the ledge, then disappeared down the other side.

"Muesli!"

Cassie rushed over to join me and we both tried to look over the wall but it was too tall.

"Oh *bugger*!" I slumped against the bricks and looked at Cassie in consternation. "What are we going to do now? I'm never going to find her."

Cassie snapped her fingers. "Doesn't Mrs Purdey's cottage back onto the tearoom? I'll bet her garden is on the other side of this wall. You'll probably find Muesli hiding somewhere there."

I pushed myself upright. "You're right! I'll pop over now."

A few minutes later, I was standing on Mrs Purdey's doorstep. When the old lady opened the door and I'd explained the situation to her, she wrung her hands in concern.

"Oh! Oh! But of course, we must find her—poor little mite!" she cried, hustling me into the cottage and shutting the door behind me.

She led me past the overstuffed sofas and

various populations of lace doilies to a glass door which led out into her rear garden. It was a rambling, overgrown patch filled with cottage garden perennials and straggly rose bushes. At the rear of the garden was a small shed, right up against a familiar brick wall—the same brick wall which encircled my tearoom courtyard on the other side.

"Muesli? Muesli?" I called softly, walking up to the shed.

There was a rustle in the undergrowth, then a pair of green eyes glowed at me from the shadows in the gap behind the shed.

"Muesli! Come out now..." I crouched down and stretched a hand out to her.

"*Meorrw!*" she said reproachfully.

"Come on, Muesli, I'm sorry about what happened... You're safe now. No more frights."

"*Meorrw!*"

I saw the tip of a grey striped tail twitch in the shadows, then more rustling. I stood up with a smile, expecting my cat to walk out, but instead I heard a scratching sound and, the next moment, Muesli appeared on the shed roof.

"Muesli! Come down—what are you doing?" I demanded, starting to lose patience.

She looked down at me, her little face sulky.

"*Meorrw!*" she said.

Then she deliberately turned around and sat down with her bum to me. I sighed. She was obviously punishing me for testing the cage trap on her. I took a deep breath and tried again. But no amount of threats, pleading, or cajoling could get my little cat off the roof of the shed. Finally I turned to the little old lady standing next to me.

"Have you got a ladder so I can climb up to try and reach her?"

The old lady shook her head.

"Then... maybe we should call the fire brigade?" I suggested, squirming at the thought.

"Oh no, dear—don't do that!" cried Mrs Purdey. "I'll tell you what: why don't you leave her here with me? I'll wait a bit and then I'll try again. Smudge used to do this too, you know, when he was put out. Sit on the shed roof with his back to me. He always came down eventually when he got hungry. I'm sure Muesli would be the same." Her eyes sparkled. "Then she can stay overnight with me, and you can come and fetch her tomorrow."

I started to protest, then changed my mind. It was a good suggestion. I didn't fancy standing in Mrs Purdey's garden for another few hours, calling to my sulking cat to come down, and Muesli would be perfectly safe here. Even if she refused to come down all night, it was midsummer now and the warm enough that it didn't really matter if she spent a night outdoors. Besides, I could see from the hopeful expression on Mrs Purdey's face that Muesli staying with her would make her day.

"All right," I agreed. "But I'll leave you my mobile

number and if she gives you any trouble at all, don't hesitate to ring me."

Mrs Purdey clasped her hands together, a big smile on her face. "Oh no, I'm sure she'll be no trouble. Muesli and I are going to have a wonderful time together!"

CHAPTER TWENTY

Cassie looked up in surprise when I re-entered the tearoom a short while later. "Where's Muesli?"

I rolled my eyes. "Spending a night on Mrs Purdey's shed roof. Well, hopefully not, actually. We're hoping she'll come down after a few hours."

I explained the arrangement to Cassie, then we turned off the lights and walked together to the front door. As I was locking up, however, Cassie grabbed my arm and said:

"Listen, you don't have to go home straight away, do you?"

"Well... no, why?"

"Remember I was asking about the maid who gave Leanne Fitch her alibi? While you were gone, I rang the hotel and she's on duty today. In fact..."

Cassie glanced at her watch. "She doesn't clock off until six. It's the perfect opportunity!"

I looked at her in bewilderment. "But Cass—"

"Come on!"

She hustled me out of the tearoom and onto my bike, then took off on her own bicycle, calling to me to follow. I had to work to keep up with her as she pedalled furiously ahead of me on the road. We drew up at last in front of a small chain hotel situated on the outskirts of Oxford. Cassie jumped off her bike, chained it to a post, and ran into the lobby. I hurriedly followed and found her at the reception desk, asking to speak to "Marta".

"Hmm, I dunno where she might be at the moment," said the receptionist. "You could try the guests' lounge out the back. She usually cleans in there last."

We found a thin woman in a faded cotton dress wearily dusting the bookshelves in the guests' lounge.

"Marta?" asked Cassie, approaching her.

The woman turned. "*Tak?* Yes?"

Cassie gave her a warm smile. "Marta—can we talk to you for a minute? It's about one of the guests: a lady called Leanne Fitch."

"Yes?" She eyed us warily.

"You know, three nights ago, a man was murdered in one of the Oxford colleges. A famous TV chef called Josh McDermitt—you know him?"

She shrugged. "I don't have time for watch TV."

"Well, the police are investigating his murder... and I believe they questioned you about Leanne's movements on that night? You told them that you took some laundry to her room at around the time that Josh McDermitt was killed and Leanne was in her room."

A flash of fear showed in the woman's eyes. "Yes. Yes, I already told police."

"But... that's not the truth, is it?" asked Cassie gently.

The woman jerked back. "What you mean?"

"You never went to Leanne's room that night, did you? She just bribed you to say that."

The woman took another step backwards, her face pale and scared now. "I don't know what you say..."

"Marta, you can't lie to protect her. You have to tell the truth."

The woman shook her head vehemently. "No! I did not lie! I see this woman, Leanne, in her room, like I say."

I looked at my friend uneasily. "Cassie, maybe we shouldn't—"

"It's really tough being a hotel worker, isn't it?" said Cassie, ignoring me. Her voice took on a warm, sympathetic tone. "Immigrants like you get a really raw deal. They probably pay you below the minimum wage and expect you to work all hours— and if you get sick, they send you home without any pay. And you never see your family... and miss them terribly..."

The woman's face softened. "Yes," she said, her voice faint and dispirited. "I have two little girls back in Poland..."

"That's why you did it, isn't it?" Cassie asked gently. "Because you needed the money badly. It would make so much difference to your little girls. And it was easy: all you had to do was tell a little lie, pretend you saw Leanne in her room... what did it matter?"

Marta hesitated but her silence was answer enough.

Cassie reached out and put a hand on the woman's arm. "Marta, you need to do the right thing. You could help the police find a murderer... You just need to tell the truth."

The woman hesitated again, licking her lips nervously. "I... I..." Then her face hardened and she took a step back from us. "I tell the police the truth. I saw the woman in the room."

"But—"

"I have to go now," Marta said, pushing past us and hurrying out of the lounge.

Cassie exhaled in frustration. "I thought she was going to confess."

"Me too," I said. I gave her shoulder a squeeze. "It was a good try, Cass. I guess I could speak to Devlin and tell him your idea about Leanne bribing Marta to give her an alibi. Maybe the police will question Marta again—"

"No, I'm not giving up," said Cassie, her chin jutting out. "I'm going to show Mabel that Leanne's the murderer if it's the last thing I do!" She whirled and dashed back into the reception.

I followed in bemusement, but when I got there, my best friend was already rushing out again.

"Where—"

"Come on!"

She grabbed my hand and yanked me after her. We came out of the hotel and instead of heading to our parked bikes, like I'd expected, Cassie dragged me towards the petrol station on the corner of the street.

"Cass! Wait, what... where are we going?" I panted as I ran after her.

We passed the petrol pumps and entered the small café attached to the service station. Cassie paused and looked around, then hurried over to an empty table by the window. She sat down and waved me to a seat.

"Cassie, what are we doing?" I asked as I dropped down next to her.

"Waiting for someone," she said with a smile.

"Who?"

"You'll see."

Grrr. It reminded me of when we were little girls and Cassie got one of her mad ideas for a new game or adventure, but refused to tell me what it was. I opened my mouth to ask her again, then froze as I spied someone in the window, walking rapidly towards the café.

A sharp-faced woman with heavy make-up and dyed blonde hair... *Leanne Fitch.*

"Hello, Leanne!" Cassie sprang up as soon as the blonde woman entered the café. She rushed forwards, a bright smile plastered on her face. "Come and sit down. Would you like a drink? Cup of tea? I think they do some juices too..." She herded Leanne over to our table and pushed the woman down into a chair.

"Where's the journalist?" asked Leanne, looking around suspiciously. "You told me on the phone that there's a journalist here, from one of the big papers. Going to write an exclusive story about me."

"Ah... about that..." Cassie gave her a shameless grin. "I'm afraid the journalist couldn't make it. But you weren't really going to tell him the truth, were you?"

"What do you mean?"

"Well, the truth would mean confessing that *you* murdered Josh."

I gasped at Cassie's bluntness.

"What are you talking about?" Leanne cried, springing up from her chair. "I didn't murder him!"

"You can't lie to us. We know you were at Boscobel College that night," said Cassie.

"I've got an alibi," said Leanne disdainfully. "I was in my hotel room the night Josh was killed. The maid can confirm it—"

"You mean, you *bribed* her to confirm it," Cassie

cut in. "That's right—she confessed. She said you offered her money to pretend that she saw you when she delivered some laundry to your room—"

"*Cassie...?*" I turned to look at my friend in astonishment.

But Cassie ignored me and kept talking, all her attention focused on the blonde woman in front of her: "I'm sure the police would be interested to know that you bribed someone to manufacture an alibi for you."

"I... I didn't..." Leanne spluttered.

Cassie continued relentlessly: "Now, why would you do that unless you didn't want anyone to know that you were really at the ball? Because you were, weren't you? You were seen going through the cloister that leads to the back of the dining hall."

She took a threatening step towards Leanne and the other woman backed away. "You went to the ball that night to get even with Josh McDermitt for dumping you and you thought of the perfect way to do it: electrocute him with his own whisk! How wonderfully ironic. Go on, admit it!"

I stared at my best friend in shock, wondering if she had gone mad. Leanne was also staring at Cassie, but to my surprise, instead of the expression of outrage I'd expected, I saw fear on her face. She opened and closed her mouth several times, her eyes darting around, then all of a sudden, she put her hands up in a defensive gesture and cried:

"All right! All right, I admit it! I was there at the ball that night. But I didn't murder Josh!"

"Of course you murdered him. Why else would you have gone to the ball?" demanded Cassie. "Don't tell me you sneaked into the dining hall just to leave him a love note? You went in there to tamper with the wiring on the whisk."

"No, I'm telling you—I didn't touch the whisk! I admit, I did go into the dining hall that night, but... but I was tampering with the food, not the wiring."

"The food?" I said in surprise. "What do you mean, tampering with the food?"

"I wanted to humiliate Josh, okay?" said Leanne with a scowl. "I wanted him to suffer, like the way he made me suffer. So I bought some laxative powder and I was going to add it to the ingredients he was going to cook with. That way, when the dishes were served afterwards, they'd give everyone diarrhoea and Josh would look pretty bad. Especially if it was all on TV."

I suddenly remembered picking up Leanne's shopping bag at the nail salon. It had been filled with various pills and drugs, including a box of strong laxatives. I also remembered how protective she had been of it, snatching it out of my hands.

"How did you get in and out of the dining hall without anyone seeing you?" I asked.

"I knew about the back way through the cloister. Josh showed me. When we first started dating, he was still at Boscobel. It was his last year and I used to visit him in college sometimes. He showed me the way through the cloister to this sort of wild garden at the back of the college that hardly anyone goes to. We used to go there to snog and stuff. It was like our secret place..." A look of sadness clouded her eyes for a moment, then her face hardened again. "Not that Josh would have probably remembered..."

"So you used the cloister to get to the dining hall... But how did you get into the college in the first place?" asked Cassie. "The ball was by invitation only."

"It was the gate-crashers, wasn't it?" I spoke up, remembering what the college porter had told me. "The lock on the side gate to the college had been broken and people were sneaking in that way."

Leanne nodded. "Yeah, it was pretty easy. I just followed the crowd. There were so many people trying to get in to see Josh. And once I was in, I knew the way."

"I must have just missed you," I said. "The Master's wife told me she saw you coming back out through the cloister—"

"Yeah, she gave me a fright! I legged it as soon as I saw her. Didn't want her asking me awkward questions about where I'd been... It was bad enough that I nearly got caught in the hall."

"What do you mean?"

"Josh and his manager came in while I was still there. I managed to duck down behind one of those long tables before they saw me and I thought I'd be stuck there until the demo was over!" She rolled her eyes. "Thank God, Josh just marched straight to the bench and started faffing around with the stuff there. And his manager was too busy talking on the phone. I waited until their backs were turned then crawled behind the tables until I was by the door and slipped out."

She shifted her weight and looked at us sourly. "So I didn't murder Josh. I wanted to humiliate him but... I wouldn't have really hurt him."

"But innocent people were going to taste those dishes," Cassie pointed out. "Laxatives can be dangerous, especially in large doses. People have ended up in hospital after an overdose. You would have hurt all those people just to get back at Josh?"

Leanne shrugged and looked away. There was a long, uncomfortable silence, then Leanne said with another scowl:

"Well, the point is, I didn't murder him, okay?"

She turned to go but I caught her arm to stop her.

"Wait, Leanne... Just now, when you were talking about being stuck in the dining hall, you didn't mention the producer. Didn't she see you?"

"What producer?"

"The producer of Josh's TV show. A short woman with brown hair and glasses."

Leanne shook her head slowly. "Never saw any woman. It was just Josh and his manager."

After she'd left, I sat in a thoughtful silence while

Cassie fumed next to me.

"...I might have been wrong about her being the murderer but I was right about one thing: she's a bloody selfish cow! I can't believe she would have harmed loads of innocent people just to get back at Josh. You'd think—" She broke off and glanced at me. "What are you so deep in thought about?"

"That thing Leanne said about Josh's producer, Maddie, not being in the hall..."

Cassie looked puzzled. "Yeah, so?"

"Well, Devlin told me that Maddie said in her statement that she was with Jerry Wallis, the manager, the whole time. Meaning, she'd gone into the hall with Josh and Jerry, and stayed in there with them until the time she and Jerry left and came out again. In fact, that's when I saw them— they were coming together out of the rear entrance of the hall."

"You mean, she lied in her statement?"

"I don't know..."

"I was so sure it was Leanne!"

"I still can't believe what you did, telling Leanne that Marta confessed."

Cassie grinned. "I know—I was bluffing."

"You were bloody good!"

She chuckled. "I could have been totally wrong and then it would have been pretty embarrassing... but I took a punt."

I shook my head in admiration. "That's some pretty good technique you've got there, Cassandra

Jenkins. Are you sure you want to be an artist? You could probably have a brilliant career as an actress!"

CHAPTER TWENTY-ONE

Cassie and I parted ways outside the hotel, she to return to her studio apartment in Jericho and me to my little cottage down by the River Thames at the south end of Oxford. I arrived home, let myself in, and shut the front door, leaning against it with a huge sigh. Saturdays were always one of the busiest days at the tearoom, and what with seeing Antonio Casa for lunch, then meeting Devlin's mum, followed by Muesli's escapade, and then the tense encounters with Marta the hotel maid and Leanne Fitch... it had been a long, long day.

Tossing my bag onto the kitchen counter, I slouched into my small living-dining room and flopped onto the old, sagging couch. I lay for a moment, staring at the ceiling, the events of the day whirling through my mind. Leanne's comment about not seeing Maddie Gill in the dining hall kept niggling at me. When the police had questioned her, the TV producer had claimed that she had been with Jerry Wallis in the dining hall the whole time. But according to Leanne, Maddie had never been in the dining hall at all. If that was true, where had she been? I knew she had to have been inside the building because I saw her coming out of the rear entrance myself. She had been walking together with Jerry... But had she not been with him inside the hall? So did that mean that she had lied to the police in her statement?

But wait... Jerry Wallis had corroborated her statement. He had agreed that Maddie had been with him. So did that mean that *Leanne* was lying? But why would she lie about not seeing Maddie? I frowned. It just didn't make sense.

I sat upright on the couch, looking around. The house seemed strangely quiet and empty without Muesli. Despite being such a small bundle of fur, Muesli's cheeky personality meant that she had a larger-than-life presence. I laughed to myself. Yes, I even missed having to cater to her loud demands for dinner as soon as I walked in through the door!

My stomach rumbled; glancing at my watch, I was surprised to see that it was past seven o'clock. With the sun not setting until nearly ten in the English summertime, it was deceptively light outside. I got up and wandered into the kitchen to rustle up something for dinner, but my enthusiasm waned when I saw the uninspiring contents of my fridge. There was a tub of yoghurt, half a bottle of milk, a couple of apples, some old lettuce, and a small crusty slab of parmesan cheese. I knew there was also some dried pasta in the pantry and a few tins of baked beans and chopped tomatoes... I had been so busy this week, I hadn't had any time to pop to the supermarket for some grocery shopping, and now I wondered how to pull together a meal from these meagre ingredients.

I was just trying to decide whether to resort to a mug of instant soup and some crackers when my doorbell rang. I looked up in surprise—I wasn't expecting any visitors. When I opened the front door, I found four little old ladies standing on my doorstep.

"Gemma, dear! Have you had supper yet?" asked Mabel without preamble.

"Er... no, I was just about to have some soup and crackers—"

"Oh good! You can have some of the shepherd's pie I made instead," said Florence, beaming and showing me a ceramic casserole dish, wrapped in a large tea towel.

"I made you some gooseberry trifle for dessert," added Glenda, indicating a plastic Tupperware container in her hands.

"And *I* made you some lace doily earrings!" said Ethel, holding up two hideous pieces of crocheted white lace and dangling them excitedly.

"Er... right... thanks." I stepped aside to let them pass. "Come on in."

A few minutes later, I was sitting at the table with the steaming casserole dish in front of me and a fork in my hand, whilst the Old Biddies fussed around in the kitchen. They made themselves a cup of tea and sat down next to me, watching happily as I consumed their offerings. I had to admit, the food was delicious and it was a much better than the pitiful dinner I had been considering. The shepherd's pie was filled with savoury lamb mince and chopped vegetables, all covered with a layer of fluffy mashed potato, and the gooseberry trifle was the perfect mix of tart and sweet, rounded off by the silky fresh whipped cream. I also had to admit that, in spite of myself, I was pleased to see the Old Biddies. The house had begun to feel lonely without Muesli and it was nice to have company.

"Now, Gemma, we have been thinking..." said Mabel as I scooped up the last mouthful of trifle. "There must be more clues hidden in Antonio Casa's luggage. Perhaps if we could look through his things again—"

"No, no!" I cried. "Do you realise how annoyed Devlin was when he found out that you had been snooping in Antonio Casa's case on the night of the cooking workshop?"

"We were not '*snooping*'," said Mabel haughtily. "We were conducting an important search. Besides, solving crime involves bending the rules sometimes—if your young man was a good detective, he would know that."

"Devlin *is* a good detective!" I said with a scowl.

"Yes, we know, dear," said Ethel in a placating tone. "But he isn't very *imaginative* sometimes, is he?"

"I blame the lack of fibre," said Mabel with an emphatic nod. "Policemen's diets are very unhealthy."

"Oh yes, I read an article in *The Mirror* about the 'blobby bobby crisis' in the U.K.," said Florence, her plump face creasing in concern. "It said that many officers are too heavy and unfit to chase crooks now, because police canteens serve too many fried chips and sausages and meat pies... Though I must say, I'm partial to a meat pie myself. Chicken and mushroom is very nice, and mince and onion too— oh, and of course, there's nothing like a good cottage pie... but I suppose they're not very healthy and we wouldn't want Devlin to start waddling, would we?"

I made an exasperated noise. "Devlin does not waddle! He's very fit and muscular and—"

"You don't want him to get too thin either, dear," said Glenda in a conspiratorial tone. "Trust me, I have known a lot of men in my life and they're not very nice when they're too skinny. You want something to hold on to in bed and—"

"Uh—right! Thanks! I'll keep that in mind," I cut

in quickly. The last thing I needed was to hear about the Old Biddies' sex lives. *Eeeuuww.*

"Look, I appreciate you trying to help on the case but you really can't go around messing with private property," I said. "And anyway, the police have searched Antonio Casa's things now. They'd be much more thorough than we could ever be and they found nothing."

"I still think Antonio is the murderer," said Mabel. "He was at the Boscobel ball... and he doesn't have an alibi. He could have easily slipped into the dining hall and tampered with the wiring on the whisk—"

"But Leanne didn't see him in the hall," I argued.

They looked at me blankly and I realised that they didn't know about the events that had happened earlier that day. Quickly, I told them about Cassie's expert bluffing and Leanne's confession.

"Aha! So I was right—it wasn't her!" said Mabel triumphantly. "That means it's even more likely to be Antonio Casa. There is no one else with as good a motive."

"He never gave a good reason for being at the ball, did he, dear?" Ethel asked.

"Well, he told the police that he was meeting a lady friend," I said. "And that's probably true. I mean, Antonio seems to spend all his time and energy 'meeting lady friends'. Even on the day we met for lunch, he had a double date: that hysterical woman he was arguing with on the phone had obviously been expecting him to meet her. She sounded so upset too—I mean, it wasn't just her pride. She sounded really hurt." I shook my head and laughed. "I just can't believe anyone could fall in love with Antonio Casa..."

"Well, dear, they do say there's somebody for everybody," said Glenda.

The Old Biddies left soon afterwards and I curled up on the sofa with a book, although I found it hard keeping my mind on the story. My thoughts kept returning to the murder. I felt like there was some connection that I was not making, some clue I hadn't recognised. The thing that bothered me the most was Maddie Gill's statement. Had she been in Boscobel's dining hall or not?

CHAPTER TWENTY-TWO

My phone rang a couple of hours later and I was surprised to hear Devlin's voice on the line. I knew he had been planning to stay late at the station to work on the case and I hadn't expected him to call me tonight.

"Fancy going out for a nightcap, Gemma? I've just finished and I can swing by your place to pick you up."

"Sounds great," I said with a smile. "I'll be waiting."

Ten minutes later, I got into Devlin's black Jaguar and leaned across to peck him on the lips.

"So where are we going?" I asked.

"Well, actually..." Devlin rubbed the back of his neck wearily. "Would you mind very much if we just went back to my place? I feel really exhausted and I think I'd rather just relax and have a drink at home." He gave me a smile. "You can stay over, if you like—and Muesli, of course. Do you want to go back in and get her—"

"Oh, Muesli isn't with me tonight—she's having a sleepover at Mrs Purdey's." I chuckled at the confused expression on Devlin's face. "It's a long story. I'll tell you about it over that drink. But what about your mum? Wouldn't you like to spend the evening with her?"

Devlin's face darkened. "Mum's gone out."

"Oh." I looked at him and said tentatively, "Um... that wine bar in Jericho?"

Devlin gave a tight nod.

"You know, Devlin... maybe... maybe you are worrying unnecessarily."

"What do you mean?" he demanded. "Don't tell me you think my mum's right? Do you think it's sensible to go off with strange men that you'd only just met?"

"Well, I..." I shifted uncomfortably. "The thing is... when you think about it, isn't that what people do all the time? I mean, lots of women go out on dates with men they hardly know. If I met you in a pub and you asked me out, I wouldn't really know anything about you either, and the first time I met you for drinks or dinner, I would have nothing to go on—other than my own judgement of your character."

"That's different," said Devlin irritably.

"No, it's not really," I said gently. "I think you've got to give your mother some credit. She's not a little girl, she's a forty-something-year-old woman—"

"She bloody well doesn't act like it," growled Devlin. "That's the problem with my mum. She behaves like a teenager! She's so reckless and... and irresponsible. She never thinks of the possible dangers or consequences—all she thinks about is having fun."

"Well, I think you're being unfair on her. I mean, she's a free spirit and that's quite nice in a way. You should see what it's like having a mother like mine, all prim and proper all the time... And okay, maybe your mum doesn't do things the way you'd like... maybe she's a bit more... er... 'relaxed' about things... but... but that doesn't mean that she doesn't know what she's doing. I think you need to trust her and have a bit of faith in her."

Devlin didn't reply and we drove in silence for several minutes. I wondered how I had ended up in this awkward position, caught between my boyfriend and his mother. As we pulled up in front of Devlin's place—a large converted barn in a country lane, just beyond the outskirts of Oxford—I stole a glance at his profile. He looked deep in thought and I wondered uneasily if this strained atmosphere was going to continue all evening. But as we were going into the house, he caught my hand and said quietly:

"Maybe you're right, Gemma... I guess it's hard for me to divorce myself from what I see at work... And when I know the dangers that are lurking out there..." He sighed, then pulled himself up and gave me a lopsided smile. "But you're right: I should have more faith in my mum. It's not as if she's gone to some acid rave—she's just gone to a wine bar in Jericho."

"And I'm sure she's doing nothing more reckless than tasting a few glasses of red," I said, smiling and squeezing his hand.

"Come on—I think it's time we had a few glasses of red ourselves," said Devlin with a grin, draping his arm around my shoulders and leading me into the house.

I was delighted to see him back in a good mood again, and we joked and bantered as we went into the kitchen and Devlin poured us each a glass of wine.

"How about a snack? I haven't had anything to eat since a sandwich at five and I'm starving..." said Devlin, opening his fridge and peering inside. "I've got some honey roast chicken slices, some Greek pasta salad, some home-made guacamole... or some tomato and basil soup I can heat up..."

It was embarrassing that my boyfriend's fridge was better stocked than mine.

"Mm... I had a huge dinner earlier, courtesy of the Old Biddies—so I think I'll just have a few crackers," I said, sipping my wine. "But you have something if you like."

"Okay, how about some cheese and crackers with the wine then... and I might heat up a bit of the soup for myself."

As Devlin started taking a saucepan out of the cupboard, my phone vibrated. I glanced down idly, then paused in surprise. It was a text message from Keeley O'Connor.

"gemma... gemma... did u know ur name rhymes with henna? lol... and vienna... and antenna... so cool... lol"

Huh? I frowned and read the message again. It made no sense. Was it some kind of joke? My phone vibrated again and another message popped up.

"vienna like vienna sausages lol... don't cook it or u'll be sorry... it's like cooking ur sister... LOL!!"

Now I was really starting to get worried. Why was Keeley sending me these strange text messages?

"Are you sure you don't want any soup?"

"Uh...?" I started and looked up to see Devlin standing next to the stove, stirring the soup around the saucepan.

"Oh... er... no, thanks." I gave him a vague smile. "Um... excuse me a moment—I just need to pop to the loo."

I scurried to the bathroom before Devlin could reply and locked myself in, then hurriedly dialled Keeley's number. She answered on the second ring.

"Gemma?" she giggled. "Gemma? ...Gemma? ...that sounds like an echo..."

"Keeley, are you all right?" I asked in a hushed voice.

She giggled. "Of course! Never better... better never... Don't you think 'better' is a really weird word? Like 'bet'... but 'better'... bet-AH..." She laughed uproariously.

Oh my God. Was she stoned?

"Keeley, what have you been doing?" I asked urgently

She giggled. "Who's doing? Are you doing?" She gasped suddenly. "Do you know... I think I can hear my hair growing..." She went off into peals of laughter again.

Oh cripes. She was high as a kite. I gulped as I thought of what Devlin would do if he knew.

"Listen, Keeley—where are you?" I hissed.

"Hmm?"

"Where are you? *WHERE ARE YOU?*"

"Gemma... are you all right?" There was a rap on the bathroom door and Devlin's voice sounded outside.

I yelped and nearly dropped my phone. "Uh... fine... fine!"

"I thought I heard you talking to someone."

"Um... no, just... that was just... er... the stupid

Siri thing on my phone... I hit it by mistake and it kept asking me what I wanted so I was telling it to shut up."

"Oh. Okay." Devlin sounded doubtful. "Well, the food's ready."

"Uh... thanks. I'll be right there!"

I waited until I heard his steps fading away, then put the phone back to my ear. I could hear thumping music in the background and the sound of talking and laughter.

"Keeley? Keeley, are you there?" I whispered.

"Gemma! Fancy you being on my phone! I thought your voice was coming from the table—*heeheeheehee!*"

I took a deep breath and tried to speak as calmly as possible. "Listen, Keeley—where are you? Are you at the wine bar in Jericho?"

"Shtupid wine bar...." Keeley said, slurring her words. "No fun... much better here..."

"Where is 'here'?" I asked desperately. "Keeley, where are you?"

"Came to dance... good music... Dancing in the bridge! In the bridge... dancing in the bridge... a bridge with weeds—hahaha!"

Weeds? "Keeley, have you been smoking pot?"

"Just a little puff," she giggled. "One little puff, two little puffs, three little puffs, four... and more!" She stopped suddenly and her voice turned serious. "Do you know, carpets can be your best friend?"

My mind was reeling. All I could think of was

that I had to find her and get her back safely as soon as possible. "Keeley, listen, are you in a club? Which club? Which club are you at?"

"I'm dancing in the bridge!" she sang. "Oops!"

Her voice was cut off suddenly and I heard the sound of rustling and thumping. *She must have dropped the phone*, I realised. Everything was now muffled. Then the call was broken. I swore and dialled her number again. It rang and rang but nobody answered.

"Gemma?" came Devlin's voice faintly from the kitchen. "Are you all right in there?"

"Um... yeah, I'll be there in a sec!"

I groaned and leaned against the bathroom wall, wondering what to do. I could just go out and tell Devlin, and let him sort it out. But I cringed at the thought of him finding out that his mother was smoking marijuana at some night club in Oxford. Okay, so it wasn't a hard drug like heroine or cocaine, and most students probably had a puff or two as part of their college experience, but nobody liked to think of their *mother* getting stoned. Besides, Devlin was a policeman now. I couldn't see him having a relaxed attitude to the whole thing. And besides, he would be terribly hurt—it would just confirm to him again how foolhardy and irresponsible his mother was. I didn't want him to be disappointed again, especially after I'd just convinced him to trust his Keeley's judgement!

I would have to go and find her myself, I decided.

If I could just somehow get her back here and into bed, without Devlin finding out where she'd been and what she'd been doing... Well, I didn't know how I was going to manage that, but I couldn't worry about it now. The first step was to find her. She was definitely at a club—I could tell that from the music in the background—but like most university towns, Oxford had several dance clubs to cater to its student population. It would take me all night to check them all! I frowned and thought back to the conversation I had just had with Keeley. She'd mentioned "dancing in the bridge"... One of the most popular clubs in Oxford was called The Bridge... what were the chances that that was where she was?

It was worth a shot. I let myself out of the bathroom and hurried back to the kitchen, where Devlin was just ladling some soup into a bowl. He looked up and smiled.

"I thought we could eat in front of—"

"Um... Devlin, I'm really sorry but I need to pop out quickly... can I borrow your car?"

"Now?" He looked astonished. "Why? What's happened?"

I squirmed. This was the second time I had to blatantly lie to him and I hated having to do it. "Cassie's just rung me and she's really upset. It's a bit of an 'emergency'—I need to pop over and see her."

"Emergency? What do you mean? Is she hurt?"

"Oh, no, no... it's... er... 'boy trouble'," I said lamely.

To my relief, Devlin had the typical man's aversion to any kind of romantic drama and he didn't ask any more questions. Instead, he reached into a shallow bowl on the counter and tossed me his car keys.

"Thanks." I caught them neatly. "Um... I might be a while so don't wait up for me!"

CHAPTER TWENTY-THREE

I wasn't very familiar with The Bridge and I had nightmare visions of stumbling through a darkened nightclub filled with throbbing music and sweaty bodies, looking in vain for Keeley. But for once, luck was on my side: as I walked into the lobby, I spotted an attractive blonde woman leaning against the wall. She was with a group of young men and they were all staring at an empty packet of potato crisps that one of the men was holding, giggling uncontrollably. A faint, sweetish smell filled my nostrils as I approached them.

"Keeley?" I put a gentle hand on her elbow.

"Gemma, luv!" She beamed and threw her arms around me. "I love you."

"Er... I love you too," I said, gently disentangling myself. "I've come to take you home."

"Home?" she pouted. "I don't want to go home...

I'm having fun!"

"But..." I started to reason with her, then realized that it was futile. Instead, I smiled at her and caught her hand. "Listen, Keeley—would you like to come and see something really beautiful?"

"Ooh! Where?"

"Come with me." I gave her hand a gentle tug and steered her towards the exit. Once outside, I hustled her towards Devlin's Jaguar, which I'd left standing on a double yellow line. I breathed a sigh of relief to see that it was still there. That would have been the final straw for Oxfordshire CID's top detective: to have his car towed for illegal parking while his mother was caught smoking marijuana!

"Oh, look!" Keeley had stopped by the car and was now staring up at a lamppost. "A beautiful star!"

"Yes, lovely..." I said, trying to bundle her into the passenger seat. "Come on... get in now..."

"But I want to see the star."

"You can see it better in the car," I said impatiently.

After several more minutes of pleading and cajoling, I managed to get her into the car and we pulled away from the night club. It was getting close to midnight now and I drove cautiously through the streets. Devlin's Jaguar XK had a powerful engine that I wasn't used to handling and it didn't help that Keeley kept yelling random words as she pointed at things out the window, making me swerve several times. When we finally pulled into Devlin's driveway, I was tense and sweating, and felt like I'd run a marathon.

Thankfully, Keeley seemed to be winding down at last. She leaned over and laid her head on the passenger door as I killed the engine.

"I think I'm going to sleep now," she mumbled as she gave a great yawn.

"Oh, not in the car!" I said quickly, grabbing her arm and trying to heave her upright again. "Come on—let's get you in the house and into bed."

I wrestled her out of the car and propelled her limp form up the pathway to the front door. The house looked dark. It was almost an hour and half since I'd left and, considering how tired he had been, I hoped fervently that Devlin might have gone to bed. I had been racking my brains all the way on the drive back to come up with an innocuous story that would explain Keeley's condition but I had come up with nothing. Now, if I could just sneak her into the sofa-bed downstairs without Devlin knowing, he wouldn't need to meet his mother again until the morning—when she would have hopefully sobered up and be her normal self again.

Slowly, I turned the key in the lock and pushed the door open, peering inside. The lights were off on the ground floor. It looked like I might be in luck! I grabbed Keeley—who seemed to have gone to sleep standing up, propped against the front door—and hauled her into the house. As quietly as I could, I crept across the living room, dragging Keeley behind me. The sofa-bed was already pulled out and some of Keeley's things were thrown across it in a rumpled heap. I pushed back the covers and steered the older woman towards the bed.

"So sleepy..." she mumbled as she tumbled onto the pillows.

I bit my lip, wondering if I should try to undress her. Then I froze as I heard a noise from above. I glanced at the open staircase which led up to the mezzanine level and Devlin's bedroom, bracing myself for the sight of his long legs descending the steps. When nothing appeared after several minutes, I relaxed again. Still, I decided that I was taking no more chances. Keeley would just have to spend the night in her clothes; I was sure it wouldn't be the first—or the last—time she did that.

Pulling the covers up and tucking them snugly around her, I whispered, "Good night!" Then I tiptoed up the staircase to the second level. Bifold doors divided Devlin's bedroom from the small living area on the landing and these were partially open. I slipped through the gap and shut the doors behind me, then paused for a moment to let my eyes adjust to the darkness.

"Gemma?" Devlin stirred in the bed.

"Hi..." I said softly, approaching the bed. "Sorry—did I wake you?"

"It's all right—I was planning to wait up for you, actually, but I kept dozing off on the couch so I decided to come up." Devlin heaved himself up on one elbow. His dark hair was sexily tousled and I could see the shadow of stubble on his chin, in the faint light from the bedroom window. "How's Cassie?"

"Cassie? Oh... Cassie! Um... she's fine... I mean, she's not really fine, you know... the chap she's seeing is a total prat... but we talked... and called him some names... and she's feeling better now," I babbled, mentally reminding myself to tell Cassie about her "romantic crisis" tomorrow, so that she wouldn't say the wrong thing in front of Devlin.

"Right..." Devlin yawned. Then he looked up sharply as we heard a noise from downstairs. "What's that?"

"Oh... that must be your mum. I... um... met her as I was coming in. A taxi was dropping her off."

"Really?" Devlin looked pleased. "I thought she wouldn't be back until well into the early hours." He smiled at me. "You were right, Gemma—I should have trusted her."

I resisted the urge to squirm. "Uh... yeah... right. Anyway, I'll just brush my teeth and get undressed, then we can get some sleep."

Devlin raised an eyebrow and gave me a sexy grin. "Oh, you can get undressed, Gemma Rose, but I can think of something much better to do than sleep..."

I laughed and decided that maybe the evening wasn't such a disaster after all.

CHAPTER TWENTY-FOUR

The next morning, Devlin and I left his place early—he to get to the station and me to stop back at my cottage for a shower and change of clothes before I headed to the tearoom. Thankfully, Keeley was still fast asleep as we tiptoed out of the house so there was no risk of awkward questions. I did wince, though, as I wondered what Devlin's mother might say to him later when he came back to pick her up for morning tea at my parent's place.

An hour later, I left my cottage and wheeled my bicycle up St Aldates Street towards the city centre. After the debacle of the night before, I felt like I needed a strong coffee this morning—proper fresh coffee, not the instant sludge that I made in my kitchen. So instead of following my usual routine of cycling straight out of Oxford, I wheeled my bike up the road to a small bakery-cum-sandwich shop which I'd often visited in my student days.

As I approached the striped awning and saw the familiar wooden A-frame sign in front of the shop, I was pleased to see that they were still offering fresh tea and coffee, accompanied by Continental breakfasts, just like they'd done for decades. The place was packed and I joined the queue at the counter absentmindedly. It wasn't until I'd got my cup of coffee and was turning away that I recognised the woman standing in the line behind me. I felt my pulse quicken—it was Maddie Gill, the TV producer.

Our eyes met and she gave me a polite smile. "Hi… it's Gemma, isn't it? You're the girl who owns that tearoom out in Meadowford."

"Yes, that's right." I gave her a wry look. "The one with the egg custard tarts."

She looked embarrassed. "I'm really sorry about what Jerry said the other day. He was… er…"

"That's okay," I reassured her. "I didn't take it to heart."

"For what it's worth, you're not the only one that he's behaved like that to. He's… he's got a reputation for being a bit… er… belligerent, sometimes."

"It must make it hard working with him," I said sympathetically.

She rolled her eyes. "You have no idea."

I waited until she had collected her coffee, then fell into step beside her as she walked back out onto the street. "Um... so what's happening with the TV show...?"

She shrugged. "I'm not sure yet. Jerry has some ideas but... well, with the police investigation still ongoing, things are sort of in limbo. Honestly, I still can't quite believe that Josh is dead. And not just dead like... like an accident. No, he was *murdered*. It's crazy!" She pointed to her chest. "I mean, it's the kind of thing that happens on TV, in shows that *I* produce, you know? Not in real life."

"Do you have any ideas why anyone would have wanted to hurt Josh?"

She shifted uncomfortably. "Well, in this business—especially when someone is as popular as Josh—you're bound to meet some unstable characters."

"What do you mean?"

"A crazy fan."

"You think a *fan* did this?" I asked. "But... that doesn't make sense. If they loved him, why on earth would they have wanted to kill him?"

She shrugged again. "Who knows? People can get obsessive sometimes... I've heard stories... fans fantasizing about a relationship with a star... and then getting upset and flipping out when they think that the celebrity betrayed them. They probably think they're being treated like toilet paper, used and tossed aside."

I frowned. *Where had I heard that phrase before?* Then it came to me: when I was having lunch with Antonio and he had got that phone call. The hysterical woman on the phone had said almost those exact same words. It was a funny analogy— not something that most people would say. What were the chances that Maddie would use exactly the same description?

I looked at the woman in front of me with new eyes. *She* had been the hysterical woman on the phone. In fact, yesterday when I had seen her in town, looking weepy and red-eyed, it had been right after the lunch with Antonio Casa. Of course, it all made sense now! Keeley O'Connor's words came back to me: *"She's crying over a man."* I laughed to myself. Devlin's mum had been right. Maddie had been upset because she'd just had a fight with Antonio Casa and had thought that he was cheating on her.

"Is something wrong?"

I blinked and came back to the present to find Maddie eyeing me nervously.

"Oh... er... nothing. Sorry. My mind wandered."

She gave me an odd look but didn't comment. Instead, she nodded a goodbye. "Well, it was nice running into you. Take care."

She began walking away. I watched her go, then on an impulse ran after her.

"Maddie! Wait!"

She turned around on the pavement. I stopped

in front of her, panting slightly.

"Maddie... you're having an affair with Antonio Casa, aren't you?"

She jerked as if she had been burnt. "I... I don't know what you're talking about."

"Yesterday at lunchtime, you had a fight with him... over the phone. You thought he was cheating on you and having lunch with another woman."

Her eyes bulged. "How... how could you know...?"

"Because I was the other woman."

She spluttered, "You? *You* were having lunch with Antonio?"

"Oh, it wasn't a romantic date," I said. "At least not on my part. I only agreed to see him because I wanted to question him about Josh's murder."

A mixture of expressions crossed Maddie's face: relief, happiness, embarrassment, and also—I noted with interest—a flash of fear.

"You know that Antonio is a suspect?" I asked.

"I heard... but really, it's ridiculous to suspect him," she said quickly

"It's not ridiculous—it's very logical, actually. The two chefs were known to hate each other and Antonio, in particular, is notorious for having a terrible temper—"

"Yes, but that doesn't mean that he would kill someone!"

"Not even in revenge? Or to get rid of a rival? Come on, Antonio thinks that Josh tried to sabotage his new restaurant... and he was furious about Josh replacing him on the next season of *Superchef*. Killing Josh would've been more than revenge, but also a way to get rid of a rival who's upstaging him. Antonio's got a background as an electrician, which would have made tampering with the wiring easy... and he was seen near the dining hall on the night that Josh was killed."

"How do you know that?" demanded Maddie.

"Because I was the one who saw him."

She looked taken aback. "Well... that doesn't mean... that's not... you... you're wrong!" she stammered.

"I'm not wrong—I know I saw him. He was skulking in the corridor which connected the kitchen to the dining hall... and I'll bet he had just come from the dining hall, where he had been tampering with the wires—"

"No! No, Antonio never went into the dining hall! You have to believe me!"

"How can you know that?"

"Because... because..." She hesitated, then said in a rush: "Because I was with him the whole time!"

"But I thought you told the police that you were in the dining hall with Jerry Wallis the whole time?" I said, watching her carefully.

Maddie hesitated again, then she hung her head and said in a low voice, "I lied."

"So you didn't go into the dining hall at all?"

She shook her head. "I knew Antonio was at the

ball—oh, he wasn't supposed to come, but he was furious about Josh's attempt to sabotage his restaurant and wanted to confront him—"

"Wait... I thought that was just an idle accusation? Josh denied having anything to do with—"

"Of course he would," said Maddie sardonically. "He was great at manipulating the media. He knew how to spin things so that he always came out looking like an angel. The truth is, Josh McDermitt was a ruthless, cold-hearted bastard who was only interested in how he could use you and he wasn't afraid to stoop to some pretty unethical practices to get what he wanted. He thought up that whole plan to sabotage Antonio's opening night and humiliate him—and I can tell you, he enjoyed it too. And then he enjoyed acting all innocent afterwards and pretending to be the wronged party, so that everyone felt sorry for him... oh, it was all part of Josh's master plan."

"How do you know all this?"

"Because I was one of the people he asked to make the bookings! He couldn't do it himself, of course—it was too risky since his voice might be recognised—and besides, Josh never does his own dirty work. So he got Jerry to make some of the calls. But then he wanted a female voice as well and he asked me. When I refused, he was really narked about it... but he needed me for his show. He knew that I was the best in the business for this kind of production and he couldn't afford to lose me. So he went and charmed some other female member of the crew instead and got her to do it for him."

"Wasn't he worried that she might tell the press afterwards?"

Maddie shrugged. "Probably not. Josh was supremely confident of his own charms and I think his arrogance meant that he never considered that anyone might betray him. He was convinced that we were all starry-eyed with love for him and would do anything for him."

"But you obviously weren't... I take it that nobody in Josh's entourage knew about your affair with Antonio?"

She flushed. "No. I... I kept it a secret. It was partly what made it exciting... like... like 'fraternising with the enemy'." She met my eyes and raised her chin defiantly. "But even if I hadn't been seeing Antonio, I would have refused to take part in Josh's scheme. It was disgusting behaviour."

"And you told Antonio about it?"

"Well, I thought he had a right to know! He was so upset... Antonio might act all tough and macho, but he's actually quite sensitive, you know," she said, her face softening. "He was absolutely crushed after his opening night disaster and I couldn't bear to see him like that. Especially when it wasn't because of anything he'd done—he was simply the victim of a low, vicious prank." She sighed. "In hindsight, it was probably a bad idea. I should have known that Antonio would be livid and would want to come and give Josh a piece of his mind."

"So that's why he came to the ball," I said. "It wasn't to meet a lady friend, like he told the police."

"Yes, Antonio got this bee in his bonnet about making Josh pay—not by physically harming him," she added hastily as she saw my expression. "He wanted to confront Josh during the live filming of the demo and tell everyone in the audience the truth about Josh's attempts to sabotage him. It was a way to humiliate Josh in public and reveal his true nature to his fans."

"How do you know Antonio didn't plan something more drastic?"

"He wouldn't!" she cried. "I know Antonio. He's all loud noise and hot air, but he's not a vicious person. It's the types like Josh that you need to worry about—the ones full of charm and smooth words, who smile to your face while they stick a knife in your back."

I digested this for a moment. Although I only had her word for it, I had to admit that Maddie's passionate defence of Antonio was convincing. I didn't like the man and found him pretty repulsive but my own instincts had also insisted that he couldn't be the murderer. There was something too straight and simple about him. With Antonio Casa, what you saw was what you got. He might thump you on the head in a temper but he wasn't the devious type to plan a cold-blooded murder.

As for Josh... I discovered that the truth about him wasn't really a surprise. Maybe Cassie's scepticism and contempt had rubbed off on me, but I wasn't that shocked to learn that there was a shark beneath that gleaming white smile.

"I did see Antonio by the dining hall, though. I'm sure of it."

"Yes," Maddie finally admitted. "He texted me and told me that he was at the ball—and that he was planning to confront Josh. I panicked. Aside from the fact that I didn't want a nasty scene, I also didn't want Antonio to reveal to everyone that I was the one who had told him. So I tried to head him off. Luckily, he hadn't gone into the dining hall yet when we got there—I saw him skulking around outside the building, obviously waiting for Josh to show up. I went in the rear entrance with Josh and Jerry but I let them go on ahead of me, into the dining hall. I hung back in the corridor to wait for Antonio and pulled him aside to speak to him. It took a bit of effort but I convinced him not to go in and confront Josh."

"But I saw you come out with Jerry," I said. "And then I saw Antonio afterwards, when I went in myself—so he was still in the building when you'd left."

"Yes, we heard someone coming back out from the dining hall, so I hustled Antonio down the other corridor—you know the hallway branched into two corridors? Anyway, so we hung around the kitchen door and saw a blonde woman come running down the other corridor and out of the building. I don't think she saw us; she was acting pretty furtively herself, actually—"

"That must have been Leanne."

"Who?"

"Nothing... never mind," I said. "So then what happened?"

"Well, about five minutes after she left, I heard someone else coming down the corridor from the dining hall, and this time it was Jerry. I got Antonio to wait by the kitchen door while I intercepted Jerry and accompanied him back out of the building. The plan was for Antonio to follow us out once the coast was clear—but of course, he hadn't expected you to come in the building straight after we'd left. He saw you and had to quickly turn around and pretend to be heading into the kitchen."

"Oh..." I thought again of the man I'd glimpsed. "So he didn't really go into the kitchen?"

"No, as soon as you'd gone into the dining hall, Antonio hurried back out and slipped out of the building. I was watching and waiting outside—he was supposed to text me once he was safely out again—and bloody hell, I was really sweating when I didn't get the message from him for ages." She looked at me earnestly. "But he was only alone for a few minutes between the time I left him and the time you saw him—there was no way he could have gone into the dining hall in that time to do anything."

I had to agree. It looked like Antonio couldn't be the murderer. But suddenly I realised that there was someone else who could be a suspect.

"You told the police that you were with Jerry Wallis in the dining hall the whole time. That was a lie—and he knew it. Why didn't he speak up? Did you ask him to cover for you?"

Maddie shook her head. "I never got a chance to speak to him before the police arrived. The detective sergeant questioned us together, and when I said that I was in the dining hall the whole time, Jerry agreed." She shrugged. "I was a bit surprised—but I figured that he probably didn't want to complicate things. I mean, nobody wants to look suspicious in a murder investigation, and I'm sure it's better for him if he can say he was with me the whole time."

It certainly gives him a rock-solid alibi, I thought. The question was, did Jerry need an alibi?

Maddie and I parted soon after and I walked thoughtfully back to where I'd parked my bike, going over everything she had told me. Could I have been looking in the wrong direction all along? If Josh's ex-girlfriend was innocent... and his arch-rival wasn't involved... then could his *manager* have been the one who had tried to murder him?

CHAPTER TWENTY-FIVE

I was so preoccupied with my new theory on Josh McDermitt's murder that I barely thought about my mother's morning tea until I was on my way there. I arrived slightly late (as usual!) and hurried in to find all her friends already in the sitting room, perched straight-backed and tight-kneed on the edges of the sofa and armchairs, sipping tea delicately from a Royal Doulton tea service. They were practically all dressed in the ubiquitous twinset, pencil skirt and pearls, with their hair carefully coiffured and their make-up subtle and discreet. And while they were pretending to make polite conversation, it was obvious that they were all listening with peeled ears, waiting for the doorbell to ring and announce the special guests.

And the most watchful of all was Helen Green, my mother's oldest and closest friend. She gave me a cool nod as I joined them, obviously still not having forgiven me for choosing Devlin over her son, then turned to Lincoln, who as usual was acting the dutiful escort, and said loudly:

"Darling, did I tell you about a recent U.S. survey I read, which said that being a police officer ranked amongst the worst careers in the world—as bad as being a maid or a dishwasher in a restaurant?"

Lincoln glanced at me, his cheeks reddening. "Er... no, you didn't, Mother."

"Well! I did think it rather surprising," said Helen, carefully smoothing a fold of her skirt. "I mean, one is led to believe that police inspectors are such great heroes—I blame all these mystery novels and detective programmes on TV—but really, it is a thankless job with poor pay and dreadful prospects. How their poor wives must suffer..."

Lincoln cleared his throat and turned to me, saying quickly, "Um... so how's the murder investigation going, Gemma? Have the police turned up any new leads?"

"I'm not sure. I haven't really had a chance to discuss the case with Devlin the past couple of days..." I leaned towards him and lowered my voice. "By the way, Lincoln—I've been meaning to ask you: is adding MSG to foods likely to be dangerous?"

Lincoln frowned. "MSG? You mean, monosodium

glutamate? Well, it used to be believed that it could cause adverse reactions or a form of food allergy— what was commonly known as 'Chinese restaurant syndrome'. People believed that you'd get headaches, skin flushes, sweating, even nausea, after eating foods with MSG... but in fact, that's a total myth. Various medical journals, such as *Clinical & Experimental Allergy*, have reviewed decades worth of research and there's no scientific evidence to support it at all. The FDA in the United States has conducted extensive investigations and they've ruled MSG as safe. It's actually found naturally in a lot of foods—like parmesan cheese, for example—and people who claim to have a problem with it have been fine when they don't realise they're eating it."

"Oh, you mean it's all in their mind?"

"Basically, yes. It's one of those pseudo-science things that gets out into the popular media and becomes an urban legend." Lincoln looked at me quizzically. "Why do you ask?"

"It was just a hunch I had. In a recent interview on TV, Josh McDermitt confessed to using MSG in his cooking, and given how controversial that seems to be, I wondered if someone might have... you know... seen the interview and thought Josh had made them sick and decided to get revenge."

"Well, I suppose someone could think that. Hypochondriacs believe all sorts of things and you know how powerful the mind can be. But... would you really murder someone just because you thought they'd given you a headache after a meal?"

I gave him a rueful smile. "I know, it sounds really farfetched. Oh well, it was just an idea..."

The front doorbell rang and my mother hurried out to answer it. A few minutes later, she led Devlin and his mum into the sitting room and everyone looked up eagerly to check out the new arrivals. I saw Helen Green's eyes bulge and I winced as I eyed Keeley's figure-hugging dress, which sported a plunging neckline that left very little to the imagination. She had a fantastic figure for a woman of her age and, from the slightly awestruck expressions on my father's and Lincoln's face, it looked like she had won the men over already. The other women in the room, however, eyed her as if she was an exotic python that had suddenly slithered into their midst.

My mother made the introductions and Keeley smiled and shook hands, completely unfazed by the cool reception she was receiving from the other women. Then she walked gracefully across the room and made a beeline for Lincoln. Helen Green looked horrified as she watched the attractive older woman smile flirtatiously at her son.

"Bloody hell, I thought dishy doctors only existed on telly," said Keeley, looking Lincoln up and down. "You could give that McDreamy a run for his money!"

Lincoln flushed to the roots of his hair and

stammered something, while his mother looked as if she was going to choke.

"Um... Mrs O'Connor, would you like some tea?" asked my mother, hovering uncertainly beside her.

"Oh, ta..." said Keeley. "I could do with a cuppa. I woke up with a blinding hangover this morning—was out late last night, you see. Had a great time, though, and I actually woke up in my bed this morning, which is a lot better than usual... I usually end up arse over tit on somebody's couch!" She laughed uproariously.

There were gasps around the room and several of the women covered their mouths, their eyes round with shock at the unladylike language. Devlin's face was stony and my mother looked at loss for words.

"Er... would you like milk in your tea?" she asked brightly. Like a true Brit, she was taking refuge in being excessively polite and pretending nothing had happened.

"Oh, cheers, luv." Keeley took the teacup that was handed to her and balanced it precariously on her knee.

Her handbag, which had been resting on her lap, fell sideways onto the floor, tipping some of its contents out. I glanced down, then my eyes widened as I saw something tucked amongst the mess of lipstick, tissues, gum, and hairpins... a long, slim roll of paper, shaped like a cigarette, with a burnt end. *A joint.*

Oh God. I lunged forwards and snatched it up,

then glanced furtively around. Keeley was talking and laughing with Lincoln, who had his eyes glued to her and was paying no attention to anybody else. My mother was making her way around the other ladies, topping up their tea, and Devlin was talking to my father on the other side of the room.

Whew. I relaxed slightly. It looked like no one had seen the joint fall out of Keeley's handbag. I sat back in my chair, clutching the limp roll of paper in my sweaty palm, and wondered how I was going to get rid of it. Unfortunately, I didn't have a handbag with me and—in deference to my mother—I had worn a dress for once, so I had no pockets either. There was no place I could temporarily hide the joint until I could get rid of it later. Then my father called across to me:

"Gemma, darling, can you come over here for a second? I want to show Devlin this marvellous magic trick that Prof Holmes in Medieval Languages showed me last week—but I need an assistant."

I swallowed. "Er... sure, Dad."

I rose as slowly as I could, wondering desperately what to do with the joint. I would probably need both hands to assist my father, and Devlin would be sure to see what I was clutching. In a panic, I turned and shoved the joint behind the cushion at the back of my armchair. Hopefully, I'd be able to slip back later unobserved and retrieve it. Then, trying to look nonchalant, I walked across the room to join my father and Devlin.

The magic trick seemed to amuse my father and Devlin a lot and it was great to see them laughing together; plus I was pleased that there was something to take Devlin's mind off worrying about his mother. Not that she needed looking after—Keeley O'Connor was more than capable of holding her own amongst my mother's friends and I felt a flash of admiration for her. It was impressive how she didn't seem to care about other people's judgement, especially in the face of such a snooty crowd.

As my father finished demonstrating his trick, I heard Helen Green say to Keeley: "Couldn't your husband make the trip down to Oxford with you, Mrs O'Connor?"

Devlin stiffened next to me but Keeley tossed her long blonde hair over her shoulder and said with a breezy smile, "Oh, I don't have a husband, Mrs Green. It's grand not having to slave over the stove for some bloke and spend half your life cleaning up after him."

Helen Green got a very pinched look on her face. "Well, I always think a woman isn't complete until she is making a home for her husband and children," she said primly.

Keeley laughed. "What are you—stuck in the 1950s, luv?"

Helen spluttered angrily.

"Er... some Madeira cake, Mrs O'Connor?" asked my mother hastily. "Or perhaps you'd like some home-made shortbread biscuits?"

"Ta!" said Keeley, reaching over to help herself from the tray my mother was offering. "These look delicious! Did you make them yourself?"

"Yes." My mother beamed at her. "Do you like to bake?"

"Hate it. Can't cook to save my life," said Keeley, grinning as more gasps sounded around the room.

"Oh." My mother looked taken aback. "Well... er... do you enjoy gardening? The roses are so beautiful at this time of the year—perhaps you'll have time to visit some of the stately homes around Oxford and do a garden tour before you go back?"

Keeley made a face. "Garden tour? Not bloody likely!" Then she brightened. "There are some great beer and music festivals nearby, though... shame there's nothing on this weekend. I would have loved to go to one of those. They've got all sorts: indie, rock, punk, blues... What's your favourite band?"

"Oh... er... I don't really know any 'bands'," said my mother awkwardly. "I do enjoy Vivaldi's *Four Seasons* and his other compositions too. I suppose you could say he's my... er... 'favourite' composer."

"Classical music?" said Keeley. "Wow, good for you. That stuff puts me to sleep!"

I squirmed and wondered when this tortuous morning tea was going to end. Then, just when I thought things couldn't get any worse, I saw my mother approach the armchair I'd just vacated and bend over absentmindedly to plump up the cushion. As she did so, a slim, crumpled tube of white paper rolled out from behind the cushion and my mother picked it up. She stared at it in puzzlement.

I gulped. *Oh. My. God.*

I fought the urge to spring up and run across the room to yank the joint out of her hand. It would only draw more attention.

"How strange..." my mother murmured, rolling the joint around in her fingers. She took it across the room to show the other ladies. "What do you suppose this is?"

My mother's friends all leaned forwards to inspect the joint quizzically. I couldn't restrain myself any longer. Springing up, I hurried across and tried to grab the joint out of my mother's hands.

"Uh... sorry, Mother. That's just a bit of rubbish... I'll get rid of it now."

"But what is it?" asked my mother, holding the joint out of my reach.

"It's... er..." I racked my brains and said the first thing that came to my mind. "It's a... a scented clothes sachet!"

"Oh, a scented sachet!" said one of the ladies, delighted. "I love those—they're marvellous for freshening up one's undies in the drawers." She squinted at the joint. "I've never seen one in that shape though."

"No," my mother agreed, turning it over in her

hands. "They're normally in little rectangular or triangular shapes."

"This is... er... a new design," I said desperately. "It's this... um... Swedish company... They make everything... you know... minimalist."

"Ooh, yes, what a wonderful idea. Takes up less space in the drawers," said another lady.

"But would it still be as effective?" asked Helen Green, eyeing the joint critically.

"Well, I imagine the herbs inside would be a more potent strength," said the first lady. "What's the fragrance like, Evelyn?"

My mother raised the joint to her nose and sniffed enthusiastically. I nearly fainted.

"Oh, it's quite pleasant," she said with a smile. "Slightly sweet... and a little bit spicy, perhaps?" She held it out for the other ladies to smell and they all passed the joint around, sniffing and nodding approvingly. I stared at them, feeling like I was having a hallucination.

My mother turned to me. "What's the fragrance called, darling?"

"Um... I can't really remember," I mumbled, as I reached across and snatched the joint out of Helen Green's hand.

"Well, you must tell me where you bought it, Gemma," said the first lady. "It's about time I stocked up on scented sachets again and I'd love to try some of this new style. It would be nice to have a change from the usual lavender and sandalwood—"

"It was a gift from a friend!" I gabbled. "I'm afraid I don't know where she bought them. Now, if you'll excuse me—I need to pop to the loo..."

I scurried out of the room and into the downstairs guest bathroom. Slamming the door behind me, I tossed the joint into the toilet bowl and hurriedly flushed it. Then I sagged against the wall, feeling limp all over. The next moment, I jumped upright again as there was a knock on the bathroom door and I heard Devlin's voice on the other side.

"Gemma?"

Hastily, I washed my hands, then opened the door as sedately as I could and said, "Oh, hi, Devlin..."

He peered at me. "Are you all right?"

"Yes, why?"

He hesitated. "I thought... that thing your mother was passing around just now... it looked like a joint?"

"My *mother* holding a joint?" I laughed shrilly.

Devlin gave me a sheepish look. "Yeah. You're right. Stupid thought. Still... it did look exactly like—"

"So... um... was there any new information waiting for you at the station this morning?" I interrupted. "On the Josh McDermitt case, I mean."

To my relief, Devlin allowed himself to be distracted. "Yes, actually, there *was* something interesting: I'd got my sergeant to do some digging into Jerry Wallis's background, and apparently he's racked up quite a lot of debt."

"Oh!" I cried. "The night we were at Brown's, I heard Maddie Gills and another member of the crew talking about him in the Ladies' toilets. They mentioned that he had the 'sharks' after him—"

"She's probably talking about money-lenders," said Devlin. "Yes, it looks like Jerry Wallis has a bit of a gambling problem: he's lost a lot of money at the races and has been borrowing heavily—from some pretty unsavoury characters—to tide him over. I wouldn't be surprised if he's been dipping into the company coffers too. I wonder if Josh ever thought to audit his manager and how his finances are being handled."

I stared at Devlin. "So... Jerry Wallis could have a motive to murder Josh after all?"

"Well, it's certainly beginning to look that way." Devlin frowned. "Although he does have a solid alibi."

"Actually, he doesn't," I said excitedly. "I spoke to Maddie Gill—did you know that she's dating Antonio Casa?"

Devlin raised his eyebrows. "Are you serious?"

"She lied in her statement to protect him. She wasn't with Wallis in the dining hall the whole time, like she said—she let him go in with Josh while she hung back to meet Antonio."

"What? But according to my sergeant, Wallis corroborated her statement—"

"Well, he questioned them together, and I think Jerry Wallis just saw an opportunity. When Maddie said she'd been with him in the dining hall the whole time, he quickly went along with it and agreed."

Devlin cursed under his breath. "I'm going to have to have words with my sergeant about this. Interviewing witnesses together... what was he thinking? He should know that we need to get independent accounts! So what was Antonio doing there?"

Quickly, I recounted my whole conversation with Maddie and also told him about Cassie's "interrogation" of Leanne Fitch.

"So it looks like both Leanne and Antonio are out of the frame," I said, "but there might be another suspect we hadn't considered so far: Josh's manager. I thought it was strange that Jerry wouldn't speak up about Maddie's false statement... but now it all makes sense! It gave him the perfect alibi! Do you think he tampered with the wires while Josh wasn't looking? I mean, if he's desperate for cash to pay off his creditors, then collecting the payout on Josh's life insurance would be the perfect answer. And especially if Josh was planning to audit him too and there was a risk that he might be found out to be embezzling funds—"

"Whoa..." Devlin chuckled. "Don't get too excited, sweetheart. If there's one thing I've learned on this job, it's that things are never as straightforward as they seem. Especially when it looks like everything is going to be tied up nicely with a ribbon on top... We don't know that Wallis was embezzling funds— or even that Josh was planning to audit him. And as for the insurance payout, that's just speculation at this point as well. I need to question Wallis again. But first, I'm going to speak to the insurance company, and other members of Josh McDermitt's entourage, to see if I can get more information. I want to make sure I have a solid case against Wallis before I tackle him again. If we jump on him prematurely, it might spook him and I don't want him doing a runner before we have enough evidence to arrest him."

He laughed at my expression. "I know... detective work in real life is a lot more plodding than what you see on TV. But I'm afraid you have to be patient. The insurance company will be closed today so I'll have to wait until tomorrow morning to speak to them... but Wallis isn't going anywhere anyway. He's been told that he has to remain in Oxford until the police give him permission to leave. Don't worry—if he's our man, we'll get him."

We heard a roar of laughter coming from the living room and voices talking animatedly. Devlin glanced in that direction. "It sounds like they're really enjoying themselves. I suppose we ought to go back to join them." He hesitated, then added, "It's actually gone better than I expected."

If only you knew, I thought silently, but I

plastered a smile to my face.

"Yes, I think your mother is a big hit."

Devlin chuckled. "That's probably going a bit far. But you know..." He sobered and came a little closer, giving me a warm smile. "I'm really touched and grateful to your mother for making so much effort with my mum..."

I slid my arms around his neck. "Well, she knows how important you are to me... *And* you did find her lost iPad," I reminded him with a teasing grin.

Devlin laughed. Then he clasped my hand in his and we walked back together to join the party.

CHAPTER TWENTY-SIX

"You hid the joint behind the sofa cushion?" Cassie guffawed. "Gemma, what were you thinking?"

I threw my hands up. "What would you have done in my place? I tell you, I lost five years off my life when my mother found it and took it over to show her friends." I gripped my forehead. "Oh my God, Cass, and they all believed me when I told them it was a scented sachet for keeping clothes fresh—they even wanted to know where they could buy some!"

Cassie went off into fresh peals of laughter.

"I'm glad *someone* is getting some enjoyment out of all this," I said with a sour look.

"You have to admit—it's bloody funny," gasped

Cassie, wiping tears of laughter from her eyes. "I'm amazed you came to work after a morning like that."

"I needed the rest," I said sarcastically.

"Oh, by the way, Mrs Purdey called and left a message: she said Muesli came down from the shed roof late last night and had a big dinner of steak and liver, then she slept with Mrs Purdey on her bed—'just like Smudge used to do'... and today, she's been helping Mrs Purdey in the garden—also 'just like Smudge used to do'..." Cassie gave me a dry look. "I think you're going to have a tough time trying to get your cat back."

I chuckled. "Maybe Muesli won't want to come home with me after spending a day spoiled by Mrs Purdey." I glanced at my watch. "I'll leave it until after we close to go over and pick her up—let the old dear have her for a bit longer."

"Well, it was probably just as well that Muesli wasn't here this morning. We were so busy, I think somebody would probably have stepped on her."

"Did you manage okay?" I asked worriedly. "The Old Biddies don't seem to be here—you weren't completely on your own, were you?"

"No, they were here earlier. They just popped out to go to Sunday afternoon bingo but they said they'd be back... ah, talk of the devil!"

The door to the tearoom opened and four little old ladies toddled in. Their eyes lit up when they saw me and they hurried over to join me and Cassie at the counter.

"Gemma, dear, there's something we must tell you!" cried Glenda.

"Yes, it's about Josh McDermitt's murder!" squeaked Ethel.

"It's a way Antonio could have done it!" said Florence.

"No, no—let me tell her," said Mabel bossily. She stopped next to me and placed her arms akimbo on her waist. "You said Leanne didn't see Antonio in the dining hall... but he could have gone in *before* she arrived. He could have slipped in, done the tampering, and then slipped out again—all before she even got there."

I shook my head. "No, that won't work. First, Devlin told me that all the equipment for the show was provided by the TV crew and had been delivered to the Master's residence earlier that day for safekeeping. When they were setting up just before the ball, a member of the crew personally took the electric whisk into the dining hall and placed it on the bench there. So the only time anyone could have tampered with it was in the ten minutes or so between the whisk being left there and Josh himself arriving in the dining hall."

"That's when Leanne sneaked in, wasn't it?" said Cassie.

"Yes. If Antonio had got in before her, it's unlikely that she wouldn't have seen him—either in the hall or on his way out. But in any case, I know he didn't go in because there's a witness who saw him outside the building when Josh and Jerry arrived."

"Who's that?" asked Mabel.

"Maddie Gill, the producer." I told them about meeting Maddie that morning, her affair with the rival chef, and what really happened outside the dining hall on the night of the ball, as well as the truth about Josh's sabotage attempts.

"Josh would never do that!" cried Glenda, looking scandalised.

"Oh, yes, he would," said Cassie grimly.

"Anyway, the point is—Antonio Casa is definitely not the murderer," I said.

Mabel looked crestfallen. "I was sure it was him."

Cassie laughed. "And I was sure it was Leanne! I guess we were both wrong."

"But... does that mean we have no suspects now?" asked Ethel, wringing her hands.

"No... I think there's someone else who had an opportunity to tamper with the whisk. Not *before* Josh arrived, but during the time he was in the hall—maybe when his back was turned." I paused as they all looked at me expectantly. "His manager, Jerry Wallis."

"Wallis? You mean that obnoxious git who came into the tearoom the other day and accused you of stealing Josh's custard tart recipe?" Cassie asked.

"Yes, him. Apparently, he's got huge gambling debts and he's the sole beneficiary in the payout on a life insurance policy for Josh."

"What? Why didn't the police consider him a suspect before?" Cassie demanded.

"Because he had a solid alibi. Maddie had told the police that she was with him the whole time. Of course, that's all different now that it's come out she was lying and she wasn't in the dining hall with Jerry at all. It means he could have—"

I broke off as the door to the tearoom opened and we all gaped as the very man we were talking about stepped in. Jerry Wallis walked up to the counter and gave me a nod. Unlike his belligerent manner on his last visit, this time he looked slightly apprehensive.

"Miss Rose? Can I talk to you for a minute? In private," he added, eyeing the Old Biddies.

I led the manager away from the others and stepped into the small shop area attached to the main dining room. It was sealed off from the rest of the tearoom by a glass door and glass walls on three sides, giving us a measure of privacy, although I could see the Old Biddies watching us, beady-eyed, through the glass.

Jerry glanced at the shelves stacked with tins of tea, shortbread biscuits, Oxford souvenirs, and other tourist paraphernalia, and said with a greasy smile: "You've got nice stuff. In fact... er... the whole tearoom is great... and I've heard fantastic things about your baking."

I eyed him suspiciously. This was a change of

tune from his last visit! Jerry was obviously trying to butter me up—and making a bad job of it—and I wondered what he wanted.

"You said you wanted to speak to me?" I prodded.

"Ah... yes... right." He shifted his weight and gave me that greasy smile again. "I've been doing some thinking, you see, and I... er... think we could come to a mutually beneficial arrangement."

I frowned. "I don't know what you mean."

"Well... it's an absolute tragedy what's happened to Josh..." He put on a mournful expression. "Especially as it has deprived the world of his great culinary talents. Like his egg custard tarts... ah, I know that everyone is desperate to taste them just once more, now that he's gone..." He made an exaggerated show of snapping his fingers. "And then I thought of you! With your delicious tarts—which taste *soooo* much like Josh's—it would be a way for people to sample his famous creations again."

He rubbed his hands together. "So here's what I propose: you produce the tarts and I'll market and distribute them. I've sounded out a few contacts in London and we could maybe even sell them in the food halls of the big department stores, like Selfridges and Harrods, and gourmet emporiums like Fortnum & Mason's... We could brand them as 'Josh McDermitt's Signature Egg Custard Tarts'— and get some fancy packaging done." His eyes gleamed. "There's a lot of activity on social media at the moment because of the murder—it's a great time to take advantage of the extra visibility. We might even be able to get a campaign to go viral. You know—'eat a custard tart in honour of Josh's memory'—something like that. Maybe get one of the celebrities in on the act. And you'll be getting free PR for your tearoom... although I'll make sure you get a good deal too, of course. Forty percent of all profits. And you don't even have to stump up for any of the advertising—I'll take care of that. You won't get an offer like this every day. So... what d'ya say?"

I stared at him with a mixture of disbelief and disgust. "You were just here last week accusing me of trying to steal Josh's recipe and exploiting his brand—and now you want me to give you my tarts to pass off as his, so you can cash in on the publicity around his murder?"

He held up his hands defensively. "Okay, okay... so I might have got the wrong end of the stick when I came in here last week, but hey, we all make mistakes right?" He gave me another ingratiating smile. "Come on, we'll make a great team. You're a good-looking girl. Maybe I could get you a TV contract, eh? Star in your own show—what do you think? And I'd be happy to be your manager, of course."

I laughed. The man was delusional!

"Was this part of the plan all along?" I demanded. "Is this why you murdered Josh at the ball, using such an unusual weapon—so you could cash in on the publicity as well?"

His eyes bulged. "*What?* Me murder Josh?"

"Yes, you," I said, taking a step towards him. "You thought you got away with it, didn't you? Especially with Maddie Gill giving you that perfect alibi... you must have been laughing! But she's told me the truth: she wasn't in the dining hall with you at all—she was outside, meeting someone by the college kitchen. She admitted that she lied to the police... which means that you lied too, when you didn't speak up. Now why would you do that? Because *you* needed an alibi. And the only reason you'd need an alibi is because *you* were the one who tampered with the wiring on that electric whisk. You murdered Josh McDermitt."

He stared at me. "You're barking," he said, shaking his head slowly. "Absolutely barking. Why on earth would I want to murder Josh?"

"For money," I said succinctly. "You've got a lot of bad debt, haven't you?"

He gave me a shifty look. "How did you know about that?"

"The police have been digging into your background. And they found out that you're desperate for cash to pay off your creditors—cash that you'll get when you receive the payout from Josh's life insurance."

He started to say something but I cut him off.

"And not only that, you were embezzling funds

from Josh's accounts, weren't you? And he was getting suspicious... so you had to do something. Murdering him would kill two birds with one stone. You'd get the insurance money and you'd keep the auditors off your back... and maybe continue siphoning from Josh's estate—"

"STOP!" he roared. "This is absolute bollocks! You're crazy if you think I murdered Josh. He was the best thing that happened to me. Do you realise how much he was worth as a client? I would have done anything to save his life if I could. The life insurance money? Hah!" He snorted. "You think I murdered him to get my hands on that? Give me a break! It's hardly a huge sum; I make far more from being Josh's manager and overseeing his career."

"Yes, but you wouldn't get all the money at once, like you would with an insurance payout," I said, although less confidently than before. His vehemence was starting to make me uncertain.

He gave me a patronising smile. "Trust me, sweetheart, Josh was worth far more to me alive than dead. My commission from his TV contracts alone is more than that measly insurance payout. As his manager—and with the way his career was going—I was looking at early retirement if I wanted to."

"But... but what about your debts...?" I blustered.

"Yeah, so I got a bit over my head, so what? Josh knew about my debts. I went to him last week and told him everything. He was pretty understanding—used to gamble a bit himself—and he even agreed to give me an interest-free loan to tide me over, just until I sorted myself out. Now he's dead... I don't have my loan, I don't have my client... I have nothing." He shook his head and gave a humourless laugh. "And you think I killed him? Bloody hell... Josh's murder was the worst thing that's happened to me!"

"But... I don't understand... why did you keep quiet about Maddie's lie then?"

He shrugged. "I don't know... it seemed like a good idea at the time. I didn't want the police breathing down my neck so I thought it would be simpler if they thought I had an alibi. No one wants any extra reason to look suspicious when there's been a murder, right?"

It was exactly what Maddie had said. It had sounded too simple, and yet now I had to reluctantly admit that it might be the truth.

"So... coming back to this deal..." said Jerry, giving me an oily smile again. "Whaddya say? I could get the paperwork to you tomorrow and we could—"

"No."

"Okay, we'll split it fifty-fifty, how about that?"

"No," I said. "I'm not—"

"All right, seventy-thirty, then, and that's my final offer. Come on—you can't get a better deal than this! Seventy percent of profits and the chance to use Josh McDermitt's name on your products—"

"No, I told you, no!" I said, looking at him in revulsion. I opened the glass door of the shop and held it pointedly. "I think there's nothing more to discuss."

"I'll let you think about it," he said with a smug smile as he walked slowly out of the shop. "I'm sure that after you've slept on it, you'll see what a fantastic opportunity this is and how stupid you'd be to—"

"Goodbye, Mr Wallis."

When he had finally gone, I returned to the counter where Cassie and the Old Biddies were waiting for me, and made a face, rubbing my arms with distaste.

"Ugh. I feel like I need a shower after speaking to that man."

"What did he want?" Cassie asked, whilst the Old Biddies gathered eagerly around us.

I told them and also recounted Jerry's explanation for his "fake" alibi.

"And you believe him?" asked Cassie.

"Yes... I do, actually," I said. "I mean... I think the man is a creep, but I think he's telling the truth. There was something in the way he got so incredulous... I don't think he was faking that. And besides, while I don't have much faith in his morals or ethics, I'm pretty certain I can rely on his greedy nature. So if it's true what he said, killing Josh would have been like killing the golden goose. Jerry would never have wanted that. Anyway, I'll tell Devlin everything and let the police check it out. I think they'll agree with me, though."

"But... if the manager is not the murderer... and it's not Antonio Casa or Leanne Fitch either... then who is it?" wailed Glenda.

"We're back to Square One with no suspects," said Mabel grimly.

"And no clues, either," said Florence mournfully. "They all seem to have led to dead ends."

The Old Biddies were right. It was disheartening to realise that after all the drama of the past few days, we were right back where we'd started with no better idea of who had murdered Josh McDermitt.

Then Ethel spoke up in her soft, gentle voice: "Maybe there is a clue in the interview."

We all turned to look at her.

"The one that was on the telly last week," Ethel explained. "In the morning."

Cassie snapped her fingers. "Yeah—when Josh went on that breakfast show. I said the other day that he was probably murdered for some deep, dark secret he revealed on the show, remember?"

"But there was no 'deep, dark secret'," I protested. "I watched the interview at my mother's house. There was nothing really scandalous. Josh just talked about a few of his recipes and then he denied that he had tried to sabotage Antonio Casa's new restaurant—"

"The show hosts kept asking him about

something he used in his cooking, though," said Mabel thoughtfully. "Monosodium glutamate—"

"Yes, MSG. It's a flavour enhancer. Some people think you get a sort of allergic reaction from it. But as Josh said on the show, there's no scientific evidence backing that up."

"Are you sure about that?" asked Cassie. "I mean, of course Josh is going to defend it on the show, but how do you know it's true?"

"I asked Lincoln about it too and he confirmed that it's just an urban myth. Besides, you're not seriously suggesting that someone killed Josh because he added a bit of MSG to their food and gave them a headache?"

"I don't know," said Cassie. "But I think Ethel is right—I think there's a clue in that interview that we're not seeing. If we can just figure it out, we'd have the answer to the mystery of Josh McDermitt's murder."

CHAPTER TWENTY-SEVEN

Once the four o'clock teatime rush was over, I left the tearoom in Cassie's and the Old Biddie's capable hands and—armed with the cat trap that Seth brought me—I set off for Boscobel College. I enjoyed the ride back to Oxford, cycling along the country lanes and inhaling the smell of freshly cut grass and the sweet scent of honeysuckle in the hedgerows. When I finally pulled up outside Boscobel, I was in a wonderful carefree mood.

My mood did sober slightly as I approached the dining hall and was reminded again of what had happened there. But I put the murder resolutely from my mind and headed down the path towards the secluded garden at the rear of the college. Right now, I just had one concern and that was to catch a

273

wily feral tomcat.

A middle-aged man was coming out of the garden just as I was walking in and I recognised him as Henry Mansell, the Master of the college. He was wearing a brown tweed jacket and a bow tie, despite the warm summer weather, and looked the stereotype of the absent-minded Oxford don, with spectacles perched on the end of his nose and a tattered textbook in one hand. He raised his eyebrows as he saw me and his eyes fell on the cage I was holding.

"Hi... er... I'm Gemma." I said, feeling the need to explain myself. "I've come to trap the feral cat. I spoke to your wife, Irene, and she said it was okay for me to come today..."

"Oh yes, that's right," he said vaguely. "Irene did mention it to me. Well, I must say, I can't understand why you'd bother..." He shuddered. "Can't abide cats—nasty, sly creatures—but I suppose one must try to do the humane thing." He looked at me again and said, "Forgive me but... you look very familiar. Have we met—?"

"Yes, just very briefly when I was shown to your house to wait for the police. I was the girl who found Josh McDermitt's body."

"Oh yes, of course, that's right." His face turned grave. "Terrible business, terrible... such a promising young man..."

"He was a student here, wasn't he?"

"Yes, yes, although mostly before my time. I

think Irene and I arrived here in Josh's last year and he was just about to graduate. However, he did return to the college a few years later... it was our centenary celebration and we were holding an Afternoon Tea Party in the Master's Garden. Josh had just started making a name for himself, so we thought it would be fitting to ask him to cater the party as his first big event. I remember he debuted his egg custard tarts that day and they were sensational. Everyone was talking about them." He gave me a whimsical smile. "I like to think that the college gave Josh his first leg up, especially in spreading the word about his custard tarts." He paused, then added, furrowing his brow: "I think I heard recently that there's a tearoom nearby in the Cotswolds which makes fabulous custard tarts too... Er... Little-something... Little Manger, I think it's called? Some friends of ours were talking about it."

"The Little Stables," I said, blushing slightly. "Yes, actually, I'm the owner of that tearoom."

"Are you really?" He looked at me with delight. "Well, I must remember to stop by the next time we're in the neighbourhood. Now, I must go..." He gave me a nod and strolled past, murmuring, "I'll let Irene know that you're here..."

I watched him disappear down the cloister, heading towards the private courtyard and the Master's residence, and wondered if he would remember to tell his wife after all. He looked so vague and forgetful that I wouldn't have been surprised if he had completely dismissed me from his mind by the time he got back and simply wandered into his study and become immersed in some academic journal.

Anyway, it doesn't matter, I thought as I heaved the cage higher and walked into the garden. I didn't need Irene to be there, and in fact, if the tomcat really was as hostile towards other people as I'd been told, I might have better success if I was alone.

I scouted the area and finally set the cage down near a large bush at the back of the garden, just by the access to the wild meadow beyond the college grounds. Carefully, I rigged the trap with the bait I'd brought—an oily, smelly can of tuna—and laid a small trail from the mouth of the cage to the trigger plate at the back. Then I walked away and found a comfortable position against an old stone sundial, where I could keep an eye on the trap.

The minutes passed. It was very peaceful, almost soporific in the garden. There was no sound, except for the soft murmur of the breeze through the tall grasses and the lazy humming of bees hovering around a large lavender bush. The warm late afternoon sunshine glinted on the handle of a pitchfork stuck into a large compost heap next to me and reflected off the central gnomon on the sundial. I shifted my weight from one leg to the other, looking idly around and trying not to be impatient.

Then, just as I was thinking of finding somewhere to sit down, I heard a familiar rustle in the undergrowth. There was a movement in the bushes behind the cage and a svelte shape stepped out of the shadows. It was the grey tabby tomcat. He paused and sniffed the air, then turned his head and looked at me with his big green eyes which were so like Muesli's. He had a fresh scar across his face and it made him look even more menacing.

"*Miaowww...*" he said.

"Hello, you..." I said softly, breaking into a smile.

He regarded me for a moment longer, then turned and prowled towards the cage. My pulse quickened as I watched him walk around it, sniffing it cautiously. I saw his whiskers quiver as he smelled the tuna, but he kept his distance from the trap, eyeing it with suspicion. Irene Mansell had been right: this tomcat wouldn't be easy to trick. I watched anxiously as he circled the cage twice more, and then, to my dismay, he started to walk away!

I took an involuntary step forwards, then stopped myself. The cat had paused a few feet away and sat down with his back to the cage. He began to wash himself in a leisurely fashion, for all the world as if he wasn't aware of the strong, fishy aroma nearby. I stared at him in frustrated bewilderment. Just as I was thinking of taking another step forwards, he suddenly got up again and strolled back to the cage. This time, he went closer, sniffing intently along the steel bars, flicking his ears backwards and forwards as he went along. He reached the mouth of the cage and paused, staring at the morsel of tuna I'd left there. His whiskers twitched. I held my breath.

He glanced quickly around, then bent and grabbed the piece of tuna, gulping it down. I felt a surge of excitement. He was taking the bait! I watched tensely as the tomcat lowered his head again and sniffed the spot where the piece of tuna had been. Slowly, he moved his head along to where the next morsel of tuna lay waiting, just inside the cage. I saw him hesitate, then lift a paw to step inside the cage...

RRRRRRING!

I jumped, then cursed under my breath as I realised that it was my mobile phone. I had forgotten to set it to 'silent', and now the shrill ringing sounded like a fire alarm in the stillness of the garden. The tomcat had jerked back from the cage and was now crouched wide-eyed a few feet away, looking ready to bolt. I fumbled in my pocket for my phone, pulled it out and frantically answered it.

"Hello?" I said in a hushed voice.

"Darling!" my mother trilled. "I'm just in Boswells and they've got the most marvellous Brollymaps. Would you like one?"

"*What?*"

My mother tutted. "Don't say 'what', darling, say

'pardon'. It's made by Fultons, the umbrella suppliers to the Queen, and it has a lovely illustrated map of central London, with all the important landmarks—"

"Mother, look—I can't talk now."

I glanced over at the cage and was relieved to see that the tomcat hadn't run away. In fact, he seemed to have relaxed and was approaching the cage again. I felt a surge of hope returning. Keeping my voice low and steady, I said:

"I'm... er... sort of in the middle of something now, Mother. Can I ring you back later?"

"Oh, I suppose so... although I'll be going to have my hair done in a moment. It's not really a convenient time but the girl making the appointments has gone on maternity leave and the lady who replaced her just didn't seem to know what she was doing—oh, before I forget, darling, do you still want me to keep that interview with Josh McDermitt? Only because your father was sorting out the recorder for me last night and he wanted to delete it."

"Oh no—don't delete it! I'd like to watch that interview again. There might be a clue as to his murder."

"Well, apparently they're going to run it again anyway. I heard that they're putting together a special commemorative programme on Josh, featuring a selection of his TV appearances and interviews." My mother tutted. "Really, I don't know what all the fuss is about. I mean, it's a terribly tragic thing to have happened to the poor boy, of course, but everyone is acting as if he's the greatest cook that ever lived."

"Aren't you a fan, Mother? I thought you would be."

"Oh no, he doesn't compare with any of the real 'greats'—the British chefs who have been household names for decades... like Delia Smith, for instance. Really, most of Josh McDermitt's recipe variations are a bit silly and some of them are downright dangerous. Like using unpasteurised cream, for example, in his egg custard tarts. He was talking about that in the interview. It's really very irresponsible—raw milk can harbour all sorts of germs, like *Salmonella* and *E.coli*... and *Listeria* is so dangerous if you're pregnant. Even if you don't show any symptoms, you can suffer a miscarriage or have a stillborn—"

"*What?*" I gripped the phone tighter. "Mother, what did you say?"

"Don't say 'what', darling, say—"

"Oh my God, Mother, I think... I think I know who killed Josh McDermitt!"

Ignoring my mother's bewildered questions, I babbled an excuse and hung up. Then I stood staring blindly into space, my heart pounding and my mind whirling like crazy.

Could I be right?

Yes, it all fit, and I couldn't believe that I hadn't

seen it before. Josh McDermitt's interview... his first big event and the debut of his famous egg custard tarts at Boscobel College... the unpasteurised cream... *Listeria* and the danger of miscarriage... a woman with a face prematurely lined from years of pain and sorrow... revenge served with a chef's own tool...

I held up my phone again and punched Cassie's number. She answered on the second ring.

"Hiya, Gemma... you just missed the funniest thing. Dora said—"

"Cassie, I think I know who murdered Josh McDermitt! You were right: it *was* because of something revealed in his interview," I said breathlessly. "Listen, the other day, the porter at Boscobel told me that this was always a bad time of year for Henry Mansell and his wife: it's the anniversary of when they lost their baby. Do you know what happened?"

"Oh, that...yes, I know the story." Cassie's voice turned sombre. "This was after I left college, of course, so I don't know the details, but I heard it from some friends who stayed on at Boscobel to do postgraduate degrees. Apparently, Irene Mansell got pregnant after a lot of difficulty—I think they had fertility treatment and stuff; she was an older mother, you know, and they'd been told that the chances were slim... Anyway, they were really happy and it was all going well... and then all of a sudden, she had a miscarriage and lost the baby.

She was six months along and she'd been decorating the nursery and everything..."

"Oh, that's awful," I murmured.

"Yeah. I heard she took it really badly. It had been her last chance to have children. She became a virtual recluse for a while. But she's been better the last few years. I think I even saw her at the ball. Why are you asking—" She broke off. "Gemma, you're not thinking that Irene...?"

"Yes," I said. "Irene Mansell is the murderer. She must have seen that interview and suddenly realised that Josh was the reason she lost her baby. The unpasteurised cream he used in his egg custard tarts caused her to contract listeriosis."

"Listeriosis?"

"It's a type of food poisoning—an infection caused by the *Listeria* bacterium. It's quite rare and it's not usually lethal, but it's really dangerous for pregnant women. I don't know the date Irene had her miscarriage but I'll bet it was shortly after the Centenary Afternoon Tea Party at Boscobel College, which was catered by Josh. He said in the interview that he first tried the unpasteurised cream at his 'first big event'—and Henry Mansell told me earlier this afternoon that Josh debuted his egg custard tarts at the college tea party... It all fits!"

"Bloody hell..." said Cassie. "So Irene was the one who tampered with the wiring?"

"She had the perfect opportunity: when the equipment was left at the Master's residence for safekeeping during the day, before the TV crew set up for the ball. We were all focusing on who could have got into the dining hall to tamper with the whisk and we never considered the possibility that it was tampered with *before* it was carried into the hall and placed on the bench!"

"I can't believe we were so wrong about everything—"

"Well, not everything. We were right about one thing: this murder *was* about revenge. You know, I met Lincoln and Jo at the White Horse pub, when I was having lunch with Antonio Casa. Jo said something which is just coming back to me now. She said women '*can bottle things up and stew on something for decades*'; she was talking about women who killed their husbands or boyfriends in revenge for cheating on them, but this isn't that different. Irene Mansell must have been carrying all this pain and bitterness inside her all these years and then suddenly, she found out why she lost her precious baby: all because a cocky young man decided to flout the rules and not tell anyone."

"Bloody hell..." said Cassie again. "She must have been livid."

"Who wouldn't be? She must have hated him— and when she learned that Josh was coming back to the college for the ball, it seemed like Fate had given her the perfect opportunity to get an eye for an eye... or a life for a life, in this case."

"You've got to tell Devlin all this."

"I will. I'll tell him as soon as—"

A noise behind me made me break off and spin around. I gasped and the phone slipped from my slack fingers. Irene Mansell stood behind me, her face pale and strained. From the expression in her eyes, I knew that she had heard everything.

"Irene..." I said nervously. I darted a look around but we were completely alone in the garden. The only other movement came from the feral tomcat, who was still hovering by the cage trap, but I barely paid him any attention now. All my focus was on the woman standing in front of me, her eyes dark and burning.

"I wondered if you'd find out in the end," said Irene pleasantly. "I could tell that you were a smart girl. I used to teach... did you know that? I was a high school science teacher before I married Henry. You remind me of some of my best students: bright, creative, and persistent. It's a shame you won't live to continue using those talents..."

She took a step towards me and my eyes bulged as I saw what she was holding in her hands: the pitchfork from the compost heap, with the sharp ends of the prongs pointed towards me. I started to back away but found that the sundial was right behind me. I was wedged against it, unable to move, with the vicious-looking pitchfork thrust towards my chest.

"Wait... Irene... uh, can we talk about this—?"

"What else is there to talk about? You seem to

know everything already," she said, still in that pleasant voice, as if we were sitting down together over afternoon tea.

"I don't know how you tampered with the wiring," I gabbled. "I mean, I don't know how you knew *how* to do it."

She laughed. "Oh, that was easy. I knew the basic principles from my teaching days. Ninth grade science *does* come in handy. And it's amazing what information can be found on the internet... Of course, sometimes one doesn't have the time to plan and prepare the perfect murder—sometimes one has to improvise..."

She raised the pitchfork slightly, so that the prongs jabbed towards my neck. I swallowed and leaned back as far as I could.

"Irene... this is crazy! You can't kill me... the college is full of people... you'll never get away with it."

"Won't I? I think you might be surprised. Term is over now and there are very few students in college, and only a skeleton staff. Most never come down here, anyway. And if your body is dumped in the meadow behind the college, you might not be found for a couple of days..."

"My friends know I'm at Boscobel," I said desperately. "They'd look for me. They'd find me very quickly—it wouldn't be days. And my boyfriend is a detective—"

"He's the handsome inspector with the blue eyes,

isn't he? Yes, I'll have to be careful with him. I can see that he's no fool. But don't worry, he'll have no reason to suspect me."

She took another step closer. The prongs of the pitchfork were almost touching my neck now and I could feel myself shaking from the effort of leaning backwards.

Irene Mansell smiled. "Now, hold still—I won't say 'it won't hurt' because I suppose it will... but hopefully it shouldn't take long, and you won't feel much once the blood loss becomes severe."

I felt panic seize me. The woman was completely mad! My hands clenched on the stone sides of the sundial behind me as I thought about heaving myself sideways. But I knew with a sinking heart that there wasn't enough space—I'd never be able to avoid the pitchfork. I might even be thrusting myself into its path. But what was the alternative? To stand here waiting while Irene Mansell impaled me like a sausage on a stick?

As if in slow motion, I saw her knuckles go white as she clenched the handle and raised the pitchfork towards me. I opened my mouth to scream, but before I could utter a sound, the air was rent by a hideous shriek.

"*YEEEEAAAOOOWWWWWWWLLL!*"

There was a bang and a clatter of steel as the cat trap next to us suddenly shook violently. Another scream sounded and what looked like a tornado of hissing, spitting fur flew around the inside of the cage as it rattled and bounced on the ground.

Irene Mansell gave a start of surprise, jerking around and thrusting the pitchfork in the direction of the cage, but the sudden movement unbalanced her and she staggered backwards.

I jumped out of her way as she lurched past me, still clutching the pitchfork. Then she tripped and fell against the sundial. I heard a sickening *crunch* as her head smacked against the side of the stone structure.

Then she slumped to the ground.

My legs felt suddenly rubbery beneath me and I sat down quickly on the grass. There was a loud roaring in my ears and, for a moment, I thought I was going to be sick. Cold sweat ran down my back and my hands were shaking. Then, slowly, the feeling passed. I sat up again, swallowing past the lingering nausea in my throat, and took a shuddering breath.

There was the sound of running footsteps, then two men rushed into the garden. It was Henry Mansell and the friendly college porter I'd met on the night of the ball. They stopped short as they took in the scene in front of them: Irene Mansell lying unconscious next to the sundial, me huddled in the grass next to her, and, on the ground next to me, a hissing, spitting tomcat giving everyone the Evil Eye from inside the cage.

"Irene!" cried Henry Mansell, rushing towards his wife. "Call an ambulance!" he shouted at the porter, who nodded and hurried away. Then he crouched next to his wife's limp form and checked her vital signs. Seemingly satisfied, he leaned back—then froze as he noticed the pitchfork still in her hand. He looked at me in bewilderment.

"What happened here?"

I hesitated, then said, "Your wife tried to kill me."

"I beg your pardon?" Henry stared at me.

"It's true. She needed to silence me because I'd found out the truth."

"The truth about what?"

"The truth about Josh McDermitt—that she was the one who murdered him."

He jerked as if he had been stabbed himself and all colour left his face. "Why... why on earth would she want to kill Josh?" he whispered.

"For revenge... for causing her to lose your baby," I said gently. I saw the expression in his eyes. "But you already knew that, didn't you?"

The Master of Boscobel College hesitated, then gave a great sigh and seemed to shrink into himself. "I... Yes... God forgive me, I did." He looked down at his unconscious wife. "I felt terrible even suspecting her but..." He shook his head and looked at me pleadingly. "You have to understand, Irene never the same after we lost our baby. I was devastated, of course, but for her, it was as if all the light went out in her world. She didn't eat, didn't sleep, didn't leave the house for months... And even after years had passed, she never managed to move on like I did. In fact, it became an obsession with her—in particular, trying to find out why she had had the miscarriage. Doctors told her that sometimes spontaneous abortions just happen but she refused to believe them. She had been so careful during the whole pregnancy, monitoring her diet, her exercise, her sleep patterns, doing nothing that might harm the baby... and she just couldn't understand how it could have happened."

"And then she found out..." I said.

Henry Mansell nodded grimly. "Yes, and then she found out... and it was as if the raging inferno, which had smouldered inside her all these years, suddenly roared to life. I knew something had changed a couple of weeks ago but I didn't realise what it was. I didn't watch that interview with her. But I noticed that Irene seemed suddenly restless and distracted—and yet full of a strange repressed energy. I suppose I should have known... should have said something—"

"You can't blame yourself," I said, reaching out impulsively to put my hand on his. "And in a way... you can't really blame Irene either."

I expected him to pull away—he was just the type to follow the classic British tradition of a "stiff upper lip" and never show emotion in public—but to my surprise, he covered my hand with his and gave me a sad smile.

"Thank you, my dear. That's kind of you to say so." He glanced at his unconscious wife again. "I hope the jury will be as understanding..." Then he squared his shoulders and looked up as the college porter re-entered the garden.

"The ambulance is on its way, sir."

Henry Mansell nodded, then said heavily, "And you'd better call the police as well."

"The police—?" said the porter in surprise.

I saw that Irene was stirring and her husband began lifting her tenderly into his arms. I stood up and walked over to the porter.

"I'll come back to the Porter's Lodge with you," I said, wanting to give the Mansells some privacy.

We walked out of the garden together, the porter still looking bewildered.

"What happened?" he asked. "When I heard that dreadful screaming, I came running as fast as I could. I didn't realise it was the cat—I thought something awful had happened."

"Something awful nearly did happen," I said, gingerly rubbing my throat. Then I gave him a watery smile. "But like once before, a cat saved my life."

CHAPTER TWENTY-EIGHT

It was rush hour and Oxford railway station was packed with commuters, as well as the usual crowds of visitors and tourists that flooded to the famous university city daily. I followed Devlin as he escorted his mother out onto the platform and we stood together to wait for the next train heading north.

"So is the case wrapped up now?" Keeley asked Devlin.

"Yes, in a way. The investigation is closed as we've made an arrest. But the trial is only just beginning and it will probably go on for a while."

"They'll be understanding, won't they?" I asked.

Devlin's gaze softened. "Yes, I think everybody will be very sympathetic to Irene Mansell. Not that it excuses her—murder is never justified—but I think we can all understand how she could have been driven to do what she did."

"The poor woman..." said Keeley. "I can remember being pregnant with you, Dev, and even though I had never wanted to be a mother, I was terrified that I'd lose you. I can't imagine what Irene must have gone through."

I turned away and gazed out over the railway tracks, thinking about the irony of life—of one woman who wanted so desperately to be a mother, she was willing to kill to avenge the child she had lost, and another woman who had never wanted motherhood, now trying to connect with the son she had carelessly brought into the world.

"It's been grand meeting you, Gemma," said Keeley, reaching over to give me a hug. "I've really enjoyed spending time together—I'm sorry we didn't have longer."

"Me too," I said with a smile, and I realised to my surprise that I was telling the truth.

For all the hassles and stresses her visit had brought, I'd really enjoyed Keeley O'Connor's company. Yes, she was flighty and impulsive, outspoken and irresponsible... but she was also warm and charming and even inspiring in a way. And most of all, she was "fun". You might feel exasperated by her but you also couldn't help enjoying being with her. It was funny: I had been worried about meeting my boyfriend's mother and I had found myself meeting what seemed like a wacky older sister instead.

Keeley glanced tentatively at her son. "Maybe you and Dev can come and visit me sometime? Dev doesn't come home much."

It was said lightly but I saw the flash of vulnerability in her eyes. In her own way, Keeley O'Connor wanted her son's love and understanding. I looked hopefully at Devlin. His blue eyes—so like his mother's—were clouded for a moment, then he smiled and slipped his arm around Keeley's shoulders.

"I'd love to bring Gemma to visit, Mum. Maybe the next time I can put in for leave—and Gemma can take time off from the tearoom."

Keeley beamed and gave her son a fierce hug just as the train pulled into the station with a rush of wind that tossed her long blonde hair in every direction. People started jostling and pushing towards the carriage doors. Devlin lifted his mum's case to help her on board and she paused by the carriage steps to give us both a smile.

"Be good, you two!"

A few minutes later, the train was gone and we were left standing on the empty platform. I glanced at Devlin: he was staring at the departing train in the distance and it was difficult to read his thoughts. I slipped my hand into his and gave it a squeeze. He turned to me and a smile lit his blue eyes.

"You know, Gemma... I think you were right about my mum."

"Me?"

"Well, you told me to give her a chance... and she does seem to be finally changing. This visit has been the quietest and nicest time I've spent with her in a long time. There were no embarrassing rescues from drunken bars, no dodgy smoke coming out of the bathroom window, no sleepless nights wondering where she had got to and what she was doing..."

"Er..." I bit my tongue on what I was going to say.

"I think she's changing at last," said Devlin enthusiastically. "Maybe now that she's in her forties, she'll calm down and behave more like other mothers."

I looked at Devlin's happy face and wondered what was the right thing to do. Let him continue his delusion of ignorance or tell him the truth about the woman who was his mother?

"Um... Devlin, you know... maybe we shouldn't expect our mothers to change," I said at last.

He frowned. "What do you mean? You've seen what my mum's like—surely you agree that she needs to become more mature and responsible?"

"Well... even if she doesn't... she's still your mother. And maybe... well, maybe you'd have a happier time with her if you didn't keep expecting her to change... if you just accept her as she is." I touched his hand. "People don't really change, Devlin—you should know that. They are who they are... and if you love them, then you take them as they are." I gave him a wistful smile. "Children are always saying they want their parents to accept who they are... well, I think sometimes, parents feel the same way." I looked back at the empty railway lines leading into the distance. "For all her faults... I think your mother's great."

Devlin looked at me disbelievingly. "You think my mother is great?"

I reached up and slid my arms around Devlin's neck, pressing my lips to his in a tender kiss. "Well, she brought you into the world, didn't she? That will always make her a wonderful woman in my eyes."

Devlin started to respond but we were interrupted by the shrill ringing of my phone. Giving him an apologetic look, I disentangled myself and pulled my mobile out of my pocket, glancing quickly at the screen. It was my mother.

"Darling!" my mother trilled. "I'm just in Debenhams getting some nail brushes. Do you think you'd like the walnut wood with ergonomic shaping or the natural wood with strong cactus bristles?"

"Huh?"

"I was thinking the walnut would be much nicer. It's got medium-strength natural bristles and it also doubles up as a mini body brush when travelling—

isn't that convenient?"

I groaned. "Mother, I don't need a nail brush."

"Oh, nonsense, darling—how else would you get your nails properly clean? Remember, a lady always takes care of her hands and having dirt under your fingernails is dreadfully unsightly!"

"Mother—" I started to growl a reply, then I stopped and thought about what I had just told Devlin. I gave a rueful grin. Maybe it was time I followed my own advice. Taking a deep breath, I said:

"You know what, Mother? If you hang on, I'll come and join you in Debenhams. I'm just at the train station now so I should be there in ten minutes. Hmm? Oh... tea with you and Aunt Helen afterwards sounds lovely too... yes, see you soon!"

EPILOGUE

"The vet said he's in remarkably good shape, considering that he'd been living rough and scrounging for food. A bit on the thin side and some nicks and scratches, but nothing serious. A dose of flea treatment, a couple of vaccinations and some worming pills, and he was good to go," said Seth. "In fact, I think they were quite glad to see the back of him. He sounds like a vicious beast—bit the vet nurse twice and nearly took the vet's eye out. I'd be careful approaching him, if I were you," he added, eyeing the tomcat in the cage warily.

I ignored Seth's warning and crouched down next to the cat carrier. The feral tomcat was sitting sulkily in the far corner, his ears flattened against his head and his eyes narrowed to slits. He lifted his chin slightly when he saw me and I saw his green eyes soften.

He let out a deep "*Miaoowww...*" and gave me a reproachful look.

"Hello, you..." I said softly. "I'm sorry I tricked

you, but we're trying to find you a good home."

"Er, yes... about that..." Seth shifted awkwardly. "I've been asking around and there's a bit of a problem finding somewhere that would take him."

"I thought you said anywhere with a bit of outdoor shelter would do... like a stable or a farm—"

"Well, yes, there are a couple of places nearby, but the thing is, one is a farm with a young family and the other is a riding school, which has a lot of children visiting... and really, given how aggressive he is, I don't think it would be fair or safe to rehome him at either place."

"Oh, he's not that bad—look!" I pointed to the tomcat, which had come towards me and was now nuzzling my fingers through the bars of the cage. "Are you sure they're not exaggerating? Maybe they're just prejudiced because of his scarred face. I think he's a big softie."

"I don't know, Gemma... I saw the bandage on the vet nurse's hand and I can tell you, she wasn't exaggerating!" Seth tilted his head and watched incredulously as I scratched the tomcat under the chin and a loud purring filled the room. "It's weird how he seems so friendly with you, though..." He brightened. "Maybe *you* can adopt him?"

I glanced across to where Muesli was hunched on top of my sofa, glaring at the tomcat, with her fur standing on end and her tail twitching angrily.

I shook my head and chuckled. "I think Muesli

might have something to say about that."

"What do you mean? I bet they'll become great friends!" said Seth. "They even look alike. They'll probably eat together and play together—"

"Play together?" I bit off a laugh. "Seth, most cats don't play together—at least, not once they're no longer kittens, and especially if they haven't grown up with each other. I think I'll be lucky if they agree to stay in the same room without fighting." I glanced at my cat again. "Or on second thoughts, if Muesli doesn't shred him to pieces..."

"Muesli?" Seth laughed. "He's twice as big as her! I'd be more worried about the tom hurting her."

"I wouldn't be so sure," I said darkly. "Size doesn't always matter. Otherwise you wouldn't have so many big dogs in the world terrified of little kittens. Anyway, no—I'm sorry, I'd love to but I can't take him."

"Well, it was worth a try," said Seth with a sigh. "I don't know what I'm going to do with him. What we need is to find someone who can see past his belligerent exterior, give him time and understanding, and love him for what he is."

I smiled suddenly. "You know what? I think I might know just the person."

***

The village of Meadowford-on-Smythe was quiet and peaceful, with the late afternoon sun casting long shadows across the cobbled lanes and onto the golden limestone walls of the cottages. In the distance, I could hear the tinkling tune of the ice cream van doing its rounds, and closer by came the trill of a robin singing. It seemed like the perfect end to a lazy summer's day and—I glanced down at the cage I was carrying—I hoped it would also be the perfect end to the story of a lonely old lady who needed someone to love.

Slowly, I walked up the path to the familiar cottage and rang the doorbell. The door swung open a moment later and Mrs Purdey looked at me in surprise.

"Gemma, dear! I didn't realise you were coming—" She broke off as she spied the cage and a big smile broke across her face. "Ooh, you've brought Muesli for a visit!"

"Er… no, actually, it's not Muesli—although he does look a lot like her." I smiled as I held up the cage.

"Ohhh…" Her eyes were round as she stared at the tomcat. "Is he… What's his name?" she whispered.

"Well, he doesn't have one… yet. He was a feral cat, you see, and he'd been living in one of the Oxford colleges and making a bit of a nuisance of himself."

"A nuisance? How could such a beautiful boy be a nuisance?" said Mrs Purdey indignantly.

"Well, he *can* be quite aggressive with strangers

and he does scratch—oh, careful!" I cried as Mrs Purdey stepped closer and put her wrinkled face up to the cage.

"*Miaoowww...*" said the tomcat.

I held my breath. There was a moment of silence as Mrs Purdey and the tom looked at each other. Then the cat put out a paw and patted the old lady's hand through the bars.

"Ooh! He wants to say hello!" squealed Mrs Purdey. "Quick, quick... let him out..."

"Wait, I don't think—"

I started to protest but my words fell on deaf ears as Mrs Purdey grabbed the cage from me and unlatched the door. A moment later, the tomcat was out and cradled in her arms. I watched them nervously, wondering what to do if the cat should start scratching the old lady, but to my relief, he seemed to enjoy being held, resting calmly in Mrs Purdey's arms and eyeing his surroundings curiously.

"Oh, he's gorgeous—he's absolutely gorgeous!" Mrs Purdey gushed. "Can he stay the night with me—please?"

"Actually..." I smiled at her. "He can stay forever, if you're happy to have him."

She stared at me, speechless. "You mean..."

"Well, he can't go back to live in the college now so he needs a new home. He's been vet-checked and vaccinated and flea-ed and wormed..."

I trailed off as I saw that Mrs Purdey wasn't

listening. She was busy talking to the tomcat, telling him what she was going to make him for dinner and asking which side of the bed he would like to sleep on. I felt a lump come to my throat as I looked at her face, suffused with happiness. Smiling to myself, I turned quietly to go. But as I picked up the empty cage, Mrs Purdey stopped me.

"Oh, wait... did you say that he doesn't have a name yet?"

"No... or if they called him anything at the college, I don't think it was anything nice," I said with a chuckle.

"Well! We must find a name for him," declared Mrs Purdey.

"Yes, something to go with his looks. Maybe something like Tiger or Bruiser—"

"Custard."

I blinked. "C-custard?"

Mrs Purdey nodded, beaming. "Yes, Custard. Because he's such a sweetie..." She looked lovingly down at the big, scarred feline in her arms. "Don't you think it suits him perfectly?"

"But given that he's such a big, macho boy, don't you think you should name him something more—" I broke off and looked at the cat. Then I thought of the egg custard tarts that had started this whole thing.

I smiled at the old lady in front of me. "Yes, Custard is perfect.

FINIS

For other books by H.Y. Hanna,
please visit her website:
www.hyhanna.com

AUTHOR'S NOTE

This book follows British English spelling and
usage. For a glossary of British slang and
expressions used in the story, as well as special
terms used in Oxford University, please visit:
www.hyhanna.com/british-slang-other-terms

EGG CUSTARD TARTS RECIPE

(created with the help of Kim McMahan Davis -
Cinnamon and Sugar... and a Little Bit of Murder
Blog)

<u>INGREDIENTS:</u>

Pastry:
- 225 g (8 ounces) (2 scant cups) all-purpose flour
- 85 g (3 ounces) (1/3 cup + 1 tablespoon) caster (granulated) sugar
- Pinch of salt
- Pinch of freshly grated nutmeg
- 150 g (5.3 ounces) (2/3 cup) cold butter, cut into small pieces
- 1 whole egg + 1 egg yolk, beaten together
- 1 egg yolk, for brushing on pastry during baking

Custard:

- 375 g (13.25 ounces) (1-2/3 cups) heavy cream
- 90 g (3.2 ounces) (1/3 cup) whole milk
- 2 whole eggs + 2 egg yolks
- 85 g (3 ounces) (1/3 cup + 1 tablespoon) caster (granulated) sugar
- 2 teaspoons vanilla extract
- Freshly grated nutmeg

INSTRUCTIONS:

Cake:

1. Don't preheat the oven since dough needs to chill before baking.
2. Place the flour, sugar, salt and nutmeg in the bowl of a food processor and pulse to combine. Alternately you can whisk the ingredients together in a mixing bowl.
3. Add the cold butter to the flour mixture and either pulse in the food processor or cut in with a fork or pastry cutter until it resembles bread crumbs.
4. Add 3/4 of the beaten egg and egg yolk to the flour mixture and pulse (or mix by hand) just until dough comes together. If mixture is too dry, add remaining egg.
5. Turn out onto a lightly floured surface and gather into a disk. Wrap in plastic wrap and refrigerate for 1 hour.

6. Roll the dough out and cut into circles large enough to fit your tartlet pan or mini muffin pan. You can do a combination of sizes. Press the dough circles into the pans.

7. Place pieces of foil over each pastry shell then refrigerate for 30 minutes.

8. Preheat oven to 180 C / 350 F degrees.

9. Remove the pastry shells from the refrigerator and place either baking beans or rice on top of the foil, filling almost to the top. This will prevent the dough from slumping during baking.

10. Bake for 15 minutes then remove the foil along with the rice or beans.

11. Return the pastry shells to the oven and bake an additional 5 minutes.

12. Remove from the oven and brush each pastry shell with the beaten egg yolk.

13. Return to the oven and bake an additional 5 minutes.

14. Remove pastry shells from the oven and reduce the oven temperature to 120 C / 250 F degrees.

Custard:

1. Place the cream and milk in a medium sauce pan over medium-low heat. Stirring very frequently, heat just until small bubbles form around the edges of the pan.

2. Whisk the eggs, egg yolks, sugar and vanilla together.

3. Once the cream is hot, very, very slowly add to the egg and sugar mixture, whisking constantly. Don't be tempted to add all at once or you'll end up with scrambled eggs.

4. Fill the pre-baked pastry shells with the custard, making sure to fill them evenly so that they cook in the same amount of time. Grate fresh nutmeg over the tops of the custard.

5. Bake 18 - 30 minutes, depending on size of the tartlets.* The custard should be mostly set but the middle should have a faint jiggle.

6. Remove from the oven and cool to room temperature before serving.

Tips:

1. *The tartlets I baked using a mini muffin tin took 18 minutes. The small tartlet pans took 20 - 25 minutes. Keep a close watch and check for doneness often.

2. You can use a large tart pan and bake for 35 - 45 minutes.

3. You may substitute your favorite pre-made refrigerated pie pastry dough (such as Pillsbury) instead of making the pastry from scratch. Just be sure to pre-bake it and brush with egg yolk so that the crust doesn't get soggy from the custard.

4. If you have any leftover custard filling, pour into small ramekins. Place the ramekins into a shallow baking dish and place in the oven.

Carefully fill the shallow dish with hot water halfway up the ramekins. Bake at 163C/325F degrees for 25 – 35 minutes, just until set and the middle still jiggles a bit. Remove ramekins from the hot water, chill thoroughly and enjoy!

Enjoy!

ABOUT THE AUTHOR

USA Today bestselling author H.Y. Hanna writes fun mysteries filled with suspense, humour, and unexpected twists, as well as quirky characters and cats with big personalities! She is known for bringing wonderful settings to life, whether it's the historic city of Oxford, the beautiful English Cotswolds or other exciting places around the world.

After graduating from Oxford University, Hsin-Yi tried her hand at a variety of jobs, including advertising, modelling, teaching English and dog training... before returning to her first love: writing. She worked as a freelance writer for several years and has won awards for her poetry, short stories and journalism.

Hsin-Yi was born in Taiwan and has been a globe-trotter all her life, living in a variety of cultures from the UK to the Middle East, the USA to New Zealand... but is now happily settled in Perth, Western Australia, with her husband and a rescue kitty named Muesli. You can learn more about her and her books at: **www.hyhanna.com**

Sign up to her newsletter to get updates on new releases, exclusive giveaways and other book news!

https://www.hyhanna.com/newsletter

ACKNOWLEDGMENTS

My initial beta readers: Connie Leap, Basma Alwesh, and Charles Winthrop are always wonderful but this time, they were really amazing, dropping everything to help me with the crazily tight schedule for this book. Their feedback has been absolutely invaluable in making this book better (and settling my pre-publishing nerves!). I'm also indebted to Heather Belleguelle for both her eagle eyes and her wise insights during the final proofread, and to my wonderful editor, Chandler Groover, who I don't thank enough but who always keeps my adverbs in check (!) and is amazing in matching my often hectic publication schedule. I feel incredibly lucky to have the support of such a fantastic team.

As before, I am so grateful to the talented Kim McMahan Davis of _Cinnamon and Sugar... and a Little Bit of Murder_ blog, for acting as my "baking consulant" and in this case, helping me provide and test the Egg Custard Tart recipe, (as well as providing U.S. measurement equivalents!)

And last but not least, to my wonderful husband for his patient encouragement, tireless support, and for always believing in me—I couldn't do it without him.

Made in the USA
Middletown, DE
28 September 2023

39683656R00187